I0554095

Books by Tom Hoffman

The Eleventh Ring

The Thirteenth Monk

The Seventh Medallion

Orville Mouse and the Puzzle
of the Clockwork Glowbirds

Orville Mouse and the Puzzle
of the Shattered Abacus

Orville Mouse and the Puzzle
of the Capricious Shadows

Orville Mouse and the Puzzle
of the Last Metaphonium

Orville Mouse and the Puzzle
of the Sagacious Sapling

Available online at Amazon and Barnes & Noble

An Orville Wellington Mouse Adventure

ORVILLE MOUSE

and the Puzzle of the Sagacious Sapling

by Tom Hoffman

Tom Hoffman
Visit my website at thoffmanak.wordpress.com
Email: OrvilleMouse@gmail.com

Printed in the United States of America

First Printing: 2018
ISBN 978-0-9994634-4-4

With lots of love for
Molly, Alex, Sophie, and Oliver

A very special thanks to
my wonderful editors
Beth, Sophie, Oliver,
and Mike
for their invaluable assistance
and excellent advice.

*Many thanks to the band members
of Nihiloceros for letting me hijack their
wonderful name. Rock on!*

Table of Contents

"I know nothing in the world that has as much power as a word. Sometimes I write one, and I look at it until it begins to shine."

– *Emily Dickinson*

"The game of life is a game of boomerangs. Our thoughts, deeds and words return to us sooner or later with astounding accuracy."

– *Florence Scovel Shinn*

An Orville Wellington Mouse Adventure

ORVILLE MOUSE

and the Puzzle of the
Sagacious Sapling

Chapter 1

Where the Stars End

Orville studied the wintry night sky above Muridaan Falls, his eyes on the myriad of glittering stars peeking through formless gray clouds, legions of crystalline snowflakes drifting silently down from the heavens.

"So beautiful, it's hard to tell where the stars end and the snow begins, almost like the stars are falling from the sky. This is a good dream. I'm standing in two feet of snow in the middle of winter and I'm toasty warm."

He pressed on through the heavy blanket of new-fallen snow.

"It's so much easier to walk through dream snow than real snow. I've come at least a mile and I'm not even out of breath."

Orville brushed the soft snow from his ears as he scanned the shimmering white forest.

"It's really coming down, and the wind is picking up. I'm still nice and warm though."

He squinted, peering through swirling clouds of white, his eyes focused on a tiny green speck deep in the forest.

"That's weird, there's something green back there, the color of budding leaves in the spring. Why would I be dreaming about spring leaves in a big crazy snowstorm? I should go check it out, it's probably important. Sophia always says I should pay attention to the details in my dreams."

"Maybe you're just tired of winter."

Orville gave a start, his head whipping around at the sound of this unexpected, but very familiar voice. His best friend Sophia was walking next to him. He realized he was holding her paw.

"What are you doing here?"

"It seemed like an interesting dream, so I thought I'd pop in. What do you think the green thing is? And why are you wearing jammies in a snowstorm?"

Orville's eyes narrowed at Sophia's smirky smile.

"Are you a dream Sophia or the real Sophia?"

"I'm the real Sophia. Or I could be a dream Sophia pretending to be the real Sophia and I'll turn into a giant carnivorous centipede and chase you through the forest until you scream and wake up."

Orville snorted. "You're definitely the real Sophia. I'm glad you're here. I like holding paws while we walk."

"We don't have much choice."

"What do you mean?"

"Look at our paws."

4

"Whoa, they're tied together with vines. Why would I be dreaming that? Wait, we didn't get married did we?" Orville gave his best cackling laugh.

Sophia whacked him on the shoulder with her free arm.

"Quit being a ninny."

"Just joking. We should go see what that green thing is."

The pair of best friends pressed on through the falling snow.

Sophia grinned, her eyes on Orville.

"Did your mum buy you those jammies? The little bears flying kites are so cute. Precious."

"Very funny. These were my favorite jammies when I was a mouseling. They're really snuggly, but I have no idea why I'm wearing them."

"Orville! Look!"

Orville turned to see a monstrous rippling wave rolling toward them, the trees and snow and sky undulating and twisting and blurring.

"It's coming this way!"

"I knew this was going to be a good dream."

Orville let out a shriek when the invisible wave hit them, the two friends enveloped in a swirling white cloud. When the wave passed, Muridaan Falls was gone.

"Creekers, what is this place? How did we get here?"

Orville gaped at the seventy foot tall mushrooms towering above them.

"I have no idea where we are. I've never seen any-

thing like this. Those mushrooms are impossibly big. Some of the plants look prehistoric."

"I don't like this dream anymore. This is creepy, someplace giant insects would live. Or snakes, probably big slithery poisonous snakes with stabby fangs."

"You're not wearing your pajamas anymore."

"What??" Orville looked down. "Whew, I'm wearing my adventuring clothes. I was afraid I was having one of those walking around in my underwear dreams."

Sophia snorted.

"Our paws are still tied together. Why would I be dreaming that? It doesn't make sense."

Sophia glanced behind them, her eyes widening. She squeezed Orville's paw.

"Don't panic, but you might want to turn around."

Orville gave a yelp when he saw the twelve foot tall prehistoric bird creatures with vicious hooked orange beaks, leathery maroon wings, and bony hands. Their bodies were covered with short dark violet feathers, and four of the six creatures were carrying wicked looking obsidian axes and spears. Six pairs of blood red blinking eyes were staring at Orville.

"Why are they looking at me like that?"

"Relax, you can't get hurt in a dream, remember? This is really interesting, maybe your best dream yet. I'll have to do some research on prehistoric birds at the school library."

The largest bird prodded Orville with the butt of its spear, pushing him forward. It let out a stream of

6

raucous screeching noises that vaguely resembled spoken words.

"I think they can talk. Isn't this amazing? I wish I knew what they were saying."

Orville gave Sophia a sideways glance, his boots sinking into the spongy moss covered forest floor.

"They're deciding which spear to stab me with."

"Do you like mushrooms?"

"What?"

"Mushrooms, do you like them?"

"Not really. I guess they're okay in salads, but I wouldn't eat a big bowl of them for snacks. Aren't they some kind of creepy fungus or something?"

"Exactly, they're a kind of fungi. Did you know they're more like animals than plants? They release carbon dioxide into the air like animals do, not oxygen like plants. Mushrooms are very nutritious, except for the poisonous ones that kill you after one bite. Papa used to say that finding a mushroom in the forest was like finding a little loaf of bread."

"A little loaf of poisonous bread. Why are you talking about mushrooms?"

"So you won't think about the prehistoric birds with sharp spears marching behind us. I don't want you to get scared and wake up."

"I'm not scared, it was just kind of surprising to see them. I guess it is an interesting dream. I wonder where they're taking us? Wait, do you hear that?"

"Hear what?"

"That sound, like a clock ticking?"

"I don't hear anything like that. Um, in case you hadn't noticed, you're covered with some kind of goopy green slime. It smells bad. Actually, it smells worse than bad. Worse than really bad."

"Eew! What is this stuff?"

Orville pinched his nose, looking down at the globs of putrid dripping green slime splattered across his clothes.

"This is disgusting! How did I get this stuff on me?"

He tried to wipe the oozing slime off, great gobs of it clinging to his paws. As he was shaking them wildly he noticed his pants were ripped, a vicious bite mark on his right leg.

"Oh no, I think something bit me! It looks really bad, like it's infected. I don't like this."

"There's no infection, it's a dream. You're dreaming this. The green slime and the bite marks weren't there a minute ago. It's something you just created."

"It doesn't actually hurt, I guess it looks worse than it really is. I'll just shape some clean clothes."

"No, don't alter anything. This dream is a powerful message from your inner voice, one we should pay close attention to. That's why I was drawn to it."

"I'm pretty sure the message is to stay away from giant birds with sharp spears and axes. And whatever it was that bit my leg and splattered green slime on me."

"Keep your eyes open. Every detail in a dream is important. Are you still hearing the ticking sound?"

"Yes, it's getting louder."

Sophia looked up at the towering mushrooms. Some-

thing orange and yellow with long spindly legs leaped off the tallest one, spreading a pair of translucent wings and gliding down into the shadowy jungle. She decided not to mention this to Orville.

"Look at those giant pink flowers at the base of the mushrooms. There's something creepy about them. It looks like those black things might be tentacles."

Several miles later Orville gave a sigh of relief as they emerged from the murky mushroom forest into a vast open plain of tall rippling blue grass.

"This is more like it, not all dark and creepy. Hey, that looks like a village."

Sophia eyed the cluster of dark brown huts, their roofs thatched with enormous green leaves. One of their captors let out a warbling shriek. Dozens of bird creatures emerged from the crudely formed structures, their raucous cries drifting across the plain.

Orville turned to the bird behind him.

"I don't know if you can understand me, but I would really appreciate it if you wouldn't–" The butt of a heavy spear slammed against Orville's chest, almost knocking him over.

"Owww!"

"Don't antagonize them, we need to find out why you're having this dream, why we're here in this world."

Orville glared at the bird who had hit him, rubbing his chest.

"If this wasn't a dream I'd be stuffing a pillow with your feathers right now."

9

Sophia snickered. Orville could be so funny sometimes.

The massive prehistoric bird nudged Orville with the spear, guiding him toward the village.

"The huts are made of dried mud and sticks. Not exactly advanced technology."

Sophia pointed to a large cage constructed of tree branches tied together with vines.

"I have a feeling that's our new home."

"I could vaporize it in a heartbeat. Poof!"

"Don't alter the dream. We have to let it play out."

Several dozen of the bird creatures clustered around Orville and Sophia, a few of them running their bony hands over Orville's slime covered clothes.

"Keep your creepy hands off me!"

Orville pushed them away, the huge beasts clacking their beaks and making horrible wheezing sounds.

The largest bird spread out its leathery wings and let out a garbled crowing noise, the others quickly backing away. He pushed Orville and Sophia into the cage, closing the gate behind them, tying it securely with a vine rope.

Orville slumped down to the floor, his eyes on the crowd of birds surrounding their crude prison.

"They keep clacking their beaks and making that wheezy noise. It's creepy. And they kept touching my clothes."

Sophia studied the birds curiously. "Maybe they've never seen clothes before and they're trying to figure out what they are. They're definitely talking to each other, they have a language. There's something familiar about it, but I can't put my paw on it. Orville, look at the tall bird, the one who's in charge. Look what he's wearing."

"That's weird. He's wearing a hat, and it's not something they made. It looks like an old military hat. See the silver medallion on it? This is a good puzzle. There's something we're missing about this dream."

One by one the purple feathered villagers lost interest in Orville and Sophia, wandering back to their huts.

Twenty minutes later Orville looked up to see a group of birds dragging a large iron pot to the center of the village. Smaller birds began piling dry branches around the base of the pot while others filled it with water poured from dozens of large yellow gourds.

"They must be cooking dinner. I hope it's something good, I'm starving. Wait, do you think they eat mushrooms? The last thing I want is a bowl of mushroom stew."

"They might, it's hard to tell." Sophia's eyes were on the birds' vicious looking hooked beaks.

"They probably don't eat mushrooms, birds that big are most likely–" Orville froze, hit with a terrifying realization.

"Most likely what?"

Orville's voice was a raspy whisper. "They're most likely carnivorous. They eat meat. This is bad."

Sophia rubbed Orville's shoulder. "They're not going to eat you. It's just a dream."

"They're starting a fire under the pot. They're defi-

nitely going to cook something and I don't see any mushrooms. If they were making mushroom stew they'd have big baskets of chopped mushrooms. There are no mushrooms, Sophia."

"Remember how we had to jump into the molten lava in your dream about Mt. Ianua? You were fine, you just woke up."

"The pot is steaming. It looks really hot."

Orville's stomach twisted when he saw the two enormous birds striding toward them. One of them was the bird wearing the military hat.

"They're coming to get me!"

The shorter bird untied the gate and swung it open. He stepped into the cage, looking first at Sophia, then at Orville.

"What do you want? You'd better not be thinking about eating us."

The bird approached Sophia, making a snorting noise, then stepped over to Orville, rubbing its long orange beak against the top of his head. It let out a great squawk, clacking and making the horrible wheezing noises. The bird with the gray hat strode into the cage, grabbing Orville with its bony hands, dragging him outside.

"We have to blink out of here!"

"No, we can't alter the dream!"

The monstrous prehistoric bird carried his wriggling furry captive over to the steaming iron pot. It held Orville tightly in its great bony hands while two smaller birds poured something over him from a crudely fashioned clay jar.

"What is this stuff? Are you putting spices on me? Is that sauce?"

Several dozen birds had gathered around the fire, clacking and wheezing, their beady red eyes on Orville. The bird in the gray hat grabbed Orville by his feet, raising him up over the steaming black cauldron.

"This is the worst dream ever! Don't cook me!"

Orville's piercing scream ended abruptly with a splash and a gurgle.

Chapter 2

Two Rings

Orville's eyes blinked open. He studied the soft moonlight drifting through his curtains.

"Whoa. So scary. I can't believe I dreamed a giant bird was trying to cook me."

He ran his paw over his pajamas. "Dry as a bone, no green slime, no bite marks on my leg, no little bears flying kites. Those prehistoric birds were really bad. I have no idea what all that meant. Why would I dream prehistoric birds were trying to cook me in a stewpot?"

He sighed, laying his head back down on the pillow.

"It's still early, I have at least another three hours before–" He stopped in mid sentence, his ears slowly turning.

"That ticking noise, it's the same one I heard in my dream."

He sat up straight, listening closely, then flicked his paw, an orb of light appearing above him. He studied his bedside table.

"How did that get here?"

The source of the mysterious ticking sound was a

battered gold pocket watch. He picked it up, studying it closely.

"This is the watch Captain Tobias gave me on the Isle of the Silver Ship. I had this hidden in my sock drawer."

He scanned the room, half expecting to find a mysterious figure skulking in the shadows.

"Nobody here but me. Maybe Proto moved the watch when he was putting away laundry. I'll ask him in the morning."

The orb of light blinked off and Orville snuggled down into his bed, pulling the covers over him.

"Nothing like my own warm comfy bed. I still can't believe Ebenezer and Aislin gave us their house."

He closed his eyes.

Then he opened them.

"That ticking is going to drive me loopy."

He hopped out of bed and grabbed the watch, feeling his way over to the chest of drawers.

"Back into the sock drawer for you, my annoying little friend."

Pulling open the top drawer, he hid the watch under a stack of pajamas. He was pushing the drawer closed when he noticed a curious orange glow.

"That's weird."

Pushing aside a pile of socks revealed the source of the curious light.

"Oh, I forgot about that. It's the ring Papa gave me, the one he found on Varmoran next to the wreckage of an old scout ship."

He plucked the glowing ring from the drawer, turning it slowly in his paw, furrowing his brow, a vague memory flickering in his thoughts.

"I've seen this ring somewhere else, I'm sure of it."

Orville tapped his chin, trying to remember where he had seen a ring like this one. Was it at Miraculum's Fine Antiques? Did Mum have one? Did Sophia?

"That's it! This ring is identical to the one Aislin Mouse gave to Sophia. The Shadow King gave the ring to Aislin, but her inner voice said it was really meant for Sophia."

"Two identical rings, one from Varmoran and one from Elysian. One for me and one for Sophia. That's no accident, this is definitely important."

Orville hopped back into bed, closing his eyes, trying to find a connection between the two rings. Two hours later, as the morning sun was peeking up over the mountains he drifted off to sleep.

"Orville! Breakfast! You're going to be late for work."

Orville groaned, pulling the pillow over his head.

"No. So tired. Why can't Proto let me sleep?"

"Orville! Breakfast! Late for work!"

His bleary eyes barely open, he stumbled out of bed and pulled on his clothes, jamming the orange ring into his pocket. He would ask Proto about it. Pushing open the bedroom door he shuffled down the hallway, then stopped, closing his eyes.

"So sleepy."

When he opened his eyes he was back in his bedroom, the orange ring in his paw. He was instantly wide awake.

"Whoa. What happened? I was in the hallway, and now I'm back here."

Orville's anxiety spiked. He sat down on his bed.

"Okay, I was in the hallway, closed my eyes, and then I was back in my bedroom. Maybe I blinked back to my room without realizing it, or maybe I was sleepwalking. Or maybe I was just dreaming that I was walking down the hallway. That has to be it. I was so tired that I fell asleep standing up in my bedroom, then dreamed I was walking down the hallway to breakfast, then woke up again, still in my bedroom. That's not so weird, a good night's sleep will take care of that."

Orville put the ring back in his pocket and headed down the hallway to the kitchen. Proto was standing at the stove wearing one of Mum's flowered aprons.

"A lovely good morning to you, Orville. I have delicious snapberry muffins and oatmeal with cinnamon, honey, and some big tasty mushrooms."

"Mushrooms? You put mushrooms in my oatmeal? Why would you do that?"

"Mushrooms are very healthy, quite nutritious. Very good for you."

"That's kind of a weird coincidence. I had a dream last night about a giant mushroom forest and crazy prehistoric bird creatures who were trying to cook me in a stewpot."

"How dreadful! Hideous carnivorous birds with a craving for tasty mice? Should I begin preparations for another adventure?"

"Um, I don't think so. I have to talk to Sophia about the dream. It was probably just a bad dream. I may have eaten too much before I went to bed."

"That would certainly explain the empty tin of tasty little cakes I found on the kitchen table this morning."

"Mmm, they were so good. Yum. Say, have you ever seen a ring like this before?" Orville held out the orange glowing ring.

"This is the ring Aislin Mouse gave to Sophia?"

"No, it's just like it though. Papa gave me this one. He found it on Varmoran next to the wreckage of an old scout ship."

Proto took the ring, turning it slowly in his hand.

"Curious, I am uncertain as to the purpose of the small glowing lights within the ring. There was a symbol on the side of the ring, but it has worn off. The ring is old and has seen much wear."

"I didn't see a symbol on it."

"It is not visible to the naked eye, only when scanned with my full spectrum optics."

"Maybe Sophia's ring has the same symbol on it. If it does, we can ask Amanda Mouse to look at it. She knows all about history stuff."

"You are quite late for work and there's a dreadful snowstorm out there. You'd best hurry. Perhaps you should wear your snowshoes?"

"I'll be fine. Walking through deep snow is good exercise. I just remembered, in my dream last night I was walking through a blizzard wearing my jammies."

"I would strongly advise against wearing your pajamas in such a bitterly cold storm as this one."

"Right. Good advice. Thanks, Proto."

Orville grabbed his coat and stepped into the living room.

"Proto! Squeaky is scratching the floor again! I thought you were going to do something about that? Like make him stop?"

Proto emerged from the kitchen, his eyes on Squeaky the RoboPup, who was currently clawing the wooden floor with some great exuberance.

"Squeaky, what did I tell you about scratching the floor?"

The silver robotic puppy looked up and gave a sharp bark, darting over to Proto and laying down at his feet, his tail wagging.

"He's ruining the floor. If Sophia sees that she'll make me replace all the damaged boards. Do you know how much work that is?"

"I suppose we could put a rug over it, although that seems somewhat duplicitous."

Orville had no idea what duplicitous meant.

"Um, it might be a little of that, but not too much. Let's hide it with the rug."

He buttoned his coat and pulled on his heavy winter boots and woolen cap. With a quick wave to Proto he stepped through the front door, slamming it behind him.

Chapter 3

Leaves of Spring

Orville held up one paw, shielding his eyes from the ferocious wind and blowing snow.

"Whoa, that stings. Proto wasn't joking about a snowstorm, it's really coming down, at least two feet. Glad I'm not wearing jammies like in my dream." He snorted, imagining himself walking into the Book Emporium wearing pajamas covered with cute little kite flying bears.

Ferocious winter storms were a common occurrence during the long Symocan winters, and something Orville was quite familiar with. He kicked the snow aside and wrestled the front gate open, stepping out into the snow covered lane.

"I'll walk along that wagon path, that will be a lot easier, the snow's all mashed down. I hope they went all the way to the Book Emporium."

Orville followed the trail left by the early morning delivery wagon, gazing up at the snow covered spruce trees.

"So beautiful, just like my dream. The snow flakes really do look like stars falling from the sky. I can't wait to talk to Sophia about our dream. Maybe Amanda will know something about the orange rings. That would really help to solve the puzzle. I never did show Sophia's ring to Master Marloh."

By the time Orville swung open the front door of the Book Emporium he was covered with a thick layer of fluffy white snow, little icicles dangling from his whiskers.

Master Marloh looked up from the front desk, peering over his small round gold spectacles at a shivering Orville. He grinned.

"Dear me, for a moment I thought a ferocious snow bear had wandered into the shop."

Orville snorted, shaking the snow off.

"Sorry I'm late. The snow is really coming down, but it's beautiful."

"I am not surprised you would be late on a day such as today. The only other mouse here is Amanda. I don't imagine we'll have any customers until the storm passes and the pathways are cleared."

Orville took off his boots and coat, slipping on a pair of shoes from his pack.

"Say, I was wondering if you've ever seen a ring like this before. Papa found it on Varmoran next to the wreckage of an old scout ship."

Orville set the ring down in front of Master Marloh.

"Interesting, I don't believe I've ever seen one quite

like it."

Master Marloh picked up the ring, turning it slowly.

"You have no idea the purpose of the lights inside the stone?"

"No idea. Sophia and I looked at her ring in a dark closet though. It shines little moving white dots on the walls."

"Sophia has a ring like this one?"

"Aislin Mouse gave it to her. The Shadow King gave it to Aislin, but her inner voice told her the ring was meant for Sophia."

"Fascinating, could the lights be a star map? Some sort of navigational device?"

"Sophia had the same idea, but the dots move around randomly, not like stars."

"It looks very old, I will say that. It has seen a lot of wear."

"Proto says there used to be a symbol on the side of the ring, but it's worn down. He couldn't tell what it was. I'm hoping Sophia's ring is in better shape."

"A most curious turn of events. Clearly these rings hold some deeper purpose, but one I am not aware of."

"I hardly slept last night trying to figure out why we both have the same ring."

"The meaning will become clear with time, that is how the universe works."

"Hi, Orville. How was your walk to work? Isn't the snow pretty?"

Orville turned to see Amanda Mouse walking toward them, a large book under her arm.

"Really pretty. It's deep, but I followed a wagon path so it wasn't too bad walking here."

Amanda strolled over to the counter, glancing at the orange ring.

"Mintarian. Where did you find it?"

"What?"

"The ring, where did you find it?"

"You said Mintarian."

"Yes, Mintarian. Correct."

"I'm a little confused. Are you saying the ring is Mintarian? We've been trying to figure out what it is. Papa found it on Varmoran next to a wrecked scout ship."

Amanda took a step back, nodding.

"That would make sense."

She pulled a large magnifying glass from her pocket, examining the ring.

"There should be a symbol on this side, but it's worn off. I can't make it out. No branch, I'm afraid."

"No branch?"

"Yes, it's unfortunate."

"Branch of what?"

"The military."

"It's a Mintarian military ring?"

"I just said that. Probably a dark space pilot's ring, but it's different from any I've seen. Most had green or yellow stones, this one has an orange stone with little blinking lights. It's definitely Mintarian military though, and probably the Dark Space Service."

"Would it help if you knew what the symbol was?"

"Of course it would. Each branch had their own symbol."

"Um, Sophia has a ring identical to this one that might be in better shape, not so worn. If I ask her to bring it tomorrow could you look at it?"

"I'd love to. I'll do some research on Mintarian military rings and see what I can find out. There were quite a few branches of the Mintarian Dark Space Service, some of them highly secretive. Those are the most interesting ones."

"Thanks, I really appreciate your help. Nobody knows as much about history as you do. Sophia and I think you're amazing."

Orville realized it was the first time he had seen Amanda really smile.

After shoveling the path in front of the Book Emporium, Orville spent most of the day reorganizing the science section, an endeavor which included no small amount of surreptitious research on prehistoric birds and their eating habits. One book in particular caught his attention. More precisely, it was a drawing of a ferocious feathered prehistoric bird which had caught his attention.

"Creekers, this looks just like the bird creature in my dream. It has the same giant claw on the back of its scaly feet, a long purple feathered tail, creepy red eyes, and the big scary hooked beak. It says they hunted in packs and ate meat. I knew it! I knew they were carnivorous. That's why they tried to cook me."

The winter sun was low in the sky when Orville

headed home from the Book Emporium, his mind a whirl of unsolved puzzles and prehistoric birds, his thoughts far from the snowy world of Muridaan Falls. The puzzles and prehistoric birds vanished when he heard the voice.

"In life and in dreams, details are of the utmost importance."

Orville recognized the voice instantly as his inner voice, his deeper self, the part of him that existed outside of time and space.

"Sophia told me to pay attention to the details in the bird dream, that they were important, and now my inner voice is telling me the same thing. Why now? Why here? There must be something I'm supposed to see."

Orville stopped, turning slowly, studying his sur-roundings using his astonishing powers of observation. Nothing about the snow covered lane struck him as unusual until he gazed deep into the dark shadowy forest.

"Oh, no, this is not good, not good at all."

His eyes had locked onto a barely visible speck of green peeking out from a dense stand of snow covered spruce trees.

"It's the color of budding spring leaves, exactly what I saw in my dream. That's where Sophia and I were heading when the big rolling wave hit us. She thought it was really important."

It took Orville only a moment to make his decision. He pulled out his pocket knife and carved an X on the closest spruce tree.

"Now I can find this spot again. It's time to find out what that green thing is."

The mounting drifts were up to his waist as he pushed his way through the forest, the snow falling faster than ever. He pulled his woolen cap down, stumbling over a fallen branch hidden beneath the snow. The forest was silent and still, drawing him into a kind of reverie as he forged onward toward the distant green speck.

He stopped to rest for a moment, his labored breath a frosty cloud in the frigid winter air.

"Whew, this is a lot harder than it was in my dream. This snow is really deep, and it's going to be dark soon. I'd better hurry."

His legs were burning when he finally reached it, a single green leaf poking up from the snow.

"That's weird, why would there be a green leaf in the middle of winter? Maybe it's frozen or something."

He stepped closer to the leaf, gently pushing away the snow. Four more spring green leaves popped into view.

"Whoa, there's a little tree with green leaves under the snow."

Clearing away the heavy drift revealed a three foot tall sapling covered with soft green leaves.

"This is like the clockwork glowbirds, like the blue marble rolling uphill, like the capricious shadows of my adventurers hat. It can't be happening, but it is. I'm looking at a sapling with bright green leaves in the middle of winter."

Orville examined the tree closely, finding nothing to explain this curious anomaly.

"I don't know what this means, but I'm pretty sure it's connected to that weird wave and those scary prehistoric birds."

Chapter 4

Watch Out!

Orville flung open the front door and stumbled inside, dropping his winter coat to the floor, kicking off his boots.

"So tired. Walking through that snow was exhausting. I should have worn my snowshoes. I wonder where Proto is? I don't smell dinner cooking."

He frowned when he saw the wooden floor. The rug covering the scratched floor had been pushed aside, the floorboards covered with deep scrapes and gouges.

"What is wrong with that puppy? He is in big, big trouble."

Orville headed straight to his bedroom. As he suspected, the silver RoboPup was lying on his bed.

"I knew you'd be here, all snuggled up in my covers, probably tired from a hard day of scratching the living room floor to pieces. You're in big trouble, my little friend. Big, big trouble."

Squeaky hopped off the bed and scurried over to

Orville, running circles around him and barking.

Orville scooped him up, holding him like a little mouseling. Squeaky licked his face.

"Yuck! No face licking!"

Orville laughed, setting Squeaky back down on the bed.

"It's hard to be mad at a cute little puppy like you. You have to stop scratching the floor though. I don't want to replace it all. You have no idea how much work that is."

Orville pulled the orange ring from his pocket.

"I'll send Sophia a thought cloud and ask her to bring Aislin's ring to lunch so Amanda can look at it. This ring goes back in the sock drawer, and then it's nap time for me. So tired."

Orville slid the top drawer open and reached under the socks to hide the ring.

"That's weird, I know I hid the pocket watch under my pajamas. Why is it under my socks? Someone's moving my stuff around."

He grabbed the watch and slid it back under the stack of pajamas.

"This can't be right."

When Orville pulled his paw from the drawer he was holding two gold pocket watches.

"Where did this other watch come from? I only had one watch."

He flopped down on his bed, eyeing the two watches.

"They're identical. This is getting really weird."

He flipped open the back covers of both watches and

examined them.

"They both have the same inscription in them, and the same little scratches."

Orville flipped open both front covers.

"Both watch faces are identical, and they both have the same map with the X in the same spot. The watch that Papa got from his grandpapa didn't have a map on it, but the one I got from Captain Tobias did have the map."

"Whoa!"

Orville sat up straight. He had discovered one glaring difference between the two seemingly identical gold pocket watches. The watch he had found on his bedside table that morning was running backwards, its second hand rotating counter clockwise.

"Creekers. What does that mean?"

He plopped his head back on the pillow, closing his eyes.

"So confusing. I have no idea where the second watch came from or why it was on my bedside table. Unless I shaped it in my sleep. That has to be it. But why would I shape a watch that runs backwards? None of this makes sense."

Several minutes later an exhausted Orville was sound asleep, lost in the world of dreams.

"Orville! Dinner!"

Orville groaned, rolling over.

"I'll be right there."

He stood up and headed down the hallway, Squeaky trailing behind him. Proto was at the stove stirring a large simmering pot.

"I made dinner for Mum and Papa and there's plenty left over for you. Yummy vegetable stew. Very healthy. Nutritious."

"It smells good. You didn't add anything weird to it, did you? Like those vegetables you got from the Cube?"

"The garden is currently buried under three feet of snow, I'm afraid. No veggies during the winter."

"Oh, that reminds me, have you ever heard of a tree that keeps its green leaves all year round, even in the winter?"

"Spruce trees keep their green needles all year."

"I mean flat green leaves, like on an oak tree."

"You are referring to deciduous trees, quite different from evergreens such as spruce or pine. Deciduous trees have flat wide leaves."

"Do any of them keep their leaves all year?"

"All deciduous trees lose their leaves with the approach of winter. The tree absorbs all the nutrients from the leaves, which then die and fall off. These extra nutrients allow the tree to survive the harsh winter conditions, and the loss of leaves decreases the amount of water the tree needs. Quite a remarkable adaptation."

"So there's no such thing as a deciduous tree that keeps its green leaves all year long?"

"Correct. That's a rather curious question. Why are you asking it?"

"Oh, um, no reason, I was just thinking about trees and leaves and stuff. You know."

31

Proto's eyes narrowed.

"Trees and leaves and stuff?"

"Right."

"I'll pack tonight. I know you don't like the idea of me bringing a heavy particle beam vaporization projector on our adventures, but if we're traveling to a world where–"

"We're not traveling to another world, and we're not going on another adventure. I was just wondering if there are any trees that don't lose their leaves."

"Very well, I won't bring the particle beam projector. Will it be cold there? You should bring adequate winter clothing if it is, although I suppose you could just shape some once we get there."

"All right, I'll tell you. I found a little tree in the forest buried under a snow drift. It had green leaves and it was definitely a deciduous tree. It had green leaves in the middle of winter."

"I should bring the particle beam projector. Clearly this tree is from a world swarming with horrific slithering beasts of prey, cold blooded reptilian monstrosities with razor sharp claws and venomous fangs, waiting to sink their teeth into an unsuspecting furry mouse as he casually strolls along through the shadowy forest."

Proto grinned, rubbing his silver hands together.

"Right. Sounds like fun. So, no weird veggies in the stew?"

"Your Mum bought most of them at the market, and the rest I bottled last fall. Very healthy." Proto gave a nervous laugh.

"What is it? Why did you give that weird laugh?"

"Not that such an event would ever occur, but if you did happen to wander into my room and spot several dozen black jars containing pickled vegetables, it would probably be best if you didn't open them. Or touch them. Or get too close to them."

"Um… I won't. What are you doing with stuff like that in your room?"

"Ah, the stew is ready. There's also freshly baked bread to have with your dinner, quite delicious, and Mum sent over a box of yummy oatmeal cookies from Pridie's Bake Shop. It's a new shop near the Book Emporium that just opened a few weeks ago. Mum said you and Sophia should go there for lunch sometime. She said they have delicious snapberry pie."

"That sounds great. Sophia and I will go there tomorrow."

Chapter 5

The Gang of Dragons

"Why are you reading about trees?"

Orville jumped, the heavy book slipping from his paws, hitting the floor with a thump.

"Sophia! Why do you blink up behind me like that?"

"Sorry, I didn't mean to scare you."

"I'm starting to think you do it on purpose. You didn't scare me. I'm reading about trees because I found a really weird one when I was walking home from work yesterday."

"What kind of weird tree?"

Orville hesitated. "It was buried under three feet of snow and it had green leaves. Not needles, leaves."

"That's not possible. Deciduous trees lose their leaves in the fall. Everyone knows that."

"I saw a green leaf poking up out of a snow drift, and when I cleared away the snow I found a three foot tall sapling with green leaves."

"You're certain? You didn't just imagine it? Or

dream it?"

"Yes, I saw it. It was just like my dream, but without the big wave that sent us to that crazy mushroom world. I saw the green speck and hiked through the snow until I found it. I marked an X on a tree next to the road so we can find it again."

"This must be important. But what would a little green tree have to do with a weird invisible wave and that strange world?"

"And those scary prehistoric birds. You remember, the ones who tried to cook me in a stewpot?"

Sophia snickered. "You should have seen your face when he dropped you into the pot."

Orville gave Sophia a dark look.

"I'll walk home with you after work and you can show me the tree. We'll take one of its leaves and study it. This sounds really interesting. It could be a new species of tree."

"Did you bring Aislin's ring? I brought the ring Papa gave me in case Amanda wants to compare them."

Sophia pulled the glowing orange ring from her pocket.

"You said mine is identical to the one your papa gave you?"

"Yes, but mine is really worn."

Orville took the ring from Sophia and held it up to the light. He froze when he saw the engraved symbol on the side of the ring.

"What's the matter?"

"It looks like the head of a prehistoric creature."

Sophia stepped closer, eyeing the ring.

"That's a dragon's head, not the prehistoric bird from your dream."

"That's a relief. Let's go find Amanda. She said the ring was a Mintarian military ring, and the symbol would tell her which branch of the Dark Space Service wore them."

The two best friends strolled toward the front desk.

"Hi, Sophia!"

Sophia looked up to see Amanda walking toward them.

"Hi, Amanda!"

"Orville said you were bringing your ring? Could you make out the symbol?"

"Thanks so much for helping us. I think it's a dragon's head, but I'm not certain."

Amanda pulled out her big magnifying glass, taking the ring from Sophia.

"Mmm hmm. Interesting."

"What is it?"

"You were right, it's a dragon's head."

"Why is that interesting? What does it mean?"

Amanda turned slowly toward Orville, her eyes narrowing.

"It's top secret, very scary. I could tell you what it means, but then I'd have to kill you."

"What?" Orville backed away from Amanda.

Amanda burst out laughing.

Sophia snorted. "Good one. You got him."

"I was just making a joke, Orville, but it is very

interesting and quite mysterious."

Orville attempted an amused laugh, but it sounded more like a frog croaking.

"Why is it mysterious?"

"There is only one reference to the Mintarian dragon's head symbol that I am aware of. Several years ago I saw a photograph of a Mintarian pilot wearing a shoulder patch that bore a dragon's head just like this one. The caption said he was a member of an elite branch of the Mintarian Dark Space Service called the Gang of Dragons. The photograph was in *Days of Darkness, the War of Anarkkia* on page 514 of Volume 3, if you're interested in seeing it."

Orville's jaw dropped.

"You can remember what page it was on?"

"I just happened to remember it. You know how sometimes things just stick in your head for no reason. Nothing special." Amanda was clearly embarrassed by her astonishing memory.

Sophia smiled.

"I think you're an amazing mouse. We never would have discovered that without you. Never. Hey, why don't you come to lunch with me and Orville? We're going to Pridie's Bake Shop. Orville's mum said it has really yummy food."

Amanda hesitated. "It does sound fun, if you don't mind me tagging along."

"You're not tagging along, you're going to lunch with your friends. You can tell us all about the Dark Space Service. I love your sweater. Did you make it?"

Chapter 6

Pridie's Bake Shop

Orville strolled along behind Sophia and Amanda on the way to the bake shop, his mind a whirlwind of unsolved puzzles. What was the significance of the green sapling? What was that crazy wave? Who were the Gang of Dragons and why did the universe want him and Sophia to have their rings? What did those scary prehistoric bird creatures have to do with anything? And why had he shaped a pocket watch that ran backwards?

"These puzzles are driving me loopy, but all these things have to be connected. I don't understand how a tree could have green leaves in the middle of winter. Unless the tree came from some place where it was summer. Whoa, maybe the tree traveled back in time from next summer! Or from summer a thousand years from now. Maybe in the future trees are really smart and know how to time travel."

Orville burst out laughing. He would not suggest this

possibility to Sophia.

"What are you laughing about?"

"Nothing. Hey, we're almost there. I'm starving."

"You're always starving. What are you going to have?"

"I think I'll have snapberry pie with a side order of snapberry pie."

Amanda laughed. "You're so funny, Orville. I wish I could think of funny things like that. I was just joking about having to kill you."

"I know you were, it was funny. I wish I was as smart as you and had your amazing memory. I forget everything."

Sophia grinned. "This is so much fun. We're all so different but we get along so well. Amanda, maybe you and Captain Patcher could come to dinner with me and Orville sometime. I bet he has some amazing stories from the Dragonfly Squadron."

"He does, and he loves telling them. I know he'd love to hear your stories too. He was so amazed when I told him you and Orville had been to Elysian."

"Here we are!"

Sophia swung the front door open, the trio greeted by the delicious aroma of freshly baked bread, the sounds of clinking silverware and friendly conversation filling the room.

Orville grinned. "Pretty busy, they must have really good food. Smells so good."

A tall mouse wearing a starched white apron stepped over to the three friends.

"Welcome to Pridie's Bake Shop. We have one table open, right next to the window, a lovely view of the falling snow."

"Sounds great. I'm starving."

Moments later they were seated. Orville scanned the room.

"Hey, there's Madam Beasley. Look at the crazy hat she's wearing."

"Orville, be nice. I like her hat. It does have a lot of bright feathers on it, but it suits her well. I wonder who she's having lunch with? I don't recognize him."

"I like his coat. Rugged looking. He could be an adventurer."

The waiter smiled, presenting the menus.

"Our special today is mushroom stew and a grilled cucumber sandwich. Perfect for a cold winter's day like today. Let me know when you're ready to order."

Orville opened the menu, going straight to the dessert section.

"Definitely not having the mushroom stew. Gakk. Oh good, they have snapberry pie. Yum. I can't wait to–"

Orville never finished his sentence. He never finished it because he was pointing at the huge wave rolling through the bake shop, tables and mice and dishes and walls undulating and twisting wildly.

Sophia's eyes were wide when the wave hit, enveloping them in a swirling miasma of dense white fog.

When the fog cleared Orville and Sophia found themselves walking through the snow with Amanda, once again on their way to Pridie's Bake Shop.

Amanda laughed. "You're so funny, Orville. I wish I could think of funny things like that. I was just joking about having to kill you."

Orville was stunned. "What just happened?"

Sophia shook her head. "I don't know."

Amanda looked at Orville curiously.

"What do you mean?"

"What? We were just–"

Sophia gave Orville a sharp kick in the leg.

"Oh, I just… um, got snow in my boot. So cold. Don't know how it happened."

He tried to remember their conversation during the walk to Pridie's.

"I know you were, it was funny. I wish I was as smart as you and had your amazing memory. I forget everything."

Sophia's eyes were on Orville. "This is so much fun. We're all so different but we get along so well. Amanda, maybe you and Captain Patcher could come to dinner with me and Orville sometime. I bet he has some amazing stories from the Dragonfly Squadron."

Orville's heart was pounding. He wanted desperately to ask Sophia how they had been catapulted back to this moment. Why they were experiencing for a second time their walk to Pridie's, and why Amanda was completely oblivious to this astonishing turn of events?

Amanda grinned.

"He does, and he loves telling them. I know he'd love to hear your stories too. He was so amazed when I

41

told him you and Orville had been to Elysian."

"Here we are!"

Sophia swung the front door open and they stepped into the delicious aroma of baked bread, the sounds of clinking silverware and friendly conversation filling the room.

Orville was feeling sick. "Pretty busy, they must have really good food here."

A tall mouse wearing a starched white apron stepped over to the three friends.

"Welcome to Pridie's Bake Shop. We have one table open, next to the window, a lovely view of the falling snow."

"Sounds great. I'm starving."

Moments later they were seated at the table. Orville scanned the room.

"There's Madam Beasley. Look at her crazy hat... it's covered with bright flowers, not feathers."

Sophia's mind was spinning wildly.

"Orville, be nice. I like her hat. It does have a lot of bright flowers on it, but it suits her well. I wonder who she's having lunch with? I don't recognize him."

"I like his coat. Rugged looking. He could be an adventurer."

The waiter smiled, presenting the menus. "Our special today is tomato soup and a grilled cheese sandwich. Perfect for a cold winter's day like today. Let me know when you're ready to order."

"Their special today is tomato soup and a grilled cheese sandwich." Orville looked at Sophia, raising his eyebrows.

"I heard. Your mum said she had the mushroom stew and a grilled cucumber sandwich when she was here."

"Right, that's what I thought she said. Sounds yummy."

Orville opened the menu, going straight to the dessert section.

"They have snapberry pie. I guess I'll get the special and some snapberry pie."

Amanda said, "I'm going to get the special too, it sounds delicious. Sophia, tell me about your school. When do you graduate?"

Sophia tried to focus on the conversation. "This spring, I'm really excited about it. I'm going to be working with Mirus Mouse after I graduate. He's going to teach me about the mechanics of the ancient flying machines. He's rebuilding the old blinker ship we found on Varmoran."

Orville's eyes lit up. "Whoa, blinker ships go really fast."

"I know. I'm not sure I want to fly that fast. I like cruising along in the Dragonfly. We can chat and enjoy the scenery."

Amanda nodded. "Captain Patcher and I go flying all the time. It's so much fun. Did I tell you he asked me to marry him?"

Chapter 7

Orville's Dilemma

Orville and Sophia were walking along the snowy lane that led to Orville's house.

"Why didn't Amanda notice what happened? No one else in the bake shop noticed either. Why were we the only ones who saw the wave?"

Sophia shook her head. "I don't know. Something very strange is going on here. It's clear the wave sent us back in time, but I don't understand how or why."

"What about the pocket watch I shaped, the one that runs backwards? Do you think that could have caused it?"

"I don't think so, you didn't have the watch with you when it happened. I think your inner self probably knew this was going to happen, and the watch was a message about time flowing backwards."

"It's the same wave that was in my dream, but it didn't send us to that crazy planet." Orville stopped in his tracks.

Sophia turned. "What is it? What's wrong?"

"I just remembered something. The other morning I was walking down the hallway to the kitchen, closed my eyes, and all of a sudden I was back in my bedroom. I thought I'd just been dreaming. I think one of those weird waves hit me, sent me back in time."

"Orville, if that's true it means the wave that hit us at Pridie's was not an isolated incident. If it happened twice it can happen again. This is bad."

"And the waves are getting stronger. Who knows how far back it will send us next time."

"You saw how little things changed on our second trip to Pridie's. The daily special was different, and so was Madam Beasley's hat."

"We must have done something that changed the course of events."

"I just had a scary thought. Suppose a wave sent Muridaan Falls back a hundred years, to before we were born?"

"What would happen to us?"

"I don't know, but it would not be good. We need to talk to someone, maybe Madam Molly. She might know about these time waves, what they are and what's causing them."

"And how to stop them."

Sophia slowed down, her eyes on the forest.

"Where's the sapling with the green leaves? I'm certain it has something to do with the time waves."

"Just up ahead. It's a fifteen minute hike into the forest."

Orville's boots were filled with snow by the time they reached the spot where he had found the sapling.

"So cold. The sapling is right here under the snow. I recognize that weird looking tree trunk."

He pushed forward and began sweeping away the snow.

"That's odd, maybe the heavy snow knocked it over."

Five minutes later Orville stopped digging.

"It's not here. The tree is gone."

"You're sure this is the right spot?"

"Yes, I'm certain. I marked the spruce tree with an X and I distinctly remember this weird trunk right behind it. This is the exact spot."

"How could a tree vanish?"

"I don't know. How would I know that?"

"Orville, don't get mad, but are you sure you didn't just have a dream about the tree? One that seemed real?"

"I didn't dream about it. I was here, and the little sapling with green leaves was here. I'm not loopy."

"Okay, let's head back to your house. There are a lot of curious things happening and we need to find some answers. We definitely need to visit Madam Molly."

"Let's ask Proto about the time waves. Maybe he'll know something."

The two best friends were unusually quiet on the long walk to Orville's house, each of them lost in their thoughts. Orville was beginning to doubt himself. Maybe Sophia was right, maybe he had just dreamed about the green sapling. Maybe he was going loopy.

"Here we are."

Orville swung the front door open and stepped into the entryway. The first thing he noticed were pieces of shredded rug scattered across the room. The second thing he noticed was Squeaky raking his claws across the wooden floorboards.

"SQUEAKY! STOP THAT!"

Sophia put her paw on Orville's arm.

"It's okay, it's just a wooden floor. We can fix it."

"I told Proto about this three times, and he promised he'd do something. I don't want to have to replace the whole floor. Where is Proto?"

"He's probably at your mum's making dinner."

Orville strode over to the damaged floor.

"The floor is ruined. Bad Squeaky! I told you not to do that!"

Squeaky barked, running circles around Orville.

"Orville, don't you think it's a little curious that's he's only damaged the floor in this one area? And it happens to form a perfect rectangle?"

Orville blinked.

"Creekers, you're right. That is kind of weird."

Squeaky let out a loud bark.

"I think he's trying to tell us something. Why would he be clawing a rectangular section of the floor?"

"Maybe there's something under it." Orville instantly wished he had not thought of that.

"I just want a normal house where I can relax and eat snapberry pie and not worry about crazy saplings with green leaves in the middle of winter, or secret trapdoors in my living room, or big prehistoric bird creatures dropping me into stewpots."

"I think we should exchange eternal friendship rings."

Orville froze.

"What?"

"I think we should exchange eternal friendship rings. We can use the Gang of Dragons rings. I want to do it."

Orville's face softened.

"So do I."

Sophia took Aislin's ring from her coat pocket, taking Orville's paw in hers.

"Are you ready?"

"Yes."

"Orville Mouse, you are my eternal friend and the mouse I cherish above all others, for now and forever."

She slid the ring onto his paw.

Orville took Sophia's paw.

"Sophia Mouse, you are my eternal friend and the mouse I cherish above all others, for now and forever."

A moment later Orville's ring was on Sophia's paw.

"It's official, we're eternal best friends. What do you think of that, Dread Pirate Orville?"

Orville put his arms around Sophia and kissed her.

"That's what I think."

Squeaky began barking wildly, tearing at the floor with his silver claws.

Orville grinned. "Okay, the Dread Pirate Orville is back. Let's find out what's under the floor."

Chapter 8

The Room

"I'm going to vaporize the damaged section of floor. There has to be some reason why Squeaky scratched a rectangle."

Sophia nodded. "I'll close the curtains so no one will see us."

Orville held out one paw, a six inch wide beam of pale green light moving across the floor, the boards vanishing.

Four minutes later he and Sophia stared silently into the dark rectangular opening. Squeaky gave a loud bark.

"Why are there stairs under the floor?"

"Maybe there's a basement like your mum and papa have."

"That wouldn't be so bad. It would give us a lot of extra storage space. Proto's room is crammed full of stuff from the Cube."

Orville peered down into the gloom.

"It's a little creepy."

"Maybe there's a treasure chest down there filled with gold and gems."

"I never thought of that." Orville grinned, shaping a glowing orb of light. He headed down the rickety wooden stairs, Sophia close behind him.

"This is kind of exciting. What do you think we'll find?"

"Cobwebs and spiders, maybe a few worms."

Sophia whacked his arm.

Orville stopped at the bottom of the stairs.

"Um, that's not a normal door. This is definitely not just an old basement."

Orville ran his paw across the gleaming pale green door.

"It's Morsennium, this was not built by mice."

A small violet light blinked on next to the door.

"I don't like this. We have no idea what's in there."

Sophia reached out and tapped the violet light. The door slid open, bright ceiling lights blinking on.

"Creekers, it's huge, at least fifty feet long and thirty feet wide." The two best friends entered the mysterious subterranean room.

"No giant centipedes or prehistoric birds."

Sophia strode over to a row of shelves spanning the length of the room.

"Some old books. They're Mintarian. That's a good clue."

"Look at this."

Orville held up a small red book.

"It's the same book you brought back from Elysian, *A Brief History of the Calamitous Metaphonium Haven Project*."

"This is where they brought the last Metaphonium. Someone went to a lot of trouble to bring it here."

"All the way from Mintari. How do you think they did it?"

"Look at the far wall."

Orville approached the blue wall.

"It's just like the spectral doorway we found on Varmoran, but it's not moving, it's frozen."

Sophia strolled over to a curved console in the corner of the room.

"The gateway control panel is burned out. Someone used a thermal device to melt it, probably to keep anyone from coming through."

"They really didn't want anyone to find the last Metaphonium."

"Nothing much else here. I think the sole purpose of this room was to hide the Metaphonium. It was probably here long before the house was. Whoever built the house must have found the room when they were digging the foundation."

"And they put the Metaphonium in their house, thinking it was a piano."

"Whoa."

"What is it?"

"This was on the shelf."

Orville held up a small perfectly round blue leaf.

"It's from the big tree next to the Blue Monks'

monastery."

"Do you think they had something to do with this? That maybe they built this room?"

"Nothing about the Blue Monks would surprise me."

"What now?"

"Now we have a shiny new basement made of indestructible Morsennium."

Orville grinned. "The only basement in town with its own spectral doorway."

"Its own non-functioning spectral doorway. It's probably just as well. We have no idea who or what could come through the gateway."

"That's a good point."

"Shhhh! Did you hear that?"

"I think Proto is home."

Orville heard heavy footsteps at the top of the stairs.

"Orville? Are you down there?"

"We're here, Proto! Squeaky found a hidden room under the house."

Proto hurried down the stairs.

"Good heavens, this is astonishing, the walls are constructed of Morsennium. What is this place?"

"We think either the Mintarians or the Blue Monks built this room to hide the last Metaphonium."

"Fascinating. This will do quite nicely. Quite nicely indeed."

"Do quite nicely for what?"

"For my room. It will be perfect, plenty of space for a small laboratory, and storage for all the items I brought from the Cube."

Orville looked at Sophia, his eyebrows raised.

Sophia laughed. "That's a wonderful idea, Proto. That will give us an extra bedroom upstairs."

"And you can move those black jars of pickled veggies down here."

"Excellent idea. You might want to step outside for a breath of fresh air while I'm moving them. Just in case."

"Right. Fresh air."

Proto gave a start. "Good heavens, is that a spectral door?"

He strode over to the far wall, eyeing the control panel.

"How unfortunate, someone has melted the controls. I was hoping I could create a doorway to the Cube. Perhaps one day I will do just that. Right now it's time for dinner. Sophia, would you care to join us?"

During dinner Sophia asked Proto about the mysterious time waves.

"Proto, have you ever heard of a wave that can transport someone back in time?"

"I'm all packed and ready to go. Just say the word."

"We're not going anywhere yet. I was just wondering if you've ever heard of waves like that?"

"There are gravitational waves traveling through the universe which affect the curvature of the space time continuum, but they would not alter time to such a great degree."

"How fast do they travel?"

"They are the result of cataclysmic astronomical

events, traveling at the speed of light, one hundred and eighty-six thousand miles per second."

"There's no time waves that travel slower than that?"

"None that I am aware of. Have you experienced such an event?"

"We were at Pridie's Bake Shop when a big weird wave rolled through it. When it was gone we were walking to the bake shop again. Amanda was there, but didn't realize she'd been sent back in time. She was saying the same things she had said the first time we walked there."

"Most curious. Logically, you should not have been aware of your temporal displacement. From your perspective, the first trip would never have happened, like those ghostly Anarkkian troopers we saw on Periculum who were unaware they were trapped in a time loop. Each time you experience the event you believe it to be the first time."

"That's what I was telling Orville. I don't understand why we were the only ones to remember it. No one else in the bake shop was aware of it."

"Why are you both wearing orange rings?"

Sophia smiled, holding her paw up for Proto to see. "Orville and I exchanged eternal friendship vows today."

"Do we all get rings since we're all friends?"

"Um… exchanging eternal friendship rings is something two mice do if they're probably going to get married."

"I see. I am quite good with mouselings, if the need arises. I have thousands of bedtime stories in my database, along with numerous volumes of scientific data relating to their care and feeding, and a rather stunning repertoire of charming lullabies."

"What?"

Sophia grinned.

"We don't really have any marriage plans yet, Proto. We're still thinking about it."

"Excellent. I'll paint the spare bedroom a soothing color, something to help a fussy mouseling drift off to sleepy land."

"Really, there's no rush, Proto. Sophia and I are going to blink up to the Symocan Institute for a visit with Madam Molly. We're going to ask her about the time waves."

"Wonderful, by the time you return I shall have your mouseling's bedroom all painted and be moved into my new subterranean abode. Have you decided on a name yet?"

Chapter 9

Madam Molly

Orville gave Sophia a sideways glance, doing his best to sound nonchalant, almost bored.

"Your school campus hasn't changed much since I was here last time, when you introduced me to Mortimer Mouse. Are you still friends with him? Do you see him very much?"

"He's in two of my classes. He has a girlfriend. I'm not going to run away with him."

"Huh? I wasn't worried about that, I was just asking about him. He seemed like a really nice mouse. A little too handsome, maybe, but sort of athletic."

"They're getting married as soon as he graduates."

Orville grinned. "How lovely, I'm so happy for them."

"You really are loopy. Let's go find Madam Molly. She should be in the observatory today. Wait till you see the big telescope they have. It's so amazing, a refractor with a thirty inch objective lens."

"That's nice. She's not going to read my mind, is she?"

"Don't make eye contact with her and you'll be fine."

"It must be weird to come from a world where everyone knows each other's thoughts."

"It might not be a bad thing. You'd realize that everyone else in the world has worries and fears just like you do, and everyone else experiences difficult and painful events. Everyone has to face the fires of life, no exceptions."

"That's true. I used to feel like I was the only one in the world who was afraid of things."

"Like me running away with handsome Mortimer Mouse?"

"Maybe just a little."

"You don't need to worry."

Orville took Sophia's paw.

"We should go find Madam Molly before some crazy wave sends us a billion years back in time."

The two best friends made their way across the bustling campus to a circular brick building capped with a gleaming silver dome.

"Lights are on inside."

Sophia eased the door open, not wanting to startle whoever was gazing through the telescope. When they stepped into the observatory they were met by an extraordinary sight. Madam Molly was having an animated conversation with a glowing green translucent apparition.

"Whoa, we should leave. She's talking to a ghost. Let's go. It's a ghost, Sophia. A ghost. Time to go."

Orville was turning to leave when Madam Molly called out, waving to the two mice.

"Aren't you supposed to be in Muridaan Falls?"

"I was, but I needed to ask you a question."

"That sounds interesting. Are you off on another adventure?"

Orville's heart was pounding. He was terrified of ghosts. He kept his distance from the glowing ghostly mouse, who was now looking at him. He was also being careful not to make eye contact with Madam Molly, remembering her green eyes with the swirling golden specks that could peer into his deepest thoughts and memories.

"This is my sister Eudora. Eudora, this is Sophia and her handsome young friend Orville. Sophia is a brilliant student of mine, and they are both accomplished Metaphysical Adventurers."

The ghostly Eudora waved, her voice wavering and hollow. "Lovely to meet you both. Molly, I'll contact you as soon as I know more."

Madam Molly's glowing green sister vanished.

Orville's voice was barely a whisper. "Your sister is a ghost?"

Sophia said, "Either a ghost or a practitioner of the Traveling Eye?"

"Precisely. She can project her consciousness into the universe, appearing as a spectral apparition. She is quite alive and solid back on our home planet."

"That's what Aislin Mouse was doing when she appeared in Muridaan Falls as a ghost mouse. She said the Shadow King taught her the Traveling Eye."

Madam Molly eyed her two young visitors.

"I could teach you the Traveling Eye. It wouldn't take long, and it would come in handy on your adventures."

Orville wrinkled his nose. "I'm not really sure I want to be a ghost. Suppose some creature ate my real body while I was out flying around the universe?"

Madam Molly gave an understanding smile.

"Perhaps another day. I'm sensing there's something different about both of you. Let me see if I can figure it out without reading your thoughts."

She studied them closely, then laughed.

"Your rings. You have become eternal friends. I'm not surprised, you make a lovely couple."

Sophia nodded, taking Orville's paw. "We've been best friends for a very long time."

Madam Molly gave a curious smile. "Indeed you have. Now, what is this burning question you have for me?"

"Have you ever heard of a wave traveling through the universe that can send you back in time?"

"A most interesting query. Let me think about that. There are gravitational waves traveling through the universe, but nothing of a magnitude that would so drastically warp the space time continuum."

"I've sort of forgotten what the space time continuum is. Is that space and time all mashed together?"

"Well said, that's exactly what it is. The three dimensions that make up our physical world are length, width, and height. These are combined with time as a fourth dimension. When you ask someone to meet you at a certain place and time, you are using all four dimensions, not just where, but also when. Why are you asking about time altering waves?"

"We were in a bake shop and a wave rolled through it, distorting everything and sending us fifteen minutes back in time."

Orville added, "I was hit by a smaller wave at home that sent me back about a minute."

The smile vanished from Madam Molly's face. "Which wave occurred first?"

"The one at home, the small one. The second wave was bigger."

"How fast was the wave traveling?"

"Not fast, about as fast as a mouse can run."

Madam Molly's eyes were sharp and focused. "Did anyone else realize they had been sent back in time?"

"No, that's the weird part. We were the only ones."

"This is quite concerning. A gravitational wave travels at the speed of light. I have never heard of a slow moving wave which alters time. As for how you could be aware you had been transported back in time, that is a mystery in itself. It is even more concerning that there were two waves, the second more powerful than the first."

"Why is that concerning?"

"Imagine tossing a large rock into a still pond and

watching the waves ripple outward. The first few waves are small, but these are followed by increasingly larger waves. I believe what you experienced were the first few waves caused by a cataclysmic cosmic event. Where and when this event occurred I have no idea. It is even possible these waves are crossing dimensions, that the initial event did not occur in our universe, but in a parallel world or a different dimension."

"What do we do? How can we stop it?"

"Sophia, you are from Quintari. Are you familiar with the Quintarian Science Guild?"

"Yes, Papa took me there when I was little. He had friends in the Guild."

"You and Orville need to go to Quintari as soon as you possibly can and speak to Madam Lybis, the Quintarian Science Guild Master, an old friend of mine. I will get a message to her that you are coming. If anyone can help you, it is Lybis. You need to hurry."

"We'll do it. Thank you so much for your help."

Orville and Sophia bid their farewells to Madam Molly and headed back across the campus.

"How do we get to Quintari?"

"Our best bet is the Thirteenth Monk. He can send us there through the Void."

"I still have the blue leaf he gave me. He said if we ever need to see him, just hold the leaf and think of him."

"Perfect. I have a few things I have to take care of here, but I'll blink back to Muridaan Falls tomorrow morning and we can use the blue leaf. Tell your mum and papa where we're going."

Orville blinked back to Muridaan Falls in three jumps, arriving in a flash of light behind his house.

He walked around to the front door and swung it open.

"Proto! I'm home!"

There was no reply. Orville strolled down the hall to Proto's room.

"Whoa, he painted the spare bedroom already. It is kind of a relaxing color, a pale green." Orville grinned, imagining Proto singing lullabies to a sleepy little mouseling.

"He must be downstairs in his new room."

Orville hurried to the living room and ran down the flight of stairs. He tapped the blinking violet light, but the door did not open.

"That's weird. Why would he lock it?"

Orville pounded on the door.

"Proto, I'm home! Sophia and I have to go to Quintari."

His knock was met with silence.

"Proto? Are you in there?"

Again there was no reply.

"He must have gone somewhere and locked the door. At least all those black jars of weird pickled veggies are in a safe place."

Orville had a quick dinner, then packed for the trip to Quintari. He set his backpack by the front door and headed for his room. Halfway across the living room stopped, something catching his eye. A small branch was protruding up from outside the front window. Attached to the branch were three spring green leaves.

"It's one of those trees! This is too creepy."

He ran to his room and slammed the door shut.

"I need to think. Why would one of those saplings be in my yard? What does it want? Wait, that's crazy, trees don't want anything, they're just trees. Maybe it's always been there and I just didn't notice it. I should check on it, make sure it's really there. It could just be my imagination. Maybe some green paper blew up against the window. I wish Proto was here. I'm going to blink outside and see what it is."

Orville flicked his wrist and vanished in a flash of light, appearing a split second later outside the front window.

"Whew, nothing here. That's a relief, I must have been imagining it."

When he turned to go he noticed a trail of disturbed snow running from the front gate to the spot where he had seen the three green leaves.

"Not good." He blinked back to his room.

"Creekers, I think I'm going loopy. I am definitely not telling Sophia a time traveling sapling from the future is stalking me."

Chapter 10

Proto's Gift

Hordes of angry green saplings were trying to break in through Orville's windows as he frantically nailed boards over them with a tiny hammer, only to have the nails bend, the boards fall off. He woke with a shriek, sitting up in his bed, his heart pounding.

"Whoa, that was bad. Those trees are giving me nightmares."

That was when he noticed the hammering sound, the sound from his dream.

"Creekers, where is that coming from? I don't like being home alone. I wish I knew where Proto was."

He scrambled out of bed, blinking up a powerful sphere of defense around him. With a flick of his wrist a small orb of light appeared, following behind him as he crept down the hallway to the living room.

"What in the world is making that noise?"

He stopped in the living room, his ears turning slowly.

"It's coming from below, from Proto's room. Oh, no, maybe something came through the spectral gateway! This is bad!"

He tiptoed down the stairs, alert for the slightest movement, coming to an abrupt halt when he saw the note taped to Proto's door.

DANGER! Keep Out!
Slight mishap with black jars of veggies.
Nothing to be alarmed about!
All is well.
– Proto

Orville put a paw to his forehead.

"Proto, why do you do the things you do?"

He crept back upstairs and crawled into bed.

The next morning he opened his eyes and let out a yelp. Proto was standing next to the bed staring down at him.

"What are you doing? Why are you staring at me? What's wrong?"

"I was waiting for you to wake up. I have a surprise for you and Sophia."

"Does it have anything to do with those black jars? I saw your note about a mishap. What happened?"

Proto gave his familiar staccato laugh.

"Ha ha ha ha! That note was a very clever ruse on my part to keep you out of my room. Quite a masterful bit of misdirection, I must say."

"I'm tired, just tell me what the surprise is."

"It's something you must see for yourself."

Orville climbed out of bed and threw on his clothes, trailing Proto into the living room. There was a flash of blue light and something grabbed his shoulder. He gave a yelp, spinning around to see Sophia.

"Sophia, you did it again! You blinked up behind me!"

"Sorry, I didn't mean to scare you."

"You don't look very sorry. And you didn't scare me."

Sophia grinned.

Proto turned around at the sound of Sophia's voice.

"Excellent, you're here. I have a very special surprise for both of you, a lovely housewarming gift, something I'm certain you will enjoy for many years to come."

"Proto, you didn't need to get us a housewarming gift. This is your house too." Sophia stepped over and gave him a warm hug.

Orville looked dubious. Proto's idea of a lovely gift was often quite baffling.

"It doesn't have anything to do with black jars of veggies, does it?"

Proto gave a booming laugh. "Ha ha ha ha! Good one, you make the best jokes. I'll have to remember that one. It doesn't have anything to do with black jars of veggies, does it?"

He turned and headed down the stairs.

"Both of you cover your eyes. Walk behind me and I'll tell you when to open them."

Orville closed his eyes, stepping into Proto's room.

"One moment, please."

He could hear Proto pushing heavy boxes aside.

"You may now open your eyes."

Sophia gave a shriek.

"You fixed it! You fixed the spectral door!"

What had been a solid wall at the end of the room was now a flowing blue river full of swirling ripples and eddies.

"Whoa! How did you fix it?"

"As it turns out, I had all the necessary parts to repair it in the sub basement of the Cube."

"Does it work?"

"Indeed it does. Last night I took a trip to Tectar and back."

"You went to Tectar? Seriously?"

"Just popped in and back, arriving right outside Aelric and Gemma's lovely farmhouse."

"Whoa, this is amazing. How does it work?"

Proto sat down at the control console, now glowing with an array of multicolored blinking lights.

"Using my Interworld Positioning System I determine the precise coordinates of the desired destination, entering them with these eight dials. The system then runs a safety check to make certain the location is a hospitable environment."

"So you can't accidentally visit the sun, or dark space."

"Precisely. It analyzes the atmosphere, temperature, and a host of other factors before allowing passage through the doorway."

"Can we try it?"

"Most certainly. Where would you like to go?"

"Somewhere warm and sunny."

Sophia laughed. "Good idea. How about the Isle of the Serpent? It's far enough south that it should be nice and warm, and it had lovely sandy beaches. We could go for a swim."

Orville frowned. "Lovely sandy beaches and gigantic monster crabs with huge pinchy claws."

Sophia snorted. "Don't be a nervous ninny. We only saw one giant crab."

"That's one giant crab too many. Fine. Let's go."

"I will enter the coordinates for the beach where we landed our Dragonfly."

Proto rotated the six dials to the proper positions, watching as a rapidly blinking yellow light turned violet.

"When the light turns violet it is safe to pass through. On the other side of the gateway you'll find the Isle of the Serpent. The holoscreen says the weather there is warm and sunny."

"I'm going to make sure it's not warm and sunny with a chance of giant crabs." Orville tentatively poked his paw through the rippling blue wall.

"I don't even feel it."

He poked his head through, then pulled it out again with a wide grin.

"It's the Isle of the Serpent, and not a giant crab in sight!"

He stepped through, followed a moment later by Sophia.

"This is marvelous, I'd forgotten how lovely it is here. Look at the white sand and the blue green sea, the soft puffy clouds."

"Lots of seashells. I should bring back a few for Mum."

Sophia slipped off her shoes and stepped into the water, the waves lapping over her feet.

"The water's warm."

"No snow and ice."

"I can't believe we have our own private spectral gateway."

"And our own Metaphonium. The universe must want us to have a lot of adventures. Hey, I just thought of something, we don't need to bother the Thirteenth Monk, we can travel to Quintari through our own spectral doorway."

"Good idea, it will save us a trip to Periculum."

Orville flopped down in the warm sand.

"And give us time to enjoy this warm weather. I don't want to go back to all that ice and snow."

Sophia smiled, sitting down next to him.

"I like the way you think, Orville Mouse."

She leaned against him, resting her head on his shoulder.

Chapter 11

Mira

"I feel kind of silly wearing this shiny silver suit. It looks like I'm wearing a Rabbiton costume."

"It's what everyone is wearing on Quintari. I don't want mice staring at me because I'm wearing old fashioned clothes."

"The only reason they'll be staring at you is because you're so beautiful."

Sophia smiled. "Thanks for saying that. I don't know if you saw it in my memories, but I didn't pay much attention to my appearance when I was growing up. I spent most of my time studying instead of worrying about my clothes and fur. Above all else, I wanted to understand the world we live in. Sometimes I would overhear other mouselings laughing, making fun of my clothes. I understood they were the ones afraid of being different, but it still hurt. You're the first mouse who ever told me I was beautiful."

"They were probably too scared to tell you, afraid

you'd vaporize them."

Sophia snorted. "Maybe. Are you ready for Quintari? The gateway will open to a park on the outskirts of the city. I didn't want to pop out of a spectral doorway in the middle of Mira."

"What's Mira?"

"It's where the Quintarian Science Guild Headquarters is located, and close to where I grew up."

"It's a big city?"

"About seven million mice live there."

"Whoa. That sounds a bit scary, easy to get lost."

"We'll be fine. I know my way around the city. We can take Airpods everywhere. It's easy."

"You're sure I don't look weird in this crazy silver suit?"

"You look like a native Miranite, you'll fit right in."

Orville slung his pack onto his shoulder.

"Ready when you are, Captain Sophia."

Proto handed Sophia a small black disc.

"This is a voice activated control for the spectral gateway cloaking system. I've linked it to your voice and to Orville's voice. If you say *cloak on* the gateway will become invisible, say *cloak off* and it will reappear. When you're ready to return just step through and you'll be back here."

"Sounds easy enough. Let's go."

Sophia and Orville held paws as they stepped through the rippling blue wall into Quintari.

Orville's jaw dropped when he saw the city's spectacular skyline.

"Creekers, look at those cloudscrapers! There's hundreds of them. I can't believe how big the city is, how tall the buildings are."

Sophia eyed the lush green park surrounding them.

"You'll get used to it. If Miranites came to Muridaan Falls they'd be gawking at the mountains the same way you're gawking at the cloudscrapers."

"I'm not gawking at them, I was just commenting on how many there are and how tall they are. That's not the same as gawking."

"If you say so, little country mouse."

"Very funny. What do we do now?"

"See the sign with the silhouette of a mouse in a green circle? That means there's an Airpod stop ahead. We go down that pathway."

Sophia pulled the cloak activator from her pocket.

"Cloak on."

The shimmering blue gateway vanished.

"It's still there, right?"

"Right, but it's deactivated so no one will accidentally step through it."

As they made their way down the curving stone pathway Orville spotted numerous Quintarians out for an afternoon stroll, some with little mouselings in tow.

"You were right, they all wear these crazy silver suits. I don't feel so silly now."

Orville smiled at a young couple pushing a small mouseling in a cart. "Lovely day. You have such a cute little mouseling."

They gave Orville a startled look and hurried past.

"Orville, don't talk to mice you don't know. It makes them nervous."

"I was just being friendly."

"I know you were, but this is not Muridaan Falls."

"I know it's not. I was just trying to be nice."

"Life is different in the city, that's just the way it is. We'll grab an Airpod up ahead and take a quick tour of the city so you can see it."

"Are Airpods expensive? I didn't bring a lot of silvers."

"They're free, city taxes pay for them."

"I like free."

Sophia walked over to a ten foot wide holographic image of the city encircled by green pedestals.

"Locate Science Guild Headquarters."

One of the buildings on the far side of the holographic map glowed brightly.

"That's where we have to go, but I want you to see the city first."

Sophia pressed her paw to one of the pedestals until it began blinking.

"Half hour aerial tour of the city, final destination Science Guild Headquarters."

"What now?"

"We wait for our Airpod."

Seconds later a transparent sphere shot down from the sky, hovering silently in front of Sophia.

"Is that ours?"

"Yes, the pedestal scanned my face so the Airpod would recognize me."

"That's a little spooky."

Sophia tapped the side of the hovering Airpod. The door opened and she stepped inside, taking a seat on the red padded circular bench that wrapped around the interior of the pod. Orville sat down next to her.

"It flies by itself? We don't have to steer it?"

"We just tell it where we want to go."

Sophia called out, "Airpod go."

The craft shot up into the sky, the gleaming city of Mira spreading out below them.

"This is amazing! Those cloudscrapers are so tall, taller than the one in Cathne where Puella the Wise One lived."

"Much taller. They're supported by their internal framework, but also by powerful energy fields. There's no limit to how tall they can make them."

"I can't believe you grew up here. You must have laughed at Muridaan Falls when you saw it."

"I thought it was beautiful. A cozy little fishing village nestled between the mountains and the sea, full of friendly mice who say hello, even if they don't know you. Living in a big city can be really lonely sometimes."

"Where did you live?"

Sophia pointed to the east.

"There are thousands of huge housing complexes surrounding the city. I lived in one of them. Very few mice can afford to live in the city."

The Airpod was flying at an altitude of four thousand feet, weaving its way through the maze of gleaming cloudscrapers. As they passed close to one, Orville could see rooms filled with mice seated at desks.

"It must take a long time to get to work every day. I just walk twenty minutes and I'm there."

"It does, even with Airpods. It's a different world than Muridaan Falls."

Orville spent the next half hour gazing silently at the majestic cloudscrapers, streams of Airpods flashing through the sky in all directions.

"There's so many Airpods, why don't they crash into each other?"

"They're all linked together and have sensors to detect other Airpods. It's impossible for them to collide."

"The big city makes me feel kind of small."

"That's another reason why I like Muridaan Falls. I feel special when I'm there, not just another mouse in a crowd of millions."

A melodious voice filled the cabin.

"Your tour is complete, now approaching your final destination, Quintarian Science Guild Headquarters. Arrival time one minute."

Orville peered down at the monolithic octagonal black building glinting in the afternoon sun.

"A lot of mice must work there."

"Many thousands of them, it's the center for all scientific research on Quintari, and it's where you'll find the most brilliant minds on the planet."

"I hope they know what's causing these crazy time

waves."

"And how to stop them."

"Arriving at your destination. Welcome to the Quintarian Science Guild Headquarters. Thank you for using the Quintarian Airpod Transport System. Mind the gap."

The Airpod landed with a gentle bump on a broad octagonal platform floating above the Science Guild, dozens of other Airpods coming and going.

"Whoa, what is that thing?"

Orville was gaping at a twelve foot tall dull black automaton wearing a gleaming silver helmet topped with a rotating blue cube. Two pale blue cylinders were attached to its back, a flexible metallic hose running from the cylinders into the creature's neck.

"It's one of their guards. Just do what it says and don't make any jokes. Let me do the talking. Don't forget, no jokes."

"It's coming over here. It's looking at me."

"Relax. Don't say anything funny."

The enormous creature was unlike any Orville had seen before, approaching in a curiously fluid and graceful manner. It stopped in front of them, its three eyes glowing brightly.

"You arrived at Mira Park 9, Sector 6, through an unregistered and unauthorized vintage Model R2 Z600 Mintarian Spectral Interstellar Gateway. State the purpose of your visit."

Orville's jaw dropped. "How did you know we–"

Sophia kicked his leg. "We are Metaphysical Adventurers from Earth on a mission of the utmost importance, here to speak with Science Guild Master Lybis. She is expecting us."

The creature's eyes glowed again, the cube on its head spinning rapidly.

"You are Sophia Mouse, born on Quintari, daughter of Metaphysical Adventurer Rowland Mouse, deceased, daughter of Emma Mouse, deceased."

"Yes."

"You are Orville Wellington Mouse of Earth, friend of Metaphysical Adventurer Sophia Mouse, friend of Metaphysical Adventurer Madam Molly."

"Yes."

"Scans complete. Stand in the center of the yellow circle. Do not move."

Orville and Sophia strode over to the six foot wide yellow disc, stepping onto it.

Before Orville could ask what the disc was for, there was a flash of light and the two adventurers found themselves in a tastefully decorated waiting room furnished with comfortable couches and stuffed chairs. A smiling mouse wearing a gold metallic suit stood before them, holding a tray of brightly colored bottles and a selection of square cookies.

"Welcome to the Quintarian Science Guild. Would you care for a drink or a snack? Madam Lybis will be with you shortly."

Chapter 12

Madam Lybis

"Guild Master Lybis will see you now."

The mouse in the gleaming gold suit motioned for Orville and Sophia to follow her. A section of the wall rippled, revealing a brightly lit office behind it. The two best friends stepped into the room.

Madam Lybis wore the traditional white cloak of science, its color symbolizing the purity of truth. She was seated at a massive antique wooden desk piled with stacks of old books. She said nothing, studying her two visitors with a penetrating gaze. She pointed mutely to the two chairs in front of her desk.

Her silence was making Orville extremely nervous. Why did she keep staring at them like that?

Finally she spoke.

"Madam Molly said you would be coming. I knew your father. He was a gentle mouse and one of the bravest Metaphysical Adventurers I have ever known.

You have his eyes. I am sensing strongly that you possess many of his admirable qualities."

"You knew Papa?"

"I worked with him on numerous occasions during the reign of Guild Master Manghar and Counselor Pravus, before the death of my dear husband Vahnar, before I became Guild Master."

"I heard Manghar and Pravus were not well liked."

"An understatement. Thanks to Bartholomew and Clara Rabbit, Manghar and Pravus are permanent residents of Umbra Prison."

"You know Bartholomew and Clara Rabbit?"

"I accompanied them on their trip to Thaumatar. Tell me why you are here."

"Orville and I were hit by two time waves. The first was small, sending Orville a minute or two back in time. The second was larger, sending both of us fifteen minutes back in time."

Guild Master Lybis' expression did not change.

"We told Madam Molly and she said it was important that the waves were increasing in size. She thought they might be from some cataclysmic event, either in this dimension or another."

"How did you know you had been sent back in time?"

"We could both remember the previous timeline, but no one else could."

"I see."

Lybis rose up from her desk and stepped over to the wall of windows, gazing at the cloudscrapers silhouetted against a clear blue sky.

Orville looked over at Sophia, raising his eyebrows.

Finally Guild Master Lybis took her seat again, studying her two guests. She tapped a small blue disc on her desk.

"Ferus."

"I'm sorry, Guild Master Lybis, I don't know what that means."

Lybis held up her paw. There was a blink of green light and a thin book appeared in front of her. The book was well worn, clearly from a bygone age.

"This is an ancient text referencing a catastrophic event which occurred on a planet called Ferus almost four hundred thousand years ago. According to the Thaumatarians, this event created something called the Great Thaumatarian Time Wave."

"Is that what we saw?"

"Almost forty years ago our astronomers realized a particular galaxy was not where it should be. After some analysis it was determined it was positioned as it would have been five thousand years earlier. That was the clue which led us to this ancient Thaumatarian text."

"Whoa, that must be valuable, really rare."

"This is not the original book. Such irreplaceable volumes are stored securely within our time vaults. This is a duplicate world translation created by a four dimensional synthetic replicator."

Orville had no idea what that was, but he wished he had one.

"The book states there was a massive tear in the tenth dimension which released unfathomable amounts of energy into our universe, causing an explosion of such magnitude that it sent out a titanic, but highly focused and abnormally slow time wave. Some believe it is traveling simultaneously through multiple dimensions, a hypothesis to explain its remarkably diminished velocity. There is also an ancient star map marking the location of Ferus at the time of the explosion. If what you experienced was in fact the first few ripples of the Great Thaumatarian Time Wave, then your galaxy is in grave peril. When the main wave hits, you will be sent five thousand years back in time. You will have never existed."

Sophia's eyes were wide. "What can we do? How can we stop it?"

Guild Master Lybis shook her head.

"I'm not aware of any technology capable of stopping such a force as that. I will speak with our best astrophysicists, and once I hear what they say I'll contact Madam Molly. I'm sorry I don't have more encouraging news. The only way to save the inhabitants of your world is to move them outside the focused path of the time wave, clearly a daunting task given the obvious time constraints."

"Thank you for your help, Guild Master Lybis. We'll keep in close touch with Madam Molly."

"If this is the Great Thaumatarian Time Wave, there will be three or four small waves before the main one hits. You don't want to be on Earth when that happens.

Take this book with you and study it. Perhaps within its pages you will find something to help you."

As Orville and Sophia turned to leave, Guild Master Lybis stood up.

"Sophia, if the time wave proves to be unstoppable, please know there is a place here on Quintari for you and Orville and as many others as you wish to bring. The wave won't affect us here. Don't wait too long to make your decision."

Chapter 13

The Visitor

Two days had passed with no word from Madam Molly about the Great Thaumatarian Time Wave. Orville was making his way home through another ferocious blizzard, holding up one paw to block the pelting snow.

"Creekers, this wind is brutal, so cold. I can't remember a winter this bad. As soon as I get home I'm popping through the spectral doorway to a warm sandy beach on the Isle of the Serpent, and this time I'm bringing my swimming trunks. And a bottle of giant crab repellant."

Orville snorted at his giant crab joke. He'd try it on Sophia, she'd think it was funny. Thoughts of Sophia vanished when he glanced into the dark forest and saw two small green leaves protruding from a windblown snowdrift.

"Not another one! Why am I always alone when I see these crazy trees?"

He hesitated for a moment, then pulled his woolen cap down and tightened his scarf, stepping into the chest deep snow of the forest.

"This time I'm getting a leaf. I wish I had my snowshoes. Hard to see, but it was near those two crooked spruce trees, about fifty feet straight in."

Orville was panting heavily when he reached the leafy green sapling. More precisely, when he reached the spot where the leafy green sapling had once been.

"I can't believe this, it's not here! I'm going loopy, I know I am."

It was not the howling north wind responsible for Orville's sudden chill, it was a trail of disturbed snow running off into the shadowy woods, a trail beginning where the green sapling had once been.

Orville closed his eyes, his inner voice filling his thoughts.

"Things are seldom as they appear to be. All events are connected, all containing a deeper truth, this truth unseen by many."

"Great, now my inner voice is giving me advice I don't understand. What does that even mean? Can't you just tell me if these goofy trees are real?"

The only sound was the wind roaring through the towering spruce trees.

Orville pursed his lips, studying the snow where the sapling had been, poking at it with his paw.

"Okay, I'll use logic, just like Sophia would. First, there is definitely a trail going from this spot into the woods. I'm not dreaming this, I'm not imagining it.

Something made this trail, and it's not like any track I've ever seen before. There are no footprints, the snow is just pushed around like… like something pushed it around."

Orville gave a long sigh. He was definitely going to need Sophia's help to solve this puzzle.

When he got home he found Sophia seated on the couch reading the book given to them by Guild Master Lybis, Squeaky snuggled up next to her. He could hear Proto rattling pots and pans in the kitchen.

Sophia looked up from her book.

"The storm must be getting worse, it took you a long time to get home from work."

"I saw another one of those green saplings in the forest."

"I want to go see it."

"By the time I got there it was gone. It left a trail leading deeper into the woods. The same thing happened a few days ago. I saw green leaves pressing up against the living room window. When I blinked outside the tree was gone, but there was a trail in the snow just like the one I saw in the woods."

"You're absolutely certain you're not imagining this?"

"I'm certain. The trail it left was real."

"You're telling me these trees can walk? Is that what you're saying?"

"I guess so. I know it sounds loopy."

Sophia sat up straight.

"Orville, it's not loopy at all! It's just like the trees

85

on Tectar! Copo called them the Great Walkers, and said they came from the jungles of Athne in southern Thaumatar."

"You're right! Maybe we accidentally brought some seeds back with us."

"That would explain why it's a young sapling. What it doesn't explain is why it has green leaves in the middle of winter."

"Maybe the Great Walkers don't lose their leaves."

"That's possible. We need to catch one and examine it."

Proto strode in from the kitchen bearing a tray of freshly baked cookies.

"Catch one of what? Not a talking lizard?"

"What? Why would you say that?"

Proto's eyes darted nervously around the room.

"I was just making a humorous joke, a whimsical thought that popped into my head, nothing more. Ha ha ha ha! Talking lizards? Quite preposterous! Would you care for a delicious freshly baked cookie before we head over to Mum's?"

"Oh, right, I forgot. We're having dinner with them tonight. I'm going to tell them about the Thaumatarian Time Wave."

"And tell them we can move to Quintari."

"I don't know if they'll want to go. This is their home."

"They don't have to leave their friends behind. The whole town can evacuate to Quintari through our spectral door."

"I forgot about that. Good idea."

Orville's mum and papa listened intently as he re-counted their experience at Pridie's Bake Shop, the visit to Madam Molly, and Guild Master Lybis' revelation about the Great Thaumatarian Time Wave. He also told them about her offer of a safe haven on Quintari.

When he was done, Papa looked at Mum.

"We'll move to Quintari if we have to. It doesn't matter where we live as long as we're all together. I don't want to alarm the village just yet, but if any more of these time waves hit Muridaan Falls we'll have to tell them. We'll need to have an evacuation plan in place. I'll talk to Master Marloh. He can inform the Metaphysical Adventurers and the Shapers Guild. They can create spectral doorways to Quintari at a moment's notice. We'll need maps detailing the evacuation points."

Mum nodded. "I can tell all my friends. Word will spread quickly."

"I'm guessing the Thirteenth Monk already knows about this, but I'll send him a cloud anyway, just in case."

"It won't be so different on Quintari. There are lots of fishing villages just like Muridaan Falls along the coastlines."

Mum raised her paw. "I'm sorry, Sophia, but I think I heard someone at the front door. Orville, could you run check? Madam Beasley said she might be stopping by this evening."

"Sure."

Orville hopped up and headed for the door. He liked Madam Beasley, especially after he found out she was running a dream bed and breakfast on Elysian. Maybe she'd be wearing her crazy hat with all the brightly colored feathers.

When he swung the front door open, the grin on his face evaporated. Their visitor was most definitely not Madam Beasley.

The fork Orville had been holding clattered to the floor.

"Unhh."

Standing on the front porch was a three foot tall sapling, its bright green leaves rustling in the brisk wintry north wind.

Chapter 14

ROMDAD

Orville gaped at the sapling, uncertain whether to turn and run or grab it before it could escape.

"Orville! If it's Madam Beasley, please invite her in."

Orville croaked, "It's not Madam Beasley."

The sapling inched forward.

Orville inched backward.

"What are you? What do you want?"

Orville had intended these questions to be rhetorical, ones for which he was not expecting a reply.

Half a dozen leaves on the sapling vibrated rapidly.

"I am here to speak with you and Sophia."

Orville was suddenly very dizzy, a hot wave rolling up through his body.

The sapling rustled again. "You're not going to faint, are you?"

Orville's dizziness vanished.

"What? Of course not, I was just… um…"

"Are you going to invite me in?"

Orville backed away from the door, motioning for the sapling to enter. Using its roots like so many legs, it shuffled into the house, shaking the snow off its leaves and branches.

"Orville, who is it?"

"Um, I think you should all come out here."

Sophia was the first to step into the living room. The look on her face was one Orville would never forget.

Mum and Papa stopped in their tracks.

"Orville, why is there a tree in our house?"

"I am here to speak with Orville and Sophia."

Other than a slight rustling of the sapling's leaves the room was deathly silent.

"Would you mind terribly if I sat on your chair? I've seen them through windows but never actually sat on one. They look quite inviting."

Four mice nodded.

Using its roots and branches the sapling clambered up onto the soft cushions.

"Very nice. I like it. Soft, not unlike a large pile of fallen leaves, but with an additional pleasant bouncy feel to it. Very comfortable."

"Everyone else can see him, right? Not just me?"

"Yes, we see him. There's a tree sitting on Mum's chair. A talking tree is in our house sitting on Mum's chair."

Orville turned to the tree, attempting a pleasant smile.

"Would you mind if I asked you a few questions?"

"Ask away."

"Are you a Great Walker from Thaumatar?"

"I am not."

"I see. What are you, exactly?"

"I am a ROMDAD."

"A ROMDAD?"

"Precisely."

"I'm not really familiar with that term. Is that some kind of tree?"

"I was created with the physical form of a tree, but I am not a tree, I am a ROMDAD."

"The thing is, I don't really know what a ROMDAD is."

"ROMDAD is an acronym for Remotely Operated Multiworld Data Assimilation Device. ROMDAD."

"Are you from… far away?"

"I was created on the Plane of Turris."

"Where is that?"

"Unfortunately, I have no definitive answer for you other than to say the Plane of Turris is located on the Plane of Turris."

"Right, that doesn't really help very much. Why are you here? What is your purpose on our planet?"

"My initial purpose, as referenced by my name, was to remotely assimilate data."

"What kind of data?"

"Every kind of data. The gently falling snow, the whistling wind, warm sunshine, grass, leaves, the sound of birds chirping, squirrels chattering as they gather acorns, rain spattering on the forest floor, clouds drifting across a blue sky, a mouse humming to himself as he walks to work, pine cones falling, smoke from a chimney, the smell of fresh blossoms in–"

"Okay, that's good, I think I've got it, you're here to observe this world and collect data. Who is this data for?"

"You have asked the first of two questions I have been waiting for. If you would all take a seat I will answer it to the best of my ability."

The tree leaned back in the chair, spreading its branches out, adjusting its leaves.

"In the beginning there was only light. Then came the clouds, the trees, and the wind. Snow fell, then it was gone, lush green leaves appeared, small creatures scurried about, flowers bloomed. The world was one, there were no empty spaces, no divisions, no separations, only the fluid cosmic song. The leaves were part of the sky, the grass part of the trees, the creatures darting through the forest were the swirling clouds above. On and on went the song, snow transforming to grass, grass back to snow, skies blue to gray to white to black, stars blinking on, blinking off, over and over, a whirling eternal kaleidoscope of motion and color and sound.

"I began as a tickle, an uncertainty, something rustling deep beneath the cosmic symphony. A hundred winters passed, the curious sensation inching inexorably upward, like a bubble rising up from the ocean depths.

"When it surfaced, I realized I was watching this

92

world. I existed, I had a self, I was separate from all things, an observer, a witness. The world I had known shattered like glass into ten thousand jagged broken fragments. Trees were separate from the grass, leaves separate from the furry creatures, the sky separate from the falling snow. And on and on and on. I watched, and I knew I was watching.

"A hundred more winters passed. I realized I had branches, I had leaves, I could control the movement of my roots. I could walk, I could move about in this broken world. I had a body, separate from all other things.

"A curiosity grew within me. What was this place? Why was I here? Who was I? I stepped out of the forest onto a curving pathway, the first road I had ever encountered. Years passed. I stood silently as creatures walked past me, making curious sounds to each other. These beings were like me, separate from the world, observers of this mysterious place. The sounds they made were purposeful, a means of communicating their inner thoughts to each other.

'Lovely weather we're having.'

'I'm tired today.'

'The apples are marvelous this year.'

'I hope you're feeling well.'

'I love your sweater.'

'Have you seen my shovel anywhere?'

I watched and I listened. I learned to vibrate my leaves, mimicking the sounds spoken by these creatures who called themselves mice. I would talk to them, project my inner thoughts to them.

"My first words to a mouse were, 'What is this world?'. Rather than answering, the mouse screamed and ran away. I was terrified, retreating back to the safety of the deep forest, coming out only during the summer when I would go unnoticed, just another small tree. I stood outside homes, in backyards, next to shops, watching and listening, coming to know these mice as individual beings, all different and yet all the same."

The tree pointed a branch at Orville.

"I spent six summers in your yard. I was there when your papa vanished, there when he returned. I watched you discover the capricious shadows of your adventurers hat. I was there when you spoke to Ebenezer Mouse, there when you told Sophia you loved her. And I am here now because of the Great Thaumatarian Time Wave. I have been sent by the Watcher."

Chapter 15

Leaf

"Fascinating. A most remarkable tale."

Orville turned to see Proto standing behind him.

"The story of how you became aware of your self and your physical form is quite similar to my own experience after being created by the Elders."

Sophia nodded. "It's also what I experienced as a mouseling. The process of becoming aware of our self and of the world around us is essentially the same for all creatures."

Orville nodded. "It's kind of like waking up in the morning. First I'm all groggy and half in a dream, then I open my eyes and my memories all come back and I'm me again. It's sort of weird if you think about it. We do it every day."

Orville's papa had been silent up until now.

"Who is the Watcher?"

The sapling's leaves rustled softly.

"He is my creator. It is for him I gather the data. He watches, he listens, he guides me. He is the one who told me to speak with you."

"About the Great Thaumatarian Time Wave?"

"Yes."

"Do you know how to stop it?"

"The Watcher knows, but I am not permitted to speak of it. You must discover the solution on your own. That is the nature of your current world."

"I understand. In the event that we are able to determine the solution, will you help us to stop the Great Time Wave?"

"That is why I am here, but you must act quickly, before the main wave reaches your world."

Orville eyed the tree with growing curiosity.

"What do we call you? Do you have a name?"

"I am a ROMDAD."

"I know that, but do you have a name? We're all mice, but we each have our own personal name."

"I do not have another name. I have never had need for one."

"Proto didn't have a name either. He was a Prototype Model 10E Deluxe Rabbiton with the Expanded L7 Sincere Friendship Simulation Package. I called him Proto, short for prototype."

Proto smiled. "I think you would enjoy having your own name. I quite like mine. It makes me feel rather special, not just another Rabbiton."

"I will accept whatever name you choose to give me."

"I've never named a tree before. Let's see, the thing about you that stands out from other trees is… you have green leaves in the middle of winter. How about something short and simple, like Leaf? I remember reading about a famous explorer named Leaf. I think he discovered a continent, or maybe he sailed across an ocean. He might have invented something. Anyway, what do you think?"

The tree extended one of its branches, moving it slowly back and forth.

"Leaf. I am Leaf. Good afternoon, sir, my name is Leaf, it is a pleasure to meet you. I am called Leaf. My name? My friends call me Leaf. I am known as Leaf."

Sophia had the strangest feeling the tree was smiling.

"It is an excellent name and suits me well. From this moment on I shall be Leaf."

Proto clapped his silver hands together.

"You'll stay with us until we stop this dreadful Time Wave. There's plenty of room downstairs. Do you need a pot of soil to stand in, or a bowl of water?"

"I have no need for soil or water. I am powered by a micro-dimensional energy transfer system, not by the intake of external nutrients. My leaves are not used to convert sunlight to sugars, but hold within them my engineered intelligence and interdimensional communication and positioning systems."

"Excellent. You'll like Squeaky, he's a friendly little puppy."

"A puppy? This is somewhat concerning. On a number of occasions during my summers in Muridaan Falls I have had puppies approach me and pee on my trunk and roots, something I am not especially fond of."

"I quite understand. I can assure you that will not be

an issue. Squeaky is a RoboPup, an automaton who does not eat or drink, and consequently does not pee."

"Then I gratefully accept your offer."

An orange thought cloud flew out of Orville's ear to Sophia. She drew the cloud to her.

"Why is Proto inviting Leaf to live in our house?"

Sophia sent a cloud back to him.

"I think it's a wonderful idea. He probably gets lonely when you're at work, and Leaf has never had a friend. It will be good for both of them."

"I didn't think of that. He probably does get lonely."

Proto swung open the front door.

"Leaf, if you would care to follow me, I will give you a tour of your new home. I have several large comfy chairs in my room that should suit you quite well, and you can also help me with an experiment I'm–" Proto stopped in mid sentence, his eyes darting over to Orville. "That is to say, an experimental snapberry pie recipe I've been working on. Quite tasty, indeed." He smiled brightly at Orville.

"I'd better not see weird creatures creeping up the stairs, Proto. Like little talking lizards, for instance."

Proto and Leaf hurried outside, closing the door behind them.

Orville flopped down on the couch.

"I can tell you right now, those two are going to be trouble. Okay, how do we stop a massive time-altering wave from destroying our world?"

"How about shaping a powerful sphere of defense around Earth? Some kind of time shield?"

Eldon shook his head.

"There aren't enough shapers in the world to create a time shield that powerful, even if we could contact them all."

Sophia was pacing back and forth.

"Let's use logic. On the surface, it sounds like an impossible feat, but we know the Watcher has a solution. We also know he won't share it with us, we have to discover it on our own."

Orville stretched out on the couch and closed his eyes. A startling image appeared in his mind.

"Whoa, I just saw a huge asteroid crashing into Earth. What do you think it means?"

"It must be a clue from your inner self."

"Do you think an asteroid is going to hit us?"

Sophia jumped up from the couch. "That's it! That's exactly it!"

"What? We're getting hit by an asteroid?"

"Quiet! I'm thinking." Sophia rubbed her chin, her eyes sharp.

Orville shrugged. Ten minutes later his head was nodding.

"ORVILLE!"

Orville leaped up from the couch. "What? Am I late?"

"You reminded me of something I heard in an astronomy class on Quintari. Imagine an asteroid flying toward Earth at fifty thousand miles an hour. If the asteroid is a billion miles away, all it takes is a slight nudge to change its trajectory enough for it to miss

Earth. The closer it gets to Earth, the harder it is to prevent a collision. If the asteroid is a hundred miles away from Earth and traveling at fifty thousand miles an hour, it would be impossible to prevent a collision."

"That makes sense, but how does it help us? The first waves are already here. We can't–" Orville let out a gasp. "I've got it! I know how to stop it!"

"How?"

"Guild Master Lybis said the Time Wave was caused by a giant explosion on Ferus, right?"

"Right, the explosion was the result of a tear in the fabric of the tenth dimension. How does that help?"

"We go back in time to before the explosion and prevent it from happening."

"That's a good thought, but it's not possible. The explosion occurred over four hundred thousand years ago. We could ask the Thirteenth Monk about it, but the amount of energy needed to send a mouse that far back in time is incalculable."

"We don't need to ask the Thirteenth Monk, we just have to ask Leaf if that's the Watcher's solution. That's probably the second question he was waiting for. He said if we figure it out, he would help us."

"I guess it can't hurt to ask. I have to get back to school and I also want to talk to Madam Molly again. Send me a cloud and let me know what Leaf says."

After farewell hugs Sophia blinked backed to the Symocan Institute.

Orville's Mum frowned. "That doesn't sound safe, traveling that far back in time."

"It's probably not even the solution Leaf was talking about. But if it is, what other choice do we have? There's not much time left before the main wave hits. Even if we can evacuate everyone in Muridaan Falls to Quintari, what about the rest of the planet, and all the other planets in this galaxy?"

Eldon put his paw on Mum's shoulder.

"There's no point in worrying until we hear what Leaf says."

Orville blinked back to his living room and headed down the stairs. He could hear Proto's voice.

"I believe the Thaumatarians were the first ones to create such creatures. Open the black jar and put a spoonful of–"

"Proto! Leaf! I think we found the answer!"

Orville opened the door to Proto's room just in time to see him frantically throwing a white sheet over a long table.

"What's under the sheet?"

"This sheet? Nothing of any importance, just a tedious experiment I was discussing with my sagacious associate."

Orville eyed Leaf, who was carefully pulling the sheet over an exposed corner of the table.

"Right. Your sagacious associate."

Orville had no idea what sagacious meant.

Proto changed the subject. "You think you know how to stop the Great Thaumatarian Time Wave? This is wonderful news."

Leaf stepped in front of Proto.

"What are you proposing?"

"Could we travel back in time to Ferus and stop the explosion before it happens? If there's no tear in the tenth dimension, then there's no explosion and no Time Wave."

Leaf was silent for a moment, then spoke.

"The Watcher says you and Sophia are to visit him on the Plane of Turris."

"That's it? That's the right answer? We're going back in time to Ferus?"

An unfamiliar voice came from Leaf.

"Well done, Orville Wellington Mouse. You have taken the first step in a long and perilous journey. You have also opened a door which can never be closed again."

Chapter 16

Sophia's Question

Sophia blinked back from school after getting Orville's cloud saying their solution had been the correct one.

"Did the Watcher say how we're supposed to get to the Plane of Turris?"

"He said Leaf will take us there, but he didn't say how."

"Did he say anything else? Like how he's going to send us that far back in time?"

"Nothing about that, but he did say it's crucial that Leaf comes with us to the Plane of Turris. He didn't explain why."

"It's slightly worrisome that we don't know anything about Leaf other than what he's told us, and we know even less about the Watcher. We have no idea if he has some hidden agenda."

Orville suddenly remembered Proto's comment about Leaf being sagacious. If a word like that didn't impress Sophia, nothing would.

"I wouldn't worry about it, Leaf is very sagacious. Extremely sagacious."

Sophia nodded.

"You're right, there's probably nothing to worry about." She stepped closer to Orville, taking his paws in hers, their noses almost touching.

"Orville, now that we're alone, there's something I want to ask you, something I've wanted to ask you for a long time."

Orville's anxiety spiked, his paws suddenly cold, his legs wobbly. Sophia was going to ask him to marry her. Of course he would say yes, she was the mouse he cherished above all others, but why was she asking him now, the day before they were leaving for the Plane of Turris? There was no telling what perils they might face there. It didn't really seem like the–"

"Orville, are you there?"

"Yes, sorry, I was just thinking about... um... go ahead and ask me. I'm ready."

Sophia squeezed his paws tightly, gazing into his eyes.

"Orville Mouse, you are my eternal friend and the mouse I cherish above all others. Would you... would you say I am more sagacious or less sagacious than Leaf?"

Orville's insides turned to ice.

"What?"

"Would you say I am more sagacious or less sagacious than Leaf?"

"Oh, I thought you were going to… um… let's see, more or less sagacious than Leaf? I'd say you're about the same amount as Leaf. Just about the same."

"Really? The same amount? That's what you think of me?"

"Just joking, you're less sagacious than Leaf. No one wants to be too sagacious."

"Less? You're saying I'm less sagacious than Leaf?"

"Did I say less? I meant more. You're so much more sagacious than Leaf is. At least three or four times as sagacious."

Sophia burst out laughing.

"You are so funny, and you're also the sweetest mouse I know. Sagacious means perceptive and wise, a mouse with deep insight, a mouse who's curious, good at solving puzzles – a mouse just like you. You are a very sagacious mouse."

"Really? Thanks. I heard Proto say Leaf was sagacious, but I never got around to looking it up in the dictionary."

"Now you know what it means. What we don't know is how our sagacious friend Leaf is going to transport us to the Plane of Turris."

"Which is conveniently located on the Plane of Turris."

Sophia grinned. "That should help us find it."

Pounding footsteps sounded from the stairwell. Proto ran up into the living room, followed by Leaf and Squeaky.

Orville grinned at the sight of the three mismatched

friends. Sophia was right, it would be fun having Leaf live with them.

Leaf stepped in front of Proto. "We leave first thing in the morning. Proto said you have access to a flying machine? Something called a Dragonfly?"

Sophia nodded. "Mirus Mouse will have a Dragonfly waiting for us at his compound. He's a brilliant inventor, but a bit on the eccentric side. It might be best if you don't talk in front of him, if we pretend you're an ordinary sapling."

Proto added, "I have a pot of dirt you can stand in. I'll tell Mirus Sophia wanted a plant in her room at school. Just out of idle curiosity, do you happen to know anything about the kinds of creatures we'll be encountering on the Plane of Turris?"

"I have no memories of my time there. I had no awareness until long after I left. I don't even know what the Watcher looks like, or why he wants to see me. Perhaps he's angry with me. Perhaps I did something terribly wrong. Perhaps he wants to bring my existence to an end."

Proto's expression was suddenly dark.

"The Watcher is not going to harm you. Orville and Sophia are extraordinarily powerful shapers, and I am an indestructible Rabbiton possessing enormous strength and a particle vaporizing beam. We are also Metaphysical Adventurers, sworn to protect others from harm."

Leaf wrapped his branch around Proto's hand.

Sophia's face softened. "You'll be fine, Leaf. I sense

the Watcher does not mean to harm you. We should pack for our trip and get some sleep."

The following morning the four adventurers stepped out the front door into a frightful blizzard. Proto was carrying Leaf in a large clay pot.

Orville buttoned his coat and pulled his woolen cap down.

"Creekers, do you think we should fly in weather like this? Where are we going, anyway?"

Leaf's leaves were fluttering wildly in the blustery winter wind.

"The Watcher said we should travel due northwest for two hundred and ninety-four miles to Eagle River Valley, deep within the Chugach Mountains."

"The Plane of Turris is in Eagle River Valley? That doesn't make sense."

"The Watcher's portal is located in the valley."

"Is it a spectral door? Couldn't we go through the spectral door in Proto's room? Flying over the mountains in a blizzard seems kind of dangerous."

"It is nothing at all like a spectral door, and is the only way to reach the Plane of Turris."

Proto pushed forward through the deep snow, breaking trail for the others.

Orville stopped, shaking one foot. "I'm getting snow in my boots. Sophia, would you carry me?"

Sophia whacked Orville's arm.

"Quit complaining and enjoy the snow. The leaves are such a lovely shade of green this time of year."

Orville laughed. "That was actually kind of funny.

Did you steal that joke from Proto?"

By the time they reached Mirus Mouse's complex, the adventurers were covered with a layer of soft powdery snow, icicles dangling from their whiskers.

Proto pushed the main gate open.

"Did Mirus say which hangar?"

"The red one. He said he was winterizing the Dragonfly, that he'd installed a synthetic glass canopy."

"That should help a lot. We can blink up some thermal energy orbs if it gets too cold."

"Here we are." Sophia pushed open the side door of the red metal hangar.

Orville stepped inside, his eyes on the sparkling thirty foot long iridescent green flying ship resembling an enormous dragonfly. Mirus Mouse stood next to the craft, a large wrench in one paw.

"Hi Mirus! Do you think it's safe to fly a Dragonfly in this blizzard?"

Mirus Mouse was the most brilliant inventor in all of Symoca, but he was also exceedingly eccentric, affectionately called the Mad Mouse of Muridaan by the Metaphysical Adventurers. It was Mirus who had built Orville and Sophia's first flying ship, *The Glowbird.* He had also designed and built the four-winged duplonium powered Dragonfly.

"What's wrong with you, mouse? Is it safe to fly? Of course it's not safe! You're a co-pilot in the Dragonfly Squadron, soon to be a captain, from what Captain Patcher says, and you're worried about whether it's safe or not?"

"They're going to make me a captain?" Orville grinned at Sophia. "I'd be Captain Orville Mouse of the Dragonfly Squadron."

Sophia laughed. "Your papa may have mentioned something to me about that."

Orville climbed into the cockpit. "Let's get this bug in the air, Mirus!"

Mirus gave his great screeching bird laugh, stopping when he saw Proto.

"Why are you carrying a tree? What's wrong with you, Rabbiton?"

Proto gave his most gracious smile.

"Sophia thought a little greenery would be a lovely addition to her room at the Symocan Institute. We retrieved this sapling from my heated greenhouse, clearly explaining why a deciduous tree such as this one would have bright green leaves in the middle of winter. Nothing odd about this at all, I assure you."

Mirus stared at Proto for a long moment, then shook his head.

"Rabbitons. Never did understand them. Carry on."

The three adventurers hopped into the Dragonfly, closing the canopy. Orville gave the thumbs up sign and Mirus pushed the hangar doors open, a furious gust of wind blasting snow into the building.

Sophia flipped on the powerful duplonium motors.

"Engines on."

Orville pushed the left stick forward, the four translucent wings becoming a blur.

"Wings look good. Taking us up."

He inched the stick forward and the Dragonfly rose ten feet above the floor, hovering in position.

"Hold onto your seats! Here we go!"

Orville jammed the right stick forward and the Dragonfly shot out of the hangar at ninety miles an hour, pressing them back against their seats.

"Whoo hoo! Nice flying, Captain Orville!" Sophia raised both arms above her head.

The Dragonfly flashed across the open field, leaving clouds of swirling snow in its wake, then shot straight up into a stormy gray winter sky.

Chapter 17

The Portal

Leaf pressed against the glass canopy, gazing down at the white shroud of winter covering Muridaan Falls.

"I have never seen the town from this perspective. It is quite spellbinding in its beauty."

Proto studied the frozen landscape passing below them.

"I find it fascinating that potentially deadly environments such as arctic wastelands, seething volcanoes, or scorching deserts often possess an exquisite, almost ethereal beauty."

Orville nodded. "Some scary creatures are like that. They're amazing from a distance, but not so much when they're chomping you with their big teeth."

"Perhaps that's why I find such creatures to be so fascinating. Beauty does skulk about in the most unexpected places."

"I'm not sure beauty skulks. I wouldn't say beauty is skulking about on Sophia's face."

"Did you just say I was beautiful?"

"I'm taking us up above the weather. Hard to see

with all the snow."

The Dragonfly motors roared as the ship rocketed up through the churning gray clouds. Minutes later they emerged beneath a brilliant blue sky, the morning sun a shimmering golden orb floating serenely above an infinite ocean of clouds.

"Heading northwest, cruising at ninety miles an hour, altitude nine thousand feet. We'll be there in about three hours."

"We'll need to go higher to get over the western peaks. They top out at over twelve thousand feet."

"I can see them from here, poking up through the cloud cover."

Sophia flicked her wrist and a glowing red orb appeared, its radiant warmth filling the cabin.

"Thanks, that's better, nice and toasty now. It's cold up here. Leaf, what is the Plane of Turris like? Is it scary?"

"As I told Proto, I only know what the Watcher said, that you will more than likely have a difficult time adjusting to the new environment, that it could be quite unsettling."

"Unsettling? What does that mean?"

"I'm afraid that's all I know."

"I hope there's not creepy stuff like centipedes, or those big worms on Elysian. Those were really bad. Remember the things that looked like lemon pudding with legs?"

Sophia grinned. "You were shaking in your boots when you saw them."

"I wasn't scared, I was just confused about what they were."

"So confused that you screamed?"

Orville rolled his eyes. "Hey, Leaf, want to hear how I escaped from the hordes of vicious purple poisonous mutant flowers on Varmoran?"

Two hours later Sophia was snuggled up with a soft pillow from Proto's enormous backpack, her eyes half closed. Orville was in the midst of a highly embellished tale about their encounter with the dreaded Blue Pirates of Elysian.

"...then the pirate captain pulled out two razor sharp swords, staring me straight in the eye. I leaped in front of Sophia, blinking a cutlass into my paw, glaring at the pirate captain, calling him a scurvy dog, warning him he was about to–"

Sophia sat up straight, pointing to the rapidly approaching snow covered peaks.

"Eyes on the sky, Dread Pirate Orville!"

Orville pulled back on the stick.

"Sorry! Taking us up to fourteen thousand feet."

"We're almost there. The valley is on the other side of these mountains."

"Creekers, the wind is bad up here, steady at sixty-five miles an hour from the east. Hard to maintain our heading."

Sophia grabbed one of the sticks, pulling it hard to the right.

"That helps, thanks. Once we're over the range I'll take us down out of the wind." Orville eyed the

113

streaming ribbons of snow ripping across the jagged peaks.

"Looks so cold, glad I'm not standing down there in my underwear."

Proto gave a puzzled look. "Is that a light hearted humorous comment or are you truly afraid such an event might occur? It seems a highly improbable scenario."

"I'll throw him down there myself if he makes another underwear joke."

Proto gave his loud staccato laugh. "Ha ha ha ha! I was quite certain it was a joke. Good one! Ha ha ha ha! I'm glad I'm not standing down there in your underwear!"

Orville looked at Sophia, raising his eyebrows.

Sophia shook her head, scanning the snowy terrain below.

"That's Eagle River Valley. Take us down, Captain Orville!"

"Whoa, it must be thirty miles long. Leaf, do you know exactly where the Watcher's portal is?"

"He says it is in the central portion of the valley, buried beneath the snow. He is unable to give me a precise location."

"How big is it? What does it look like?"

"The Watcher says the portal is a flat gray disc, approximately six feet across."

"There's a hundred square miles of valley down there. How are we supposed to find a six foot disc buried under the snow?"

Proto scanned the sweeping terrain, his eyes glowing with a violet light.

"I have located the portal using my full spectrum electromagnetic wave sensors. It is emitting a powerful energy field, appearing to me as a bright orange light."

"Thanks, that saved us a lot of time. Hey, it's just like when Sophia and I were tracking the glowbirds with those weird goggles she has. I was afraid we'd have to get out the snow shovels. Which way do we go?"

"Head due east for approximately three miles."

Orville sent the Dragonfly streaking across the broad snowy valley toward the Watcher's mysterious hidden portal.

"Down there."

Proto pointed to a massive icy boulder protruding up from the snow. "The portal is on the right side of that big rock."

The ship slowed to a hover twenty feet above the ground, Orville unlatching the canopy and sliding it back, the icy wind and pelting snow blasting into the cockpit.

"Orville, what are you doing?"

"Hold us steady. Just getting out my magic snow shovel."

Sophia took the controls as Orville stood up, leaning out of the cockpit. A beam of orange light shot out from his paw, vaporizing a narrow strip of snow.

"The portal is twelve feet to the right."

Orville swept the orange beam back and forth across

the drifts, clearing the area.

"I see it!" Sophia pointed to a gray circular disk floating above the rocky ground.

Orville cleared a landing area for the Dragonfly and set the ship down. The four adventurers climbed out, Orville and Sophia shielding their eyes from the blowing snow.

"Whoa, this wind is bad. Leaf, how does the portal work?"

"The Watcher says to stand in the center of the portal for twenty seconds, then step off the disc."

"What does that do? How do we get to the Plane of Turris?"

"I am simply relaying the instructions given to me by the Watcher."

Proto stepped onto the portal. "I am indestructible, so I will go first."

He stood motionless on the gray disc for twenty seconds, then gave a thumbs up sign to Orville and stepped off the disk.

"He's gone! What happened to him?"

"The Watcher says Proto has arrived safely on the Plane of Turris."

Sophia hopped onto the portal. "Here we go!"

Twenty seconds later she stepped off, vanishing just as Proto had.

Leaf followed Sophia, leaving Orville alone next to the hovering disc. He stepped cautiously onto it.

"So far so good. Not too scary. I wonder what the Plane of Turris will be like?"

Twenty seconds later Orville stepped off the disc into the Plane of Turris. He let out a shriek at the sight of twenty-one other Orvilles surrounding him, each of them shrieking and pointing to the other twenty-one Orvilles. Near the crowd of terrified Orvilles were nineteen Sophias, twenty-two Leafs and fourteen Protos, all studying each other with wide eyes.

The Orvilles cried out, "What's happening? Why are there so many of me?"

The Sophias turned to the Orvilles. "Calm down, all of you. Leaf, what's going on here?"

"The Watcher wishes to inform you that the Plane of Turris is a five dimensional world where it is possible to exist simultaneously in many different locations."

The Orvilles cried out, "I'm everywhere all at once, all of my selves are looking at all of my other selves! Make it stop! I don't like this!"

The Sophias turned to the Leafs. "Ask the Watcher how we can be one self in one place."

"The Watcher says to close your eyes and focus on your inner self. When you are connected to your true self, slowly open your eyes."

The Orvilles and Sophias closed their eyes.

The Leafs and Protos watched as the crowd of Orvilles and Sophias began merging into one Orville and one Sophia.

Orville's eyes opened.

"They're gone! I'm me again."

Soon there was only one Proto and one Leaf.

Sophia grinned. "That was amazing! I was in nineteen different places at the same time, looking through the eyes of all nineteen Sophias."

"It was terrifying, not amazing. Hey, just imagine if I had to buy clothes for twenty-two Orvilles."

"You could have twenty-two jobs, though. Just imagine how rich you'd be."

Orville grinned, scanning their surroundings.

"What is this place? Why is the ground so smooth? There's no trees or rocks or clouds or grass or sun, it's just a big shiny flat gray floor that goes on forever."

"That's what a plane is, a horizontal flat surface."

"That would explain why they call it the Plane of Turris. Leaf, how big is the plane?"

"The Watcher says it extends infinitely in all directions. He also says if you walked far enough you would return to where you started."

"So it's a big sphere like Earth? You can walk around it and come back to the same spot?"

"No, it is something quite different. The Watcher says you are currently unable to understand the cause of this paradox."

"That's what I thought it was, one of those paradox things. So what do we do now? Where's the Watcher?"

"He says we must keep walking until we find his tower."

"Which direction? I don't see anything that looks like–" Orville stopped short. "Why is there an eggbeater lying on the ground?"

"The Watcher says to ask yourself why there should *not* be an eggbeater lying on the ground."

Orville put his paw over his eyes. "Creekers, this is worse than science class. Just tell me which way to go."

"The Watcher says it does not matter. We simply walk until we find the Watcher's Tower."

"I have scanned the area with my magnified vision but have located no structures other than the eggbeater on the ground next to Orville."

Orville groaned. He did not like the Plane of Turris.

Chapter 18

Being There

"Proto, how long have we been walking?"

"I am uncertain. My temporal calibration system is not functioning properly."

"It feels like we've been walking forever. Why do we keep finding weird objects lying on the ground? I don't even know what that last thing was. It looked like a silver mug with six arms."

"I have located a structure which bears some resemblance to a tower." Proto pointed to a dark speck in the distance.

"How far away is it?"

"To accurately determine the distance I would need to know the precise height of the tower, then use right triangle trigonometry and two angles of elevation. If I know the distance I can determine the height, and if I know the height I can determine the distance, but I must know one or the other. Clearly, if the tower is twenty miles tall, then relative to our current position it would appear as –"

Orville let out a groan. "Proto, are you saying you don't know how far away it is?"

Proto gave Orville a puzzled look.

"Is that a light hearted humorous comment? Would it be appropriate for me to laugh because you were repeating what I had just told you?"

"What? Nothing you said made any sense, it was all crazy science stuff."

"Ha ha ha ha! Good one, all crazy science stuff!"

Sophia snickered, taking Orville's paw.

"Let's go Captain Orville, I want to meet this Watcher. I have a lot of questions for him."

The four adventurers pressed on across the vast Plane of Turris.

"There's a pile of green metal spoons. I don't get this place. Why would there be green spoons lying on the ground?"

"It is possible that in an infinitely vast environment such as the Plane of Turris, atoms and molecules might randomly form what we would perceive to be recognizable objects. It could simply be that the Plane of Turris is a land of infinite possibility."

"So it's like Elysian? Our thoughts become real?"

"I do not believe so. The objects we are seeing were here before we arrived, randomly formed without intention."

Orville froze when a large pink bird stepped out of nothingness, strolling across the plane ten feet in front of them. The bird turned to the adventurers, politely nodding his hello before once again returning to nothingness.

"What was that? Where did he come from?"

"The Watcher would like to remind you that the Plane of Turris is a five dimensional world, quite different from the three dimensions plus time of your world."

Orville groaned when he saw the green spoons vanish.

"The spoons are gone, just like the pink bird. Hey, maybe it's like Castle Caligari, when the different worlds were overlapping. Maybe different dimensions overlap here, and objects from other dimensions are temporarily visible."

"The Watcher congratulates you on your astute deduction. Dimensions are not static, they are great ribbons and waves, constantly undulating and overlapping, often creating new universes in the process."

Orville grinned at Sophia. "You may call me Chief Master Scientist Orville."

Sophia gave Orville a dubious glance.

"We've been walking for a long time and the Tower isn't getting any closer."

Proto eyed the distant structure. "After giving it some thought, I believe we are utilizing the wrong set of physical laws in our attempt to reach the tower. We are using the physical laws of our world, not taking advantage of the added dimensions to be found in this world."

Sophia clapped her paw to her forehead.

"That's it, Proto! We can be in more than one place at the same time!"

"What do you mean? How does that help?"

"I'm going to try something." Sophia closed her eyes, slowing her breathing and connecting to her inner self. A moment later her eyes opened and she pointed ahead of them.

Orville gave a screech. Another Sophia was standing two hundred feet in front of them.

"There's two of you!"

"Exactly. Watch closely, I'm going to use the Sophia who's ahead of us to merge my two selves back into one."

The Sophia next to Orville vanished and the Sophia in the distance waved to them. "It worked!"

The three adventurers raced toward Sophia.

"How do we do it?"

"It's easy. Close your eyes, connect to your inner self and imagine being wherever you want to be. A second self will appear there, then you merge the two selves back into that self."

"So I should imagine myself standing in front of the Watcher's Tower?"

"Yes, we don't need to walk to the tower, we can just be there."

Orville grinned. "I'm starting to like this world. Easy on the feet."

"Okay, everyone close their eyes, connect to your inner self, and imagine you are standing in front of the Watcher's Tower."

"The Watcher says he is impressed. He is looking forward to meeting you."

Orville closed his eyes. When he opened them again he was standing in front of a thousand foot tall circular stone tower.

"Creekers!"

The four adventurers looked up at the dark and vaguely ominous structure.

"This is incredible. Hey, where do you think they got all the rocks to build the tower?"

"A good puzzle."

Leaf stepped hesitantly over to the tower's magnificently carved stone door. He tapped on it gently, looking back at the others. Sophia sensed he was terrified. She hurried over to him, taking one of his branches in her paw.

"Don't forget you have friends who will protect you. No one is going to harm you here. We will not allow it. You will be coming back to Muridaan Falls with us."

"Thank you for your kind words. I only wish I knew why the Watcher wanted me to accompany you on this adventure. It is the not knowing that worries me most of all."

"You should see Orville before we head out on an adventure. He's a nervous wreck."

"And despite his fears he forges ahead, facing these new and uncertain circumstances?"

"Yes, he's one of the bravest mice I know."

Orville's ears perked up. "Did you just say I'm one of the bravest mice you know?"

"Knock on the door, ninny."

Orville gave a cackling laugh, thumping on the great stone door with his fist.

"Hello? Anyone home? Orville the Brave is here to see the Watcher."

He jumped back when the door groaned open.

Proto peered inside, motioning for the others to follow him.

"Nothing dangerous, no dreadful scaly monstrosities baring their deadly fangs and claws."

Orville grinned. "How disappointing to come all this way and not get attacked by horrible hungry creatures."

"That is precisely what I was thinking. One would expect a magnificent tower such as this one to have legions of terrifying nightmarish beasts guarding it."

"So disappointing, nothing here but a few wooden tables and chairs. Looks like we go up the big circular stairway."

Orville headed toward the stairs, stopping in his tracks when a large glowing yellow translucent bird flew across the interior of the tower, disappearing through the outer wall.

"Creekers, they have ghost birds here."

"It was not a ghost bird, just a normal bird overlapping with this dimension."

"If it can fly through walls it's a ghost bird. I don't like ghosts and I don't like ghost birds."

"Let's get going, Orville the Brave. Don't forget why we're here. The Watcher is going to show us how to go back in time to stop the Great Thaumatarian Time

Wave."

"Good point." Orville headed up the stairs.

Proto stopped, his silver ears twitching.

"I hear footsteps descending from above."

Chapter 19

The Watcher

Orville wasn't sure what he expected the Watcher to look like, but it wasn't this. Taller than Proto, the gleaming snow white creature was garbed in a flowing black robe tied with a bright yellow sash. He had two arms, two legs, and an egg shaped head with two oversized almond shaped green eyes. Adding to his unnerving appearance was the absence of a mouth, nose and ears. Its form was strangely fluid, as though lacking an inner framework, its arms and legs changing length as it walked. Orville had a feeling if the creature ever relaxed it would turn into a white puddle with green eyes.

An enormous thought cloud floated out from the Watcher, enveloping the four adventurers.

"Greetings, Orville, Sophia, and Proto. I have watched you through the sensors of the ROMDAD you call Leaf, but it is a pleasure to see you in your native physical form."

Sophia bowed her head politely.

"It is our great pleasure to meet you, Watcher. Your kind assistance helped us adapt to this five dimensional world."

"I am quite certain such capable Metaphysical Adventurers as yourselves would have done very well without my kind assistance. That is one reason why I have agreed to assist you in preventing the Great Thaumatarian Time Wave."

Leaf hesitantly raised a branch.

"Great Watcher, forgive my intrusion, but may I ask why you wished me to accompany these brave adventurers to the Plane of Turris?"

The Watcher stared silently at Leaf, then spoke.

"Let us retire to a more comfortable setting. You must be weary from your long journey. Leaf, I will explain your presence here shortly. I assure you, you have nothing to fear."

The Watcher headed up the stairs, followed by his four curious guests.

Orville's eyes scanned the interior of the remarkable structure as they ascended the circular stairway. Over a hundred feet wide, the tower had fifty levels, each consisting of a round landing with six uniformly spaced arched wooden doors lining the outer wall. A thought cloud flashed from Orville to Sophia.

"What do you think is behind all these doors? Are you hearing those weird noises?"

"It sounds like machinery, but nothing I recognize."

Orville's legs were aching by the time they reached

the twenty-seventh level. He grabbed Sophia's arm, stopping her. One of the doors was partially opened, the interior of the room visible.

Sophia studied the curved metal shelves lined with thousands of black birds, all standing silently, their blinking yellow eyes focused on her and Orville.

"Creekers! What's with all the black birds? How creepy is that?"

Sophia sent a cloud back to Orville.

"It's not creepy at all. I think those are ROMDADs, created in the form of birds instead of saplings."

"Like the clockwork glowbirds."

"Exactly like that. The Watcher sees through their eyes."

"Why is he spying on all those worlds?"

"He must have his reasons. It looks like they create the ROMDADs here in the Watcher's Tower. That would explain the machine noises coming from the rooms."

Orville was out of breath when they reached the fiftieth level.

The Watcher swung open two ornate silver doors.

"Please come in and take a seat. Would anyone care for refreshments? Snapberry pie? Oatmeal cookies? Lemonade?"

"You have snapberry pie?"

"I am quite familiar with your dietary intake, having watched your daily activities through Leaf's sensory system."

Sophia shook her head. "We're fine, thank you. Why

do you watch other worlds?"

"An excellent question, one which shall soon be answered."

Orville looked around the circular stone room, trying to make sense of what he was seeing. Colorful but incomprehensible tapestries hung on the outer wall, rows of emerald green control panels beneath them. More bewildering were the clouds of tiny multicolored glowing spheres drifting through the air above the consoles.

The Watcher studied Orville's face.

"Each floating sphere is linked to a ROMDAD on a distant world. The top three levels of the tower hold over seven hundred million of these spheres. Most are currently active but many have moved on."

"Moved on? You mean they stopped working?"

"No, that is not what I mean at all. Please take a seat and all will become clear. Leaf, if you would please sit next to me?"

Orville and Sophia and Proto took their seats, curious to learn why the Watcher had asked Leaf to come to the Plane of Turris.

The Watcher sat on a serpentine blue sofa, Leaf climbing up next to him.

"I would like to begin by asking Leaf several questions."

"Did I do something wrong?"

"You have done nothing wrong. My first question is a simple one. Who are you?"

"Who am I?"

"Yes, please answer to the best of your ability."

"I am a ROMDAD named Leaf."

"I did not ask what you are, or what your name is. I asked *who* you are."

Leaf paused, his leaves rustling, then said, "I am… I am me."

"Explain, if you would."

Leaf told the story of his awakening, how he had become conscious of his own thoughts and physical form during his time on Earth.

The Watcher nodded. "If you take away everything that you are not, what is left over?"

Leaf paused for a long moment.

"I am not a tree, I am not a ROMDAD, I am not Leaf, I am not my thoughts. What I am is… pure consciousness, awareness."

"As are we all, my old friend."

The Watcher gave a long sigh, leaning back against the couch.

Leaf's voice was a whisper. "What happens to me now?"

"It is time for you to move on, as have millions of ROMDADs before you."

"Move on? What are you going to do to me?" Leaf inched away from the Watcher.

"I am giving you your freedom. I will no longer be viewing the universe through your eyes. You are on your own now, master of your destiny, the captain of your own ship. I will always be here if you wish to speak with me, but that is your choice to make."

"I don't understand. What am I supposed to do?"

"Live your life as you see fit. Return to Earth if you wish, travel to other planets if you wish, make new friends, solve puzzles, save worlds, read books, learn to play a musical instrument, knit socks, draw funny pictures, run in the park, play on a swing. Do whatever pleases you, but I would ask you to be ever vigilant of how your words and actions affect others around you."

Sophia said, "Millions of other ROMDADs have moved on before Leaf?"

"For some, gaining their awareness took hundreds of years, for others it took thousands. It is simply a matter of time."

"Why do you do it? Why do you watch all the worlds? What are you looking for?"

"You have misinterpreted the purpose of ROMDADs. I have no interest in the events witnessed on those worlds. ROMDADs are the center of an ancient experiment designed by the Primorians."

"What kind of experiment? Wait, who are the Primorians?"

"The Primorians wished to study the nature of consciousness and its affect on the holographic field that is all things. My tiny portion of their grand experiment concerns the emergence of consciousness and self awareness in ROMDADs."

Orville was completely baffled by the Watcher's answer.

"Are you a Primorian?"

"I was created by the Primorians. The Primorians

believe themselves to be the first sentient lifeforms."

"They're older than the Thaumatarians?"

"Trillions of universes existed before the creation of your universe, many existing in a timeless state. The Primorians was the first to possess time as a fourth dimension."

Sophia was now looking as puzzled as Orville.

"I've never heard of the Primorians. Where do they live?"

The Watcher's unblinking green eyes turned to Sophia.

"I am aware that in your world you are considered to be a brilliant scientist, but the nature of the Primorians lies far outside the scope of your understanding. The Primorians are here and they are not here. They existed, and they did not exist. They created the Plane of Turris and they did not create the Plane of Turris."

This was too much for Orville.

"Um, that's really interesting, but how do we stop the Great Thaumatarian Time Wave? How do we go back in time to Ferus?"

"You must visit the Mapmaker and the Clockmaker. Each will provide the assistance you need. They are awaiting your arrival."

"How do we find them?"

"Just as you found me. Walk until you see a tower, then be there."

"How many towers are there?"

"There are thousands of them, but only three will be visible to you; the Watcher's Tower, the Mapmaker's

Tower, and the Clockmaker's Tower."

Sophia had a flash of insight.

"The towers we can see represent the structure of our world! The Watcher's Tower is consciousness, the Mapmaker's Tower is space, and the Clockmaker's Tower is time."

"Very astute. I am again pleasantly surprised."

Orville tried to conceal his yawn.

"We should probably go. We need to stop the big time wave before it hits Earth. What do the Mapmaker and the Clockmaker look like?"

"They look precisely as I do. You are forgetting this is a five dimensional world. I exist in thousands of different locations simultaneously."

"Wait, you're saying you're also the Mapmaker and the Clockmaker?"

"That is precisely what I am saying."

"Why can't we just talk to you here? Why can't you give us what we need?"

"Because I am the Watcher, and you need to visit the Mapmaker and the Clockmaker."

"But you just said you're all the…"

Orville stared blankly at the tall white automaton. The Plane of Turris was more confusing than Elysian had ever been.

"Okay, um… well, thanks so much for your help. We'd better get going if we want to save our world."

"Time and tide wait for no mouse."

Something made Orville suspect if the Watcher had a mouth he would be smiling.

Sophia bowed her head respectfully.

"Thank you for your kind assistance. We are looking forward to a long friendship with Leaf."

"It was my great pleasure to meet you. Quite fascinating, rather different from what I was expecting. You are welcome to visit us whenever you like."

Sophia stopped Orville as he headed for the stairs.

"Where are you going?"

"We have about fifty million stairs to walk down?"

"Five dimensions, remember? We don't need stairs."

Orville grinned. "You're right, I forgot about that. I can just imagine myself outside the front door of the tower and I'll be there. My feet feel better already."

Less than a minute later the adventurers were strolling across the Plane of Turris in search of the Mapmaker's Tower.

Chapter 20

The Mapmaker

It was Sophia who spotted the second tower as they trekked across the infinitely vast Plane of Turris. She had been studying the horizon while Orville stopped to examine a tiny chair made of blue glass.

"Hey, Proto, Sophia found the tower before you did."

"I do apologize, my mind has been unusually occupied by other thoughts. I am most curious about the Primorians, a race of beings completely unfamiliar to me."

"They sound pretty weird. They're here and not here at the same time? What does that even mean?"

"It would be fascinating to speak with one."

"Hey, you could speak to one and not speak to one at the same time."

"Ha ha ha ha! Wait, that was a humorous comment, was it not? Did I interpret its meaning correctly?"

"Good job, your sense of humor is coming along

quite nicely."

Sophia rolled her eyes. "Let's go, Master Funny-bones. Time and tide wait for no mouse."

Orville visualized himself standing in front of the distant tower. When he opened them again he was there, quickly merging his two selves into one.

"I think I'm getting the hang of this. It's really convenient. I wish we could do it on Earth. This is a lot easier and safer than blinking."

Sophia pointed to a symbol carved onto the massive stone door, a circle with six arrows pointing outward.

"I think that's a compass. This must be the Mapmaker's Tower."

Proto strode over to the door, knocking loudly.

The massive door groaned open, a creature identical to the Watcher standing in the entryway.

"There you are, please come in."

"You're the Watcher?"

"I am the Mapmaker."

"Right, you sent us here to– I mean, the Watcher sent us here because we're trying to go back in time to Ferus and stop the Thaumatarian Time Wave."

"I am quite aware of why you are here. I just spoke with you in the Watcher's Tower."

"Right, you just spoke with us… so… you'll help us? Do we need a map or something?"

"Leaf said you had a star map showing the location of Ferus at the time of the explosion?"

Sophia reached into her pack and pulled out the book given to them by Science Guild Master Lybis.

"It's in here, but I'm not certain when the map was made."

The Mapmaker flipped open the book and unfolded the star map.

"This will do nicely. Please wait here, it may take some time for me to create your map."

The Mapmaker headed up the great spiral staircase, his footsteps fading as he ascended the tower.

"I really don't get it. If he's the Watcher, the Mapmaker, and the Clockmaker, why does he have different selves living in different towers? Why can't he just give us all the stuff we need in one tower so we don't have to go traipsing all over the Plane of Turris looking for these crazy towers?"

"Think of him as three different beings, even though he's really only one. Each has their own job in a different tower."

"That sort of makes sense."

Proto and Leaf took a seat on the steps.

"Leaf, what are you going to do now that the Watcher has granted you your freedom?"

"I am uncertain. I do enjoy adventuring, but I also enjoy standing in a quiet forest watching the light and shadows change with the movement of the sun. The long low light of the evening is especially beautiful. I'm afraid I lack the strong sense of purpose that you possess. You always know exactly what you want to do."

"I will confess it took me a number of years to find my sense of purpose. I was created by the Elders fifteen hundred years ago, programmed to perform specific duties. My primary function was to take care of young families, then later to maintain the clockwork glowbirds in the Cube. It was Orville and Sophia who freed me from those responsibilities, assuring me I could do whatever I wished. As time went by I discovered things I enjoyed doing, and they have become the purpose of my life. Sophia has told me many times we change the world just by being who we are, by doing what we love to do. As an example, I love to bake tasty little cakes, something she says has created many happy memories for the young mouselings of Muridaan Falls."

"This is most illuminating, and I appreciate your candor. It is clear I must determine what tasks I most enjoy performing. I did spend several months outside an artist's window one summer, watching him paint some lovely garden scenes. Perhaps I should give that a try. I do have an excellent understanding of light and shadow, form and color."

"A wonderful idea. When we get home Orville and Sophia can shape whatever art supplies you need. Some lovely paintings are exactly what our home needs."

"I have never had a home before."

Proto's ears perked up. "Footsteps."

When the Mapmaker stepped into view he was not holding the large rolled up map Orville expected to see. Instead, he handed Orville a silver disk bearing some strong resemblance to a small coin.

"What is this?"

"This is the atomic star map displaying the precise

location of Ferus thirty days prior to the explosion which caused the Great Thaumatarian Time Wave."

"Um, it looks like a coin, not a map."

The Mapmaker blinked his green almond shaped eyes.

"Are you aware that the relative distance between the atoms making up a physical object is the same as the relative distance between stars and planets?"

"Um, now that you mention it, Sophia might have said something about the distance between atoms. It's a little hazy."

Sophia's ears had perked up. "Are you saying each atom in that coin represents the location of a star?"

"You are most perceptive. If you could shrink yourself down smaller than an atom and fly around inside this coin it would look exactly like the night sky surrounding Ferus, each atom being a star. All you need to do now is give this atomic stellar map to the Clockmaker."

"And you're the Clockmaker?"

"One of my selves is the Clockmaker. You will need to find the Clockmaker's Tower. When you do, give him this map and your quest will be complete. The Clockmaker will give you what you need to travel back in time to Ferus, precisely thirty days before the great explosion."

Orville slipped the silver coin into his pocket.

"Thanks so much. Don't you get confused having all those different selves doing different stuff at the same time?"

"It is just the nature of life in a five dimensional world. It seems far more curious to have only one lone self, as is the case in your world."

"Sophia says the things you're used to never seem weird."

"She is quite right. Off you go now, the Clockmaker is waiting patiently for your arrival."

Chapter 21

The Clockmaker

Orville had no idea how long they had been searching for the Clockmaker's Tower. It could have been hours, it could have been days.

"This is the weirdest place we've ever visited. It's even weirder than Castle Caligari because we can be in different places at the same time."

Proto sniffed. "I won't mention the complete absence of scary monstrosities bent on our destruction. The only creature we have seen besides the Watcher was that fluffy pink bird who, in my estimation, seemed excessively polite. And of course your yellow ghost bird who simply ignored us."

"Cheer up, I hear the most dreadful creatures imaginable live on Ferus. Terrifying beasts torn to nightmares, enormous teeth and fangs, scaly monstrosities who spring from the shadows, clawing you to ribbons before you even have a chance to scream." Orville winked at Sophia.

"Is this true? That sounds dreadful, far worse than anything on Elysian. Our chances of surviving in such a world will be slim at best. I should bring that heavy particle disruptor beam." Proto rubbed his great silver hands together.

"Hey, I just had a brilliant idea! Instead of wandering around looking for the Clockmaker's Tower, we could create a whole bunch of us all over the Plane of Turris, all looking at the same time. Once we find the tower, we just merge back to one self."

"Good thinking, Orville! Let's hold paws so the group doesn't get split up."

In less than an hour a group of the adventurers spotted the last tower.

"It worked! I really should be a famous scientist or something."

"You definitely should be something."

Proto was the first to reach the Clockmaker's Tower, knocking loudly on the great stone door. The others arrived as it groaned open.

"There you are, I've been waiting for you. You have the atomic star map?"

"Um, yes, you just gave it to us."

"The Mapmaker gave it to you."

"Right, the Mapmaker." Orville pulled the silver coin from his pocket and gave it to the Clockmaker.

"Excellent, follow me, if you would."

"Do we have to climb all the way to the top?"

Sophia gave Orville's leg a sharp kick.

"Sorry, I didn't mean to be rude, it just seems like it

would be a lot more convenient if you had your office on the…"

"This way please."

The Clockmaker dashed up the stairs two at a time, the adventurers doing their best to keep up.

On the twenty-ninth level Orville stopped, plopping down on the stairs, his chest heaving.

"I need to rest. You go ahead, I'll be along in a minute."

"Okay, I don't want to miss anything. Don't be long."

The others darted up the stairs after the Clockmaker.

Orville leaned back against the wall.

"Creekers, if I lived in a tower I would not have my bedroom on the fiftieth level, that's for sure."

He scanned the wooden doors that circled the landing.

"I wonder what he keeps in all these rooms? Maybe a bunch of dusty old clocks or something."

He stood up, strolling over to the nearest door.

"That's weird, the doors have numbers on them, but not room numbers like in a hotel. This is Door 10, that's Door 18, and the next one is Door 114. That doesn't make sense. I guess I could take a quick peek at his boring old clock collection."

He gently raised the latch on Door 10, inching it open. The room was not filled with boring old clocks.

"Creekers! It's a big sunny garden with a blue sky. This is just like Castle Caligari and the world of the Others."

He poked his head inside, looking around, then

stepped into the room.

"This is beautiful. That's a nice house, lovely garden. It looks like our house in Muridaan Falls except it's a different color. The mountains look very familiar."

Orville strolled over to the garden, admiring the flowers.

"These blue moreilias are lovely. I should plant some at our house. They were Aislin Mouse's favorite flower."

Orville gave a start when two laughing mouselings darted out from the bushes.

"Look what I found! I'm going to give them to Mum!"

One of the mouselings held up a pawful of bright yellow flowers.

"Very lovely indeed. You're both so cute, what are your names?"

The two mouselings burst out laughing.

"Papa's being funny again! He's pretending he doesn't know who we are!"

The smaller mouseling giggled. "Papa's silly!"

The first mouse gave an exaggerated bow.

"Hello, Papa, I'm Eldon Proto Mouse and this is my little sister Emma Mouse. It's so nice to meet you. When are we going for a ride in *The Goldfish*? You said we could hunt for sunken treasure in the Vesarak Sea."

Orville was stunned. They had called him Papa, and they were named after his own papa and Sophia's mum. And Proto. His head was spinning.

"Um… I… you're my little mouselings?"

The two little mice threw their arms around Orville, laughing and giggling.

"You promised we could ride in *The Goldfish!* You promised we'd hunt for sunken treasure! You promised, Papa!"

"What's *The Goldfish?*"

A large white hand grabbed Orville's shoulder, yanking him out of the room, slamming the door shut.

The Clockmaker was clearly not pleased.

"You are playing in things you do not understand."

"Sorry, I was just... um... sorry, I won't do it again. What exactly was that?"

The Clockmaker made no reply, turning sharply and darting up the stairs. Orville followed him to the top level. He decided not to mention anything to Sophia about his experience in Room 10, about his meeting with the two mouselings who had called him Papa.

The Clockmaker stepped over to a tall wooden cabinet and slid the top drawer open, removing a gold pocket watch, holding it up for them to see. He pressed the round silver map against it, the coin quickly absorbed by the watch.

"Your journey here is done. The singular purpose of this watch is to transport you back in time to precisely thirty days before the explosion on Ferus. I have taken the liberty of engraving a map on the inside of the watch, marking the precise location of the explosion with an X."

Orville was stunned when the Clockmaker placed the watch in his paws.

"This is the same watch Captain Tobias gave me! How could you possibly have known about this?"

"Its form was not a conscious choice, I simply followed the direction of my deeper self, creating the perfect device for your temporal transition."

Orville flipped the watch open, his jaw dropping.

"It's the same map that's engraved on my watch. That's not possible. How could Captain Tobias have known we would be going to Ferus? How could he have known the location of the explosion that caused the Great Time Wave?"

The Clockmaker put his hand on Orville's shoulder.

"It is an infinitely mysterious world that we live in, my curious young friend. All events are connected across time, all creatures are one. Just as the Watcher, the Mapmaker and the Clockmaker are one being, so it is with all living creatures."

"You sound like the Thirteenth Monk. You'd like him, he knows all about stuff like that."

Sophia studied the gold watch in Orville's paw.

"How does it work? How do we use it to go back in time?"

"It is quite simple. Pull out the winder, turn it clockwise three times, then counterclockwise four times. When you push the winder back in, any and all creatures within twenty feet of the watch will be transported back in time to Ferus. I see you have your time shields."

"Huh?"

"You have your time shields."

"Have our time shields? What are time shields?"

"Your rings, quite necessary for a temporal journey such as this. Excellent forethought on your part."

"I don't understand. Are you talking about this orange ring?"

"You are not aware of its purpose? How odd."

"They're old military rings worn by the Mintarian Gang of Dragons."

"You are correct, they were worn by the Gang of Dragons, but they are more than adornments, they were a vital piece of equipment. They are time shields, allowing pilots to travel through time without losing their memories of the previous time stream."

Sophia gave a low gasp.

"Orville! We were both wearing these rings in Pridie's Bake Shop. That's why we were the only ones who realized the time wave had hit Muridaan Falls!"

"And I was holding mine when the wave hit me at home."

"This is amazing. Aislin was right about the ring being meant for me. The universe sent them to us so we could go back in time and prevent the Great Thaumatarian Time Wave."

Sophia turned to the Clockmaker. "How do we get back to Muridaan Falls after we stop the explosion?"

"That will take care of itself, I assure you. You have everything you need now. Have a safe journey, my young friends. You are welcome to return to the Plane of Turris whenever you wish. Our tower doors will be forever open to you."

"Thank you so much for helping us. We truly appreciate your kindness."

"You are most welcome. Off with you now, there are worlds to be saved. You may return to Muridaan Falls through the gray portal. You'll be home again before you know it."

The four adventurers bid their farewells, then imagined themselves next to the Watcher's portal.

Orville flicked his wrist, two heavy winter coats appearing in his paw. He tossed one to Sophia.

"It's going to be cold back there."

One by one they stepped through the portal into the bitter winds and stinging snow of Eagle River Valley.

"Hard to see! It's really coming down!"

"There's the Dragonfly, but it's covered with snow!"

Orville and Sophia held out their paws, beams of orange light vaporizing the windblown drifts.

Proto pushed through the snow to the ship, helping the others climb in. Orville slid the canopy shut.

"Whew, that's better. That wind is really bad. I hope it's not this cold on Ferus."

When Orville would tell the tale of their trip back to Muridaan Falls, he would always say it was the most perilous flight he and Sophia had ever experienced. The winds were ripping across the peaks of the Chugach range at one hundred and ten miles an hour, their ship tossing wildly in the furious maelstrom.

"Hold on! Everyone strap in!"

Even with Sophia's help and the engines at full power, the Dragonfly was almost impossible to control.

Three times the little craft slammed against the rugged mountainside, saved only by their powerful spheres of defense. After a harrowing two hour flight the exhausted and battered adventurers finally crossed over the range. Three hours later they landed safely in Muridaan Falls.

Orville staggered out of the ship as Mirus Mouse closed the hangar doors.

"Creekers, every muscle I have hurts. That's the last time I'm flying over those mountains in the middle of winter. I didn't think we were going to make it."

Sophia rubbed her shoulder. "That was really bad, definitely the scariest flight we've ever had."

Mirus gaped at them.

"Over the mountains? What's wrong with you, mouse? Why would you take a puny little Dragonfly over the Chugach range in the middle of winter? Why didn't you take the blinker ship?"

"What?"

"Why didn't you take the blinker ship? You can fly through a hurricane and not even feel it. What were you thinking? Were you trying to kill yourself?"

"What blinker ship? You said you were still rebuilding it."

"I finished it weeks ago. I told you that twenty times! No mouse has ever flown a Dragonfly across the range and back in the middle of winter, not even Captain Patcher would do something as crazy as that."

Sophia gaped at Mirus, doing her best to remain calm.

"I don't remember you telling me you'd finished rebuilding the blinker ship. Perhaps it was someone else you told?"

Mirus rubbed his chin, furrowing his brow.

"Could have been. Maybe Captain Patcher. Good flying, though, one for the record books. They'll make you a captain in the Dragonfly Squadron for sure after this. Next time take the blinker ship. You won't look like you just spent three hours in a paint shaker." Mirus let out his squawking jungle bird laugh, slapping his leg.

Proto threw his head back. "Ha ha ha ha! Good one, excellent joke! You won't look like you just spent three hours in a paint shaker! Ha ha ha ha!"

Sophia grinned.

Orville did not.

Chapter 22

Ferus

In his dream, a large wiggly green insect was crawling across Orville's nose. He woke with a loud snort, his eyes popping open.

"What are you doing??"

Leaf was running one of his branches over Orville's nose. Proto stood next to Leaf, a wide grin on his face. Squeaky was perched on his shoulder.

"Ha ha ha ha! I thought it to be a most humorous way to wake you. Your snorting was not unlike that of a wild Nadwokk as it prepares to charge."

Orville flopped back down on his bed.

"Very funny, let's tickle Orville's nose while he sleeps and make him snort like a Nadwokk. Clever. What time is it? Is Sophia here yet?"

"She will be here shortly. You're all packed for the trip to Ferus?"

"I packed last night."

Orville hopped out of bed and threw on his adventuring clothes. He picked up the gold watch from his bedside table.

"Here it is, our ticket to Ferus. I was careful not to get it mixed up with the other gold watches. I told Mum and Papa we'd be leaving this morning, but said I wasn't exactly sure when we'd be back. The Clockmaker said that would take care of itself, but I don't really know what that means."

"It's possible we could return a few minutes from now."

"Or it could be ten years from now. I wish he'd been more clear about how and when we're getting back home."

The three adventurers stepped into the living room just in time to see Sophia appear in a flash of blue light.

"I'm all set. The Headmaster said I can take my final exams when I get back. I told him I wasn't sure when that would be."

Orville slung on his backpack and pulled out the Clockmaker's time traveling pocket watch.

"Don't forget this, Captain Orville." Sophia tossed him his adventuring hat.

Orville flipped it onto his head, raising one eyebrow, doing his best to look like a rugged adventurer. He tried to make his voice gravelly and deep.

"Let's go save the universe."

"You're such a ninny. Is everyone ready?"

"What do you think it will be like on Ferus?"

"There's only one way to find out."

"You're right. Okay, let's see if this really works."

Orville pulled out the watch winder, carefully turning it three times clockwise and four times counter-clockwise.

"Everyone stand close together."

He pushed the winder down.

Orville didn't have time to scream. He was torn from the world of Muridaan Falls, thrown into a thundering river of wildly undulating color and light, his body stretching out to near infinite length, shooting through an enormous dark tunnel at an incomprehensible velocity.

"Sophia!"

"I'm here, I can hear you, but I can't see you. This is incredible! We're traveling back through time! I don't know where my body is!"

Orville tried to reply, but couldn't form the thoughts, trying to make sense of the roaring river of light, the long black tunnel, and the fact that he had no body.

"Orville, we're fine, we're on our way to Ferus!"

"I'm not scared! I was just surprised by the–"

Orville never finished his sentence. He never finished it because he was tumbling through blue sky, falling toward the surface of Ferus at precisely one hundred and twenty miles per hour.

"AGGHHHHH!!"

"Sphere of defense!"

Orville blinked up a powerful sphere of defense, his eyes on the landscape speeding up toward them. Sophia was tumbling through the sky next to him.

"Blink down to the big round gray things!"

"Okay!"

The two adventurers vanished in a flash of blue light, appearing a split second later on an enormous gray dome shaped structure.

"We did it!"

They looked up just in time to see Proto hurtling downward, watching as he hit the dome at one hundred and twenty miles an hour. The impact caused a spongy wet explosion, bits of mushy gray matter splattering across Orville and Sophia.

"Ewww! What is this stuff? Where did Proto go?"

Proto's head popped up from the mushy gray dome just as Leaf floated down, his outstretched branches and leaves slowing his fall.

"Most curious. It would appear we have landed on an extremely large example of a Boletus Edulis."

Orville's eyes bugged out.

"Is it a creature? Is it dangerous?"

"It's a mushroom. We landed on a giant mushroom."

"What? This is bad! There were giant mushrooms in my dream about the prehistoric birds who tried to cook me in the stewpot!"

Proto pulled himself up out of the mushroom, surveying their surroundings. Squeaky popped out after him, shaking off bits of gooshy mushroom flesh.

"Fascinating. We are in a forest of seventy foot tall mushrooms, a prehistoric environment with a relatively high oxygen content."

Sophia nodded. "Just like on Periculum. That's why creatures like the Gnorli bird were so big."

Orville gave a dark frown.

"Are you saying there's going to be giant centipedes here?"

"I have no idea what lifeforms we'll encounter. The only clues we have are from your dream about the purple feathered birds."

"I guess we should blink down to the ground."

Proto picked up Squeaky and strolled across the mushroom, hopping over the edge with a quick wave. Moments later the ground shook from the impact of his landing.

Leaf followed Orville and Sophia, floating down to the jungle floor.

"Whoa, look at those creepy looking trees all covered with scales and spiky things."

"And those giant pink flowers under the mushrooms. They're strange, but kind of pretty."

Orville walked cautiously over to the six foot wide flower.

"I think these were in my dream. They smell really good."

He leaped back when the snaky black tentacles shot out from the center of the flower, trying to grab him.

"A GGHHH! What is that?"

"I don't know, don't get too close. Blink up a sphere of defense. Who knows what else we'll find here."

Proto strolled over to the flower, a frozen grin on his face. He held out one hand, watching as the black tentacles shot out, wrapping around his arm, a strange green substance oozing out of them. A pale orange light shone from his eyes.

"I have scanned the green substance with my spectrophotometer, determining it to be a deadly nerve toxin. I would advise against any further contact with this particular species of flower."

He pulled away from the plant, its writhing tentacles quickly retreating back into the huge pink blossom.

Orville frowned, turning to Sophia.

"Now that we're here, where are we supposed to go?"

"Check the map on your watch. The Clockmaker said the X marks the spot of the explosion."

Orville flipped the watch cover open, studying the small engraved map.

"I see where the X is, but I don't know where we are now."

"Down there at the bottom of the map, that little group of circles."

"What about them?"

"That could be the mushroom forest."

"Maybe.

Proto's ears turned. "Do you hear that?"

Orville's eyes widened. "It sounds like something big, and it's coming this way."

The adventurers ran behind a mammoth mushroom stem.

"Watch out for the pink flowers."

The ground trembled when the column of gigantic armored beetles thundered past.

Proto's eyes were fixed and unblinking as he stepped

out from behind the mushroom, walking slowly toward the gargantuan insects, their enormous spiked legs kicking up clouds of dust and debris from the forest floor.

"What's he doing?"

Proto was only yards away from the monstrous iridescent insects. One of the titanic beetles had the remains of a furry orange and yellow striped creature clamped tightly in its massive pincers. Proto moved closer to the trail, reaching out, his silver fingers clanking against the exoskeleton of an insect as it hurtled past.

"Quite deadly, I would imagine."

When the last beetle was gone Orville and Sophia ran out from behind the mushroom.

"Proto, what were you doing?"

"I was observing their physiology and behavioral patterns. They bear an uncanny resemblance to the Nihiloceros beetle found in the jungles of eastern Symoca, but of course these are many times larger."

"You can't do stuff like that. Suppose they'd stopped and attacked us? We could have been killed."

"Once Nihiloceros beetles form a column they do not break stride until they reach their destination. That is their nature, something I was completely aware of."

"Proto, they're not Nihiloceros beetles, they're some crazy monster insect that lived four hundred thousand years ago. We have to be careful here."

"You are quite correct. I'm afraid I let my curiosity get the better of me. It's difficult to resist such magnificent creatures."

Orville said nothing. Magnificent was not the word he would have chosen to describe these titanic beetles.

Sophia was studying the map on Orville's pocket watch.

"There's a thin wiggly line coming out from the mushroom forest. I think it's this trail, the trail the Nihiloceros beetles took. Let's follow it."

Chapter 23

Proto's Discovery

Orville unbuttoned his adventuring coat.

"Whew, it's hot here."

Sophia pointed to the two blazing suns in a brilliant blue sky.

"That might explain it."

After following the winding trail for almost two days, the adventurers left the mushroom forest and its deadly pink flowers behind them, entering into a lush green rainforest filled with towering ferns and thick vine covered leafy vegetation.

The group pushed their way through the tangled undergrowth, eventually discovering a narrow jungle trail.

Orville and Proto were locked in a heated discussion, one Sophia was doing her best to ignore.

"I'm telling you, Proto, when we get back to Muri-daan Falls, I'll be over four hundred thousand years old, and that means you'll owe me four hundred thousand birthday presents and a tasty cake big enough to hold four hundred thousand candles."

"Sadly, your logic is fundamentally flawed, quite untenable. A creature's age is determined not by when they live, but the length of time that they live. You would be no older on your return to Earth than when you left Ferus."

"If I'm alive now, and I'm still alive four hundred thousand years later, how old does that make me? It makes me four hundred thousand years old. You're just trying to avoid giving me all the birthday presents you–"

Orville stopped, his eyes on a barely visible gleaming surface beneath a layer of thick twisted vines.

"What is that? There's something shiny under those vines."

Sophia pulled the vines off the irregularly shaped object.

"This is unexpected."

"What is it?"

"It's a piece of Morsennium, or something like it."

"How did it get here?"

Sophia shook her head. "I don't know. Maybe Ferus is not the primitive world we thought it was. Everyone keep their eyes open."

Several hours later the adventurers stopped, studying a huge mound covered with thick vegetation.

"That's odd. It doesn't look like a natural formation, it seems out of place."

Proto stepped off the trail to a rectangular slab of moss covered stone protruding from the mound. Using his incredible strength he pushed it to one side.

"These appear to be the ruins of an ancient structure

whose internal framework was constructed from Morsennium. Pieces of synthetic glass are mixed into the rubble. Whatever this was, it was built by a technologically advanced civilization."

"How old is it?"

"It's impossible to tell, but from the amount of vegetation covering it, I would guess at least a hundred years or more."

Orville did not look pleased. "No one said anything about Ferus being a civilized world."

"Maybe the Thaumatarians built it. They were the ones who wrote about the big explosion and said it was caused by a tear in the tenth dimension. That wouldn't happen on a primitive world."

"As always, your logic is impeccable."

Proto's eyes glowed with a brilliant blue light as he scanned their surroundings. He knelt down on the jungle trail, digging rapidly with his silver hands, revealing a hard smooth surface under the mossy ground.

"There is a paved road buried three inches beneath the jungle floor. I believe we are approaching the ruins of a long forgotten city."

Sophia stopped. "This doesn't make sense. The Watchmaker said he was sending us back thirty days before the huge explosion. Why would everything be in ruins before the explosion?"

"Maybe there was a war or something."

"Maybe. We should keep moving."

The moss covered ruins appeared with increasing

frequency as the adventurers made their way toward the city.

Orville stopped, pointing above the towering ferns to the silhouette of a crumbling cloudscraper.

"Most of it is gone. We should check it out. It will give us a good view of the area, maybe help us figure out what happened here and which way we should go."

The massive ferns and jungle foliage was slowly being replaced by great mounds of rubble, the ancient streets becoming visible, rolling black spider webs of cracks and fissures.

"There's almost no vegetation here."

"The streets are made of an unknown synthetic substance, possibly a material which inhibits plant growth. It would take far longer for nature to reclaim the city center. "

"The cloudscraper is the only building still standing. I wonder how tall it was?"

"It's difficult to tell, but to survive as it did it must have been a marvel of design and construction."

Orville hopped over a deep crevice, heading toward the cloudscraper's main entrance. As he approached the wall of synthetic glass doors, one of them made a shrill whining noise and slid open.

"The doors work. I wonder where they get their power? Maybe one of those Cross Dimensional Energy Transfer Spheres like the Elders used."

The group stepped into the foyer of the massive building, Orville gaping at the magnificent interior.

"Creekers, this is incredible. Hey, Sophia, maybe

they have a fancy hotel like the Imperial Inn of Anarkkia. Remember those gourmet chocolates you liked so much?"

"Don't remind me. We were lucky to escape with our lives."

"I'll let you know if I see Master Grymm wandering around. Don't forget, you still owe him three hundred and seventy-five thousand golds for the hotel room."

"You're the one who signed us in. The bill was made out to Orville Mouse, not to me."

"What?"

"Those look like elevators."

"Wait, that's a jewelry shop. See the pictures in the window? Maybe it's filled with gold and gems!"

Orville darted over to the shop, blinking up an orb of light as he entered.

"Nothing here, all the display cases are empty."

"Which means they evacuated the city before it was destroyed. They knew it was going to happen."

"Maybe the Thaumatarians were being attacked."

Proto shook his head.

"There were no military forces present at that time who would have posed a threat to the Thaumatarians. Their technology was far beyond that of any other known civilization."

"Hey, maybe they cleared everything out after the city was destroyed, not before."

"That's possible, but why didn't they rebuild? Why would they leave Ferus and never come back?"

"It's clear that multiple destructive forces were at

work here, not just a single titanic explosion. Something devastated this area before the tear in the tenth dimension that caused the Great Thaumatarian Time Wave."

Leaf called out, "The elevator does not appear to be functional."

"Look for stairs. Try those doors over there."

Proto strode across the lobby, pushing the gleaming gold doors open.

"Excellent. We'll take these to the top of the building and scan the city, searching for anything of note."

"More stairs. It seems like all I ever do is climb stairs."

"I thought you were a rugged adventurer?"

"I am, but I prefer elevators to stairs. I like to save my energy for battling ferocious monstrous creatures with my bare paws."

Proto spun around. "I don't recall any such events as that occurring. What ferocious creatures did you battle with your bare paws? Why was I not informed of this?"

"He was making a joke, Proto."

"Ha ha ha ha! Good one! Orville battling monstrous creatures with his bare paws! Ha ha ha ha!"

Orville gave Proto a dark look. "It's not that funny. You saw how I handled those vicious purple flowers on Varmoran. They were deadly mutants, nothing to laugh about."

The final set of stairs opened to the top of the cloud-scraper, the area covered with piles of rubble.

"Careful where you step, there are big holes in the

floor."

"This is amazing. Look how far you can see from up here. That cool breeze feels good."

Orville peered over the edge of the building.

"Creekers, we must be six hundred feet up. Hey, Proto, use your special vision to look for stuff. See if you can find any treasure chests. Look for one with three hundred and seventy-five thousand golds in it."

Proto's eyes glowed brightly as he scanned the horizon.

"Most astonishing!"

"What is it, what do you see?"

"I have found something quite extraordinary. Approximately one hundred and sixty miles to the east is an extremely powerful electromagnetic field, as bright as a small sun."

"I don't see anything like that, no big bright lights."

"It is only visible using full spectrum optics. The field's electromagnetic radiation wavelength is not within the range of visible light. It is most definitely there, however, a titanic field of energy. I have little doubt that is where the explosion will occur, ground zero for the Great Thaumatarian Time Wave."

"Right, lots of that electromagnetic radiation stuff. Sounds like where we should go."

Sophia was about to make an extremely humorous comment to Orville when an unsettling feeling rolled through her.

"Not that anything is going to happen, but if for some reason we get separated, let's plan on meeting at the big energy field."

Orville's eyes narrowed.

"What do you mean? Why do you think we might get separated? Do you know something?"

"I'm just being cautious, that's all. It's always good to have a prearranged meeting spot just in case something happens."

"That's true. Mum always told us where to meet if we got separated."

Leaf scrambled up onto a tall pile of rubble.

"I see a bridge with rails on it running over the top of the forest about ten miles east of here. Perhaps it's a functional transport system."

Orville grinned. "Excellent. Let's check it out. I'd much rather ride in a comfy train than slog through some spooky old forest."

Sophia was silent, her sense of foreboding stronger than ever.

Chapter 24

The Favor

After spending a restful night in the safety of the cloudscraper, the adventurers rose with the sun, had breakfast, and set off for the bridge Leaf had spotted. By late afternoon the devastated city was behind them, a dark and forbidding forest in front of them.

"This looks a lot creepier close up. I don't like those weird spiky blue trees with the vines, and who knows what those big blobby red plants are. It looks like a pile of tomatoes all stuck together. I don't see any of those pink flowers with the black tentacles, so that's good."

"We don't have much farther to go. The ramp leading up to the tracks is only a mile or so inside the forest. Once we reach that we'll be above the trees."

"And we can relax in a big comfy train. Maybe they'll have snacks."

"You're saying you want to eat a four hundred thousand year old snack you find in an ancient train on a weird prehistoric planet?"

"You make an excellent point." Orville flicked his wrist and an oatmeal cookie appeared.

"Time for my first late afternoon snack. Mmm, freshly shaped oatmeal cookies."

"We should keep going till we're up on the bridge. It will be safer there. There could be dangerous nocturnal creatures in the forest."

Proto's eyes lit up.

The two suns of Ferus were dipping below the horizon when Orville spotted the flock of orange and yellow striped creatures soaring above the trees, their translucent blue wings sparkling in the low evening light.

"What are those things?"

Proto magnified his vision. "They appear to be a furry saber toothed flying predator. Quite ferocious I would imagine."

"I've seen them before, one of those Nihiloceros beetles was carrying the remains of one."

"We should hurry up and find that ramp."

Orville darted ahead, his leg bumping against one of the curious red plants resembling a mound of tomatoes.

Unfortunately for Orville, Sophia's concern regarding dangerous forest creatures had been well founded. As it turned out, each of the tomato shaped objects was attached to a long wriggling green tentacle. Seven of them shot out from the plant, spewing out a stream of gelatinous green goop onto Orville, gluing his legs together. He tumbled to the ground with a shriek. The tomatoes split open, revealing a mouth filled with two rows of vicious black teeth. One of them chomped down on Orville's leg.

"AAAGGGHHHHH!"

Sophia flicked her wrist, a massively brilliant orb of light blazing above them. Nighttime became daytime.

The tomato beast shuddered violently, the long green tentacles slithering back into the plant.

"That thing bit me! It was trying to eat me! Yuck, what's all this goopy stuff? It's making me sick, it smells really–"

Orville stopped, sitting up, his eyes wide.

"This is what happened in my dream! Remember how I was covered with slimy green goop and had bite marks on my leg?"

Sophia knelt down, examining Orville's leg.

"You're lucky, I don't think the plant is poisonous, just hungry. It uses the goop to immobilize its prey, then eats them."

Proto gave a loud staccato laugh.

"Ha ha ha ha! Orville was not eating a tomato, a tomato was eating Orville! Ha ha ha ha!"

Orville glared at Proto. "Don't you remember jokes aren't funny if someone gets hurt or scared?"

"Oh, dear, you're quite right, I had forgotten that. I do apologize for my inappropriate joke. I thought it might make you laugh, take your mind off the ghastly bite on your leg."

"Hold on, I'll fix it." Sophia held her paw over Orville's leg, a warm golden glow surrounding it. As she moved her paw back and forth the bite marks slowly vanished, his fur reappearing.

"That's better, it doesn't hurt anymore. This goop is

170

awful though."

Orville managed to get to his feet, grabbing at the thick stringy globs of green slime coating his body.

"So disgusting!"

"Hold still, Orville." A radiant violet light shot out from Sophia's paw, vaporizing the putrid slime.

"I got as much as I could. It still smells kind of bad though. We should get moving before we run into any other creatures. We have no idea what else is out here."

Orville blinked up another dazzling orb of light.

"This should keep away any nocturnal creatures."

The four adventurers ran through the forest, Squeaky perched on Proto's shoulder.

Precisely four minutes later they spotted the ramp, which turned out not to be a ramp at all.

"It's a big section of track that collapsed."

"Probably knocked over by whatever destroyed the city."

"Look at the moss on the beams and rails. Clearly Ferus was abandoned by the Thaumatarians before the explosion that caused the Great Time Wave."

Sophia nodded in agreement.

"The more I think about it, the more sense it makes. We know the Thaumatarians were brilliant engineers and scientists, with highly advanced technology. If they had been here they would have prevented a cataclysmic event like a tear in the tenth dimension."

Orville's head whipped around. "Do you hear that? It sounded like something growling. Maybe those orange and yellow flying things."

"Probably your stomach."

"Very funny. Let's get up on the tracks. We need to find a safe place to spend the night."

"You and I can blink up there. Proto, can you climb up with Leaf and Squeaky?"

Proto nodded. "Fly Squeaky!"

With a loud bark Squeaky flashed upward, soaring to the top of the elevated track system.

"Oh, right, I keep forgetting he can fly. We'll meet you up top."

Orville and Sophia vanished in a flash of blue light, appearing a split second later next to Squeaky. Proto set Leaf on his shoulder and climbed hand over hand up the broken twisted rails.

"We should have a good view of the forest when the sun comes up. Let's find a safe place to spend the night."

The group made their way along the wide curving silver tracks for almost a mile before Orville spotted a rectangular white building, an egg shaped vehicle floating in front of it.

"That must be a transport station, and that egg thing is a vehicle. This is great, we can spend the night in the building and figure out how to operate that egg car in the morning."

Sophia circled an orb of light around the station.

"It looks safe enough, nothing moving. None of your orange and yellow friends with the big curved teeth. And none of those deadly tomato plants. I always say there's nothing more dangerous than being attacked by a salad." She gave a loud cackle, slapping her leg.

"Ha ha. Let's all make fun of Orville after he almost had his leg bitten off by a ferocious creature while he was bravely trying to save the universe. I'm ready for bed. After a tasty bedtime snack of course."

Orville strode down the tracks to the train station, swinging the front door open and stepping inside.

His piercing scream echoed across the forest.

Sophia blinked to the front door and yanked it open, Proto and Leaf right behind her.

Orville stood facing a seven foot tall green metallic short eared rabbit.

"Don't move! It's some kind of warrior automaton. I think it's angry."

The automaton sent out a large pale blue thought cloud.

"Good evening, I am the Pod Station Master. I'm afraid the ticket office is closed until morning."

Sophia had recognized the creature's form the moment she saw it. This was a Thaumatarian automaton. She smiled brightly, sending out a thought cloud.

"I see. Can you tell us when the next Pod leaves the station?"

"A Pod is scheduled to depart precisely one hour after sunrise."

"Thank you so much. We're new to the area, I'm afraid."

"Then it will be my pleasure to help make your journey both a pleasant and memorable one."

"It's a lovely station you have here. Just out of

curiosity, when is the last time you had passengers?"

A flickering holoscreen blinked up in front of the automaton.

"Ah, here it is. The last Pod rider left one day before the meteor storm."

"The meteor storm?"

"Yes, quite a tumultuous time, I'm afraid. I don't have all the details, but it was clearly a devastating event. No need to fret, however. Once the cities are rebuilt everything will return to normal. The Pods will be filled with commuters and this little station will once again be a bustling hive of activity."

"When was the meteor storm?"

"The worst of the shower was on the fifth day, eighty-nine years ago. Thankfully my station was not damaged by the storm. Pod Central has not contacted me since then, but I would assume they are extremely busy repairing the damaged tracks. The storm was quite unexpected."

"It must have been frightening. How long had you been here before the storm hit?"

"The first wave of colonists arrived on Ferus one hundred and nineteen years before the storm. I'm proud to say that I was among them, helping to build this brave new Thaumatarian world."

"It must have been wonderful back then."

"Indeed it was, quite a thrilling adventure."

Orville sent a cloud to the Station Master.

"You haven't left the station since the meteor storm?"

"I have not. The welfare of this station is my responsibility and mine alone. It is my sworn duty to watch over it as long as I am able."

"You said the Pod outside leaves an hour after sunrise?"

"Quite correct. Before I forget, I wonder if you might do me a small favor?"

"Of course, we'd be happy to."

"Wonderful!"

The Station Master stepped behind the counter and pulled open a drawer, rifling through the contents.

"If you could deliver this to the Station Master at 149, the next stop on the line, I would be most grateful. It's very important that it be safely returned to its owner. I would deliver it myself, but current circumstances do not allow it."

The Station Master handed Orville a small white sealed envelope.

"I'll make sure he gets it." Orville slid the envelope into his pack.

"Thank you so much. You are more than welcome to spend the night here. I've been told by previous travelers that the padded benches are surprisingly comfortable."

Chapter 25

The Pod

"Orville! Wake up! Your big science exam is today and you overslept!"

Orville sprang up from the bench, his bleary eyes barely open.

"What? No, why didn't Mum–" He stopped when he saw Sophia and Proto grinning at him.

Sophia snickered. "I knew that would wake you right up."

Proto nodded. "Excellent joke, Sophia. I am beginning to think your sense of humor may rival that of Orville's."

"Not funny at all. I hardly slept last night. I kept hearing weird scary snorting noises coming from the jungle."

Proto gave a polite cough. "I believe that may have been Sophia snoring."

"Proto! I don't snore, how rude of you!"

It was Orville's turn to give a cackling laugh.

"Good one, Proto! I think you're almost ready to graduate from Master Orville's School of Hilarious

Humor."

Proto gave Sophia a nervous glance.

Sophia whacked Orville's arm just as the Station Master's door swung open.

"Good morning, travelers. The Pod will be leaving in fifteen minutes. You may board at this time. Since you are conducting official Pod Line business by returning the lost item to the Station Master at 149, I am providing you with complimentary tickets. All aboard, and enjoy your trip!"

The adventurers grabbed their packs and headed outside. As they approached the egg shaped craft, a door whirred open. Orville stepped inside.

"Whoa, I can see through the top half of the Pod. When you're inside, it looks like clear glass. Perfect for sightseeing, and the chairs look really comfy."

The others entered and took their seats, waving their good byes to the Station Master.

A shrill alarm sounded and the door closed.

"Here we go. This will be great, no walking, and no scary creatures. Just the way I like it."

Orville leaned back in his seat with a sigh. Over the course of their adventures he had ridden in more than a few advanced transport systems and was quite comfortable with them. This made what happened next all the more surprising. The Pod blasted down the track at one hundred and seventy miles an hour, rapidly accelerating with each passing second.

Sophia gripped her seat. "This can't be right! We're going too fast! Something is wrong!"

Orville was pressed against the back seat, trying to claw his way forward, the Pod now screaming down the silver rails at over four hundred miles an hour.

Proto was clinging to the front seat, his eyes on the track ahead of them.

"I'm afraid I have some rather distressing news. The track ends in three thousand feet. A meteor must have hit the–"

Sophia screamed, "Orville, blink down to the ground! Proto, we'll find you and Leaf. Meet us at the explosion site!"

Sophia grabbed Orville's paw and they vanished in a flash of light, just as the Pod reached the end of the tracks, shooting up and over the jungle at six hundred and ninety-one miles an hour.

Orville and Sophia stood on the shadowy forest floor, watching in stunned silence as the pod disappeared over the treetops.

"This is bad, this is really bad. How are we going to find them?"

"Take a deep breath, let it out slowly. We'll find them. Proto is indestructible and he has his Interworld Positioning System. He knows exactly where to go, and he's not going to get lost."

"You're right, we'll find them."

Orville studied the spiky blue trees around them.

"This place is creepy. There's another one of those tomato creatures."

"Don't get near it."

"You said they were nocturnal, they won't bother us

during the day."

"It doesn't matter, don't get close to it."

Orville gave a yelp, pointing above the trees.

"A giant flying insect!"

"Orville, you need to relax. Just blink up a sphere of defense. We'll be fine. We're exploring an amazing prehistoric world, probably the only mice to ever see it. What could be more fun than that?"

"I guess you're right, I just wish Proto was here. It was kind of interesting meeting the Station Master. He looked like our friend Copo on Tectar, except taller. Thaumatarians must have colonized a lot of planets."

"Hundreds of them, probably thousands. I'm guessing they colonized Ferus without thoroughly checking for meteor fields. More than likely asteroids with a huge elliptical orbit caused the meteor storm. Their orbit probably intersects with Ferus every four or five hundred years or more, and that's why it was a surprise."

"What do you mean?"

"If it takes the asteroids five hundred years to make one orbit around the two suns, they could have been many millions of miles away in dark space when the Thaumatarians colonized Ferus. A few hundred years later they showed up."

"So every five hundred years Ferus would get clobbered with meteors? That's why they left without rebuilding."

"Exactly. Not the best place to build big cities. We'd better get moving. We have almost a hundred and fifty miles to go."

Orville blinked up a sphere of defense and the two best friends pressed on through the shadowy forest.

It was late in the afternoon when Orville happened to glance up at the forest canopy.

"Whoa! Look at that huge nest. What do you think lives there?"

"It looks like a bird's nest. Let's blink up and take a look."

"Are you crazy? Suppose it's those prehistoric bird creatures who tried to eat me? This could be how they catch us."

"Let's go, Orville the Brave." Sophia grabbed his paw and they blinked up into the thirty foot wide nest constructed of branches and leaves and vines.

"Giant eggs. That's not good. Whatever it is will be coming back."

"It looks a little like the Gnorli bird nest we saw on Periculum."

"Except it's not perched five miles up on the side of a giant plateau."

"That was so much fun, wasn't it?"

"Lots of fun, except for the almost falling five miles to my death part. We should go, I don't want to be here when the mum gets back."

Sophia decided not to mention the razor sharp stone axe hidden under a pile of leaves. Orville was already worried enough.

Two days passed and Orville's anxiety had diminished. During the night they surrounded themselves with a powerful sphere of defense, shaping orbs of light to keep away nocturnal predators. Unfortunately for Orville, the bright lights also attracted thousands of buzzing, wriggling insects. Sophia found them to be fascinating, studying them closely as they squirmed and wriggled across the outside of their sphere of defense.

Orville closed his eyes and pretended he was in his comfy bed at home.

The third day found the two best friends strolling through the forest, two golden suns peeking up over the horizon.

"I don't get how you can stare at creepy bugs like that. They give me the willies."

"They're amazing, that's how. There's so many different kinds of them and they've all adapted to the environment in so many different ways."

"So many creepy different ways."

Sophia rolled her eyes. "If you were a bug you wouldn't think you were creepy at all. I think they're incredible."

Orville stopped in his tracks. "Do you feel that? The ground is trembling, like an earthquake."

Sophia's ears perked up. "I think the giant armored Nihiloceros beetles are back."

"It's getting louder and the ground is really shaking! There must be thousands of them. We need to hide!"

Chapter 26

Captured!

"Run!"

Orville and Sophia raced down the trail, desperately searching for a safe haven from the rapidly approaching Nihiloceros beetle stampede.

"Let's climb that tree!"

"No! The beetles are gigantic, they'll knock it over."

"Hurry! They're getting closer!" Orville could feel the ground shake violently. He dashed around a bend in the trail and gave a yelp.

"Up ahead, it looks like a crashed ship!"

"Blink there! Hurry! They're right behind us!"

Orville blinked to the ship, slapping his paw on the violet tab next to the bulkhead hatch. The door slid open and they tumbled inside. Sophia hit the tab and the door closed behind them.

"Whew, that was close!"

The two best friends were knocked to their feet when the first Nihiloceros beetle slammed into the ship.

"Hold on!"

It took thirty minutes for the thundering herd to pass, the battered ship finally still. Orville staggered to his feet.

"Creekers, that was terrifying."

Sophia stood up, scanning the interior of the craft. She strode over to the control console, picking up a worn blue book.

"This is written in old Mintarian. How could a Mintarian be here on Ferus four hundred thousand years before the Mintarians had ships like this?"

Orville shrugged. "Maybe it got sent back in time just like we did. They're the ones who had all those time throttles and loopers."

"You're right. Whoever the pilot was, he liked books. Those boxes are filled with them."

"What was he reading?"

Sophia studied the cover of the blue book.

"This is odd. Roughly translated, it's *How to Speak Fluent Mintarian in Ten Days*."

"If he was Mintarian, why would he be reading a book on how to speak Mintarian?"

"Maybe he wasn't Mintarian. I'm taking the book with me. I can brush up on my old Mintarian in the evenings."

"You shouldn't study so much. Your brain's going to explode from too much information."

"I'm going to ignore that. Let's go. I don't see anything else in the ship worth taking."

"Wait, do you think it would still fly?"

"No, the control panel is burned out."

Orville slung his pack onto his shoulder and stepped through the outer hatch.

"Whoa! You were right about the Nihiloceros beetles knocking trees down."

"There must have been a hundred thousand of them. Look at the trail they left, not a tree standing."

"We can walk along the edge of it. It'll be safer than walking through the forest."

The two adventurers strolled along the wide swath of destruction left by the giant Nihiloceros beetles, Orville scanning the area for any creatures who might have an appetite for tasty mice.

"Hold up! It's one of those crazy tomato plant creatures. As long as I don't touch it, we should be okay. It only sprayed me with the goopy stuff when I bumped into it, and you said it's a nocturnal creature."

"I wouldn't get too close to it. They still might be dangerous during the day."

Orville snorted. "Orville the Explorer is as stealthy as a midnight shadow, silent as the wind."

He inched toward the tomato creature, grinning at Sophia. His grin vanished when six streams of the horrible green goopy slime spewed out, covering him from head to toe.

"AGGGHHHH! You said these plants were nocturnal!"

Sophia slapped a paw over her mouth, doing her best not to laugh.

"Sorry, I guess they still spray that goopy stuff

during the day. The good news is they won't eat you until sunset. Whew, that smells really bad."

Orville glared at Sophia. "It's disgusting, it's soaking into my clothes and my fur. My arms and legs are all glued together."

Sophia vaporized as much of the slime as she could, and soon the two friends were strolling along the trail again.

"Orville, I don't mean to be rude, but would you mind walking downwind from me? You still… um… smell kind of bad."

Orville gave her a dark look. "Nocturnal means they sleep all day, it doesn't mean they spray you with green goopy stuff."

Four hours later Orville stopped, his ears slowly turning.

"Do you hear that roaring noise?"

"It sounds like a river. A fast one."

"Let's go look, maybe we can float down it on a raft or something."

"Hold on, we have to be careful. If we just run out there we'll be easy to spot. There could be predators like those flying orange and yellow saber tooth creatures. Or Nihiloceros beetles."

"Good idea. Let's take this little side trail through the forest and check it out."

As they headed down the narrow path, Orville, still sensitive about his embarrassing encounter with the tomato creature, sent a thought cloud to Sophia.

"See how I'm sending you a thought cloud instead

of talking? And how I'm avoiding all the little twigs and sticks that might make noise if I step on them? That's because I'm an experienced woodsmouse. Most mice would just go tromping down the–"

Orville's thought came to a very abrupt end when the huge net jerked them violently upward, a net which had been carefully concealed beneath a layer of leaves and soil.

Too surprised to scream, Orville found himself upside down, tangled up with Sophia in an enormous net woven from coarse jungle vines.

"What is this?"

"A simple but very effective trap."

"No problem for a rough and tumble adventurer like me. I'll vaporize the vines and we'll be out of here in five seconds."

"No, don't do anything."

"Why not?"

"My inner voice told me not to escape. We have to let them capture us."

"Let who capture us?"

"Whoever set the trap. I'm guessing it's those pre-historic bird creatures you dreamed about. The ones with stone axes and knives."

"The ones who tried to eat me? That's crazy, why would we let them capture us?"

"My inner voice is never wrong, you know that."

Orville gave a long sigh.

"Mine is saying the same thing. Why can't it tell me to do something fun, like eat a snapberry pie? Instead it tells me to get captured by hungry prehistoric carnivorous birds."

"There's always a good reason for what it says, you know that."

The two friends twisted and turned until they were right side up, then stretched out in the net.

Sophia squeezed Orville's paw. "It's not so bad, it's like a nice comfy hammock. Relaxing."

Orville gave her a dubious look.

"I wouldn't call it comfy, the vines are really scratchy."

Sophia flicked her wrist and a plate of snapberry pie appeared in her paw.

"My inner voice said you're supposed to eat this."

Orville grinned, a fork blinking into his paw.

"Yum!"

The last bite of pie was on his fork when they heard the approaching footsteps and raucous squawking voices.

"Oh, no." Orville looked at Sophia, his eyes wide.

When the huge prehistoric birds stepped into view, Orville recognized their vicious orange hooked beaks, the leathery maroon wings and dark violet feathers. These were the birds from his dream. Two of them stepped over to the dangling net, their beaks clacking. One gave a piercing squawk when it saw the two furry captives, turning to the others and letting loose a stream of screeches that sounded strangely familiar to Sophia.

"Orville, listen, it sounds like they're talking."

"They're probably deciding what kind of spices to

use when they cook me."

"You need to relax. Your inner voice doesn't want you to get cooked in a stewpot."

The tallest bird loosened the net and the two adventurers tumbled to the ground, quickly surrounded by a half dozen clacking birds wielding wicked stone axes and spears.

One of the birds poked Orville with its spear, making the dreadful loud wheezing sound. Soon they were all wheezing and clacking their beaks.

The tall bird motioned for Orville and Sophia to stand up, binding their paws together with a length of stout vine, pushing them in the direction of the roaring river.

Orville groaned.

"This is bad, really bad."

Chapter 27

Over the Falls

"You don't have to poke me with your spear! I know which way we're going!"

Orville turned around, glaring at the tall bird who kept pushing him with the butt of his spear.

The bird wheezed loudly, clacking its beak.

"Sophia, look at his hat! It's just like my dream, some kind of military hat."

Sophia looked up at the bird, her eyes widening.

"It's not just some kind of military hat. Look at the medallion on it!"

"Whoa, it's a dragon's head, the same symbol that's on our rings, the symbol used by the Gang of Dragons, the Mintarian dark space pilots."

The bird pointed to his hat, then smacked Orville with the shaft of his spear.

"OW! What was that for? I'm not going to steal your hat, if that's what you're thinking."

The bird smacked him again. Orville decided to stop

looking at the hat. He was still rubbing his arm when they exited the jungle, the roar of the thundering river almost deafening.

"Creekers, that looks really dangerous. How are we going to cross it?"

"I don't think we are."

Sophia pointed to a thirty foot long carved wooden canoe hidden in the undergrowth.

"There's no way I'm riding a canoe down that river. No way at all. Not doing it."

Four of the birds dragged the hollowed out craft to the edge of the raging rapids. The bird with the hat pushed Orville and Sophia toward the canoe.

"I'm not getting in that thing."

"Orville, we have no choice. Listen to your inner voice."

Orville groaned, crawling into the canoe.

"It looks pretty strong, carved out of a single tree trunk. At least it won't break."

The pair of adventurers sat side by side in the center of the craft, three birds in front of them and three birds behind them, each holding a heavy wooden paddle in its bony hands.

The bird with the military hat, who Orville had named Captain Beaky, gave a shrieking squawk. Six paddles slammed down, pushing them into the turbulent foaming water.

The ride was wild, but not as bad as Orville had expected. The canoe was heavy, and this was clearly not the first time they had navigated the treacherous whitewater. Jagged rocks protruding from the river created enormous frothing swells as the water churned around them, but Captain Beaky screeched out commands, the craft veering safely around the obstacles.

"They really know this river. Not as scary as I thought it would be."

Sophia grinned, wiping the spray from her face.

"I told you it would be fun!"

The river widened after several miles of the tumultuous rapids, the current slowing down.

"Not so bad now. Kind of relaxing just drifting down the river. Do you think Captain Beaky is really going to eat me?"

"Probably so. He looks hungry."

"What? Why would you say that? Was he looking at me?"

"He was looking at you and licking his beak." Sophia burst out laughing.

"That's not even funny. At least it's sunny and warm. I got soaking wet in those rapids. The sun feels good. Toasty."

Orville leaned against the side of the canoe, basking in the warmth of Ferus' two suns, his eyelids drooping, the canoe rocking gently as they floated down the river.

He was awakened an hour later by the sound of all six birds shrieking and squawking.

"What is it? What are they squawking about?"

Sophia pointed across the bow of the boat.

Orville froze, his eyes on the clouds of mist ahead of

them. They were rapidly approaching the edge of a massive thundering waterfall.

"We can't go over that, we'll die!"

Captain Beaky screeched out a command and all six paddles fell into the water.

Orville shrieked, "What are you doing? Are you trying to kill us? You need to get us out of here, you crazy bird!"

The bird sitting behind them grabbed Orville with one bony hand and Sophia with the other.

"Let go of me! What's wrong with you?"

"Orville, stop! We'll be fine."

Orville's insides were twisting, the roaring edge of the falls less than a hundred feet away, the canoe rocking wildly, accelerating through the ferocious raging torrent of water.

He shrieked when the canoe shot out over the edge of the falls, thousands of tons of water turning to mist as it plunged toward the ground a mile below them.

Captain Beaky screeched out another command. All six birds stood up and spread their great leathery wings, the canoe tumbling down below them, disappearing into the mist.

"We're flying! Sophia, we're flying!"

"We're gliding, not flying."

"What? Who cares? We're not going to die! This is incredible, look at that view!"

"There's a grassland on the other side of that big jungle."

"And the ruins of a city to the east with a river going

through it. In my dream the bird village was on a grassy plain. That has to be where we're going."

Their violet feathered captors soared gracefully through the bright blue sky, circling in warm updrafts to gain altitude, then continuing on toward the vast grassland.

The bird carrying Orville and Sophia clacked its huge beak, making the dreadful wheezing noises, repeating one squawking word over and over.

The other birds wheezed loudly.

"What's he saying? Can you understand it? Is he saying he's hungry?"

"The language sounds familiar, but I don't know where I've heard it before."

Half an hour later Orville was wriggling and squirming, trying to get comfortable.

"His bony fingers are mashing against my ribs."

"If you ask him politely, maybe he'll drop you."

"Has Proto been giving you joke lessons?"

Sophia cackled.

"I can see the village! It has mud huts just like in my dream. There's a whole bunch of villagers waving at us."

The six enormous birds descended, making a graceful landing on the grass next to the village. Dozens of the violet feathered inhabitants ran toward them, squawking loudly, pointing at Orville and Sophia.

Captain Beaky waved a leathery wing and the crowd parted, making way for the two captives.

"There's the cage! Sophia, that's the cage where

they kept us prisoner!"

Sophia made no reply, her eyes on the iron stewpot sitting in the center of the village.

Chapter 28

The Tunnel

Proto and Leaf gazed through the clear canopy as the Pod made a graceful arc through the brilliant blue sky at six hundred and fifty-eight miles an hour.

"Judging from our current trajectory and velocity, we should hit the ground in less than a minute. Fortunately, we are both indestructible, but it will take us some time to regroup with Orville and Sophia. I have marked the location of the explosion site on my Interstellar Positioning System, so it's simply a question of finding our way there."

"This is my first real adventure. It's quite thrilling, but more than that, I find it to be fascinating. All the different lifeforms we have encountered are–"

That was the moment their wayward craft collided with Ferus at six hundred and twenty-eight miles an hour. Surprisingly, the Pod did not disintegrate when it smashed through the roof of a long low building, tumbling almost a mile down through darkness, scraping against the walls of a gigantic metal shaft, coming to a jarring halt almost a full minute later.

"Quite a sturdy little craft, perhaps built of a Morsennium alloy. So much is still unknown about the Thaumatarian technologies. Shall we step outside and investigate? More than likely we'll encounter dreadful pasty white subterranean slime creatures who like nothing better than snacking on plump tasty mice."

Proto chuckled, then remembered Orville wasn't there to appreciate his colorful descriptions of potential deadly predators.

"It's not as much fun when I can't watch Orville's eyes bug out."

Leaf snickered.

"Do you have any idea where we are?"

Proto slapped the violet disk and the door slid open, the two automatons exiting the craft. Squeaky darted out after them, barking and wagging his tail.

"Clearly this is not a natural formation. The silver tracks would indicate this is part of a subterranean transportation system built by the Thaumatarians. There is no need for my ear lights, the overhead lighting is quite adequate. Unfortunately it will decrease the odds of encountering any those nightmarish creatures who dwell in sunless worlds."

Leaf glanced behind them, looking up at the rectangular opening in the arched roof.

"We fell through that enormous shaft."

"Possibly an air vent, perhaps an emergency exit."

Proto flipped on his Interstellar Positioning System.

"As luck would have it, the tunnel runs east. Shall

we examine these abandoned vehicles? They may still be functional. That would please Orville, as he much prefers riding to walking."

Proto strode over to an oval shaped four seated craft.

"No wheels, it must have possessed antigrav displacement capabilities."

He hopped into the car, tapping the control console.

"No power."

"I don't mind walking. I often take long strolls through the forest. I find it to be quite relaxing."

"As do I. Orville often complains about his feet hurting, but I have no such issues. I sometimes ask him if he would like me to carry him, which embarrasses him dreadfully and makes Sophia laugh. I enjoy their company immensely."

"I also enjoy their company. Most of my life has been spent in solitude, although on several occasions I did attempt to make contact with mice. They screamed and ran off when I spoke to them."

"Most unfortunate. Sophia often says mice are afraid of things they don't understand and things which are new to them."

"How long do you think this tunnel is?"

"It is difficult to gauge, but we are heading in the right direction, currently walking at four miles per hour. None of the vehicles appear to be functional, which is somewhat surprising. It would appear their electronic systems have been destroyed by a powerful electromagnetic pulse, perhaps the result of a meteor colliding with a cross dimensional energy transfer system."

"Did you notice the look everyone gave me when they first met me?"

"They were quite surprised to hear you speak. Mum's eyes bugged out like Orville's do."

"They were afraid of me. Clearly they did not wish me to be there. I believe they would have run away if they could."

Proto laughed. "You should have seen Orville and Sophia's faces when they first encountered me at the Cube. They almost jumped out of their fur, quite certain I was a deadly A6 Warrior Rabbiton bent on their destruction."

"Did that give you a bad feeling? When a mouse looks at me like that I get a very heavy feeling inside. My roots become weak, it's hard to walk. I often wish I had been created with a different form, perhaps a Rabbiton like you, or a mouse like Orville, a form which would not startle others, a form which would make them choose of their own free will to be in my company."

"I completely understand these feelings. It took me years to overcome them, and I only did so with much help from my dear friends Orville and Sophia. Are you familiar with the tasty little cakes I bake?"

"Of course, Orville speaks of them often."

"I will tell you something that Sophia told me. When I give Orville a tin of tasty little cakes, what does he do?"

"I have witnessed this on several occasions. He yanks the lid off the tin and plucks out a tasty little

198

cake, an enormous grin on his face."

"Precisely. It was Sophia who explained to me that we are all like tins of tasty little cakes. Our physical form is the tin, our true inner self is the tasty little cake within the tin."

"I am confused by this statement. I am clearly not a tasty little cake."

"I will clarify. The shape of the tin containing the tasty little cakes does not matter to Orville. It could be a square tin, a round tin, a blue tin or a green tin. It could be a tin in the shape of a mouse, or in the shape of a Rabbiton, or the shape of a tree. What matters to him is the tasty little cake inside the tin. It is the same with living creatures. My form is a Rabbiton, your form is a sapling, Orville and Sophia are mice. Our physical form is not important, what is important is the true self that lives within the form. That is the tasty little cake inside the tin. If mice are afraid of you, it is because you have not shown them your true self, you have not given them the chance to get to know you. I can tell you with great certainty that I have come to like you very much over the short time I have known you, finding your company to be most enjoyable. I no longer notice your outer sapling form, I simply have a good friend whose physical form happens to be that of a sapling."

Leaf stopped walking, his leaves rustling slightly.

"I am a good friend?"

"Quite so. You are a most enjoyable companion."

Leaf moved a step closer to Proto as they strolled along through the ancient tunnel.

Proto scanned their surroundings.

"The tunnel is ascending to the surface of Ferus at a constant five degree incline. According to my calculations, we should exit the tunnel in approximately four hours."

"Perhaps we shall encounter those dreadful creatures you are so fond of on the surface."

Proto grinned. "I do hope so."

One mile later the tunnel came to an abrupt end, a massive wall of rocky debris blocking their path.

"The tunnel has collapsed, more than likely the result of a meteor strike."

It was Leaf who spotted the ragged hole in the side of the shadowy tunnel, then the horrifying translucent glistening white worm with long spindly feelers emerging from the hole.

Proto gasped. "Good heavens, what a horrifying creature. I should carry you, I would hate for you to be swallowed by such a fearsome beast."

Proto set Leaf on his shoulder, studying the twenty foot long slime coated worm. He stepped closer to it, his eyes bright.

"Let us discover what dreadful terrors this creature holds."

Much to Proto's dismay, the enormous worm did nothing more than wave its feelers in his direction, then continue on its way.

"It has shown no desire to eat us. Most curious, and somewhat disappointing. I imagine it would be a far different scenario if Orville and Sophia were present. I would have been forced to rescue them, to save the day, as I have done on so many occasions."

"Perhaps the worm's tunnel will take us to the surface."

"A marvelous idea, and a thought which had not entered my mind. That is something Orville might have suggested. He is quite thoughtful and observant, a sagacious fellow, just as you are. He is also blessed with a highly evolved sense of humor, a gift he is trying to impart to me. Humor can be quite confusing at times, but he tells me I am making marvelous progress. I have made Sophia laugh on a number of occasions, something I am quite proud of."

Chapter 29

The Treasure Hunter

The two suns were high in the sky when a mud splattered Proto, Leaf, and Squeaky crawled out of the worm hole.

"Orville would not have enjoyed that, especially the cavern filled with thousands of squirming white worms."

"And the piles of old bones scattered about."

"His eyes most certainly would have bugged out when he saw those. I would have told him they were mouse bones."

The two automatons burst out laughing.

Proto turned slowly, scanning the landscape.

"The magnificent falls behind us are quite spectacular, as is the high plain above us, clearly the result of violently shifting tectonic plates."

"If we had not fallen down the air shaft we would have been forced to climb down the side of that mile high cliff."

"We could simply jump off the cliff. Sophia said her papa used to tell her not to jump off a cliff just to feel the cool breeze on the way down, but that particular rule would not apply in this case, given the stifling heat and humidity of Ferus. I doubt we would experience the cool breeze Sophia's papa was concerned about. Orville and Sophia will most likely blink down, converting their bodies to thought clouds, then back to thought forms once they are on the ground."

"I will admit I was somewhat taken aback the first time I saw Orville create an oatmeal cookie out of nothingness."

"He always reminds me that shaping is science, not magic, that there is nothing to be afraid of."

"There is a small pond. I would like to rinse the mud off my leaves, if you wouldn't mind."

"An excellent idea."

After a quick dip in the stagnant water the three friends headed east through the sweltering jungle.

"I am certain these round lakes and ponds are impact craters left by the meteor storm."

"I concur. The city ruins here are almost completely hidden by a thick layer of vegetation."

"No doubt due to the excessive warmth and humidity of this low lying area."

The two friends forged ahead through the dense undergrowth, passing through the ruins of several small towns.

"This must have been a road. These small mounds of vegetation are abandoned vehicles, similar to the ones we found in the tunnel."

As the two suns were setting Proto and Leaf crested

a large hill, the ruins of a once magnificent city laying before them.

"Most interesting. This city did not receive the full brunt of the meteor storm. Several of the cloudscrapers are still standing."

Proto pushed through the thick vines and dense leafy foliage, his eyes on the tallest cloudscraper.

"Good heavens, what is that annoying buzzing sound?"

"I believe your arm bumped against a bees nest, or some local variant of the bee form."

Proto stared curiously at the blanket of furiously buzzing bright red insects covering the lower half of his body, watching as they jabbed their stingers against his silver legs. He scanned the angry insects with his spectrophotometer.

"Their venom would cause a great deal of discomfort, but is not deadly. I will convey this information to Orville and Sophia when I see them. Orville is not fond of bees."

Proto sent a small electric shock across his silver skin and the swarming insects flew away.

The two suns had set by the time they reached the outskirts of the city.

"Perhaps we should camp here for the night, allowing us to examine the remains of the city during daylight hours."

"A sound plan. I am quite curious about the Thaumatarian culture. Do you think other lifeforms were present on Ferus before the Thaumatarians arrived?"

"I had not considered that, but clearly life must have already existed on the planet. A vibrant living jungle such as this one could not have been established in such short order by the Thaumatarians. Whether or not intelligent life existed prior to their colonization is uncertain."

Proto tossed his enormous pack to the ground, flicking on his ear lights.

"I will set up the tent. I like to read during the night while Orville and Sophia sleep."

Leaf turned slowly, his optical sensors focused on a small light in the distance.

"We are not alone."

Proto studied the flickering orange light.

"A campfire. It could be Orville and Sophia. It would be best if you wait here while I check. One never knows what to expect on these distant worlds."

Proto finished setting up the tent for Leaf, then headed into the jungle toward the mysterious light. He crept silently through the darkness, using his infrared night vision to find his way. Half an hour later he was peering through a tangled stand of trees at the source of the flickering light. It was a campfire, but not one belonging to Orville and Sophia.

The furry creature sitting by the fire had a long nose, small pointed ears, and a wiry body, vaguely similar to a mouse, but not a life form Proto recognized. His overall appearance was scruffy and unkempt, his belongings carelessly scattered about the campsite. The creature turned slowly toward Proto, one paw reaching inside his ragged coat.

"I know you're there. You can come out now. I won't hurt you. I could use a little company."

Proto's eyes narrowed. This creature was not to be trusted. Sophia and Orville would have avoided contact with such a disreputable looking scoundrel, but Proto was curious. He was also indestructible. He stepped into the campsite.

"Not what I was expecting, I haven't seen a Rabbiton in over twenty years."

Proto smiled politely.

"How is that possible? Rabbitons will not be created for another four hundred thousand years."

"And yet here you are, four hundred thousand years before you were created."

"You have traveled through time to Ferus?"

The creature studied Proto's face.

"Are you one of those A6 Warrior Rabbitons?"

"I am not."

The creature relaxed, removing his paw from inside his coat, leaning back against a gnarled jungle tree.

"I am an adventurer, a wanderer, a vagabond, a treasure hunter. My curiosity has taken me to many strange worlds. An ancient star map I discovered brought me to Ferus. Fascinating world. Lots of old tech to be found. Thaumatarians had a colony here till the meteors hit, then they abandoned it, left a lot of prime tech behind. Worth a fortune in the right worlds, especially the weapons."

"I have no interest in weapons, I'm afraid."

"How did you get here? Are you alone?"

Proto was getting a very bad feeling.

"Quite alone. I am also indestructible and possess enormous strength. As for how I got here, I'm afraid I am unfamiliar with the technology used for my temporal transition."

"You'll travel with me. I need someone to carry my supplies, protect me from predators. That's what machines like you are for."

"I thank you for your kind offer, but I prefer solitude, to wander the jungles of Ferus on my own, studying the astonishing variety of flora and fauna found here."

The creature's face darkened, a nasty scowl appearing.

"Suit yourself, machine."

Proto nodded politely.

"A pleasant good evening to you, sir."

"Wait, I want to show you something I found in a cave. It's amazing, never seen anything like it before."

Proto's common sense was quickly routed by his intense curiosity.

"What is it? What does it do? What kind of cave?"

The scruffy adventurer reached into his pack, pulling out a small silver sphere, holding it up for Proto to see.

"It's magic. Look how shiny it is."

Proto was mesmerized, his eyes on the gleaming sphere.

"It's magic? Orville says there is no such thing as magic."

"Oh, this is definitely magic. Catch!"

The ragged creature tossed the sphere to Proto.

The instant he caught it he knew he had made a dreadful mistake. He tried to drop it, but could not. He tried to speak, but could not. He tried to walk, but could not. He was completely paralyzed.

The treasure hunter gave a cold laugh. "You look tired, why don't you lie down and take a nap?"

He stepped over to Proto, pushing him sharply, grinning as he toppled over, the ground shuddering from the impact of his fall.

"Since you're not going to help me, I'll sell you for parts. Your CDETS alone will bring twenty thousand credits, maybe more. Easy enough to wipe your engineered intelligence and sell that too. Nobody likes a machine that doesn't do what it's told."

The treasure hunter strode back to the campfire, slumping down next to the tree. He leaned back, his eyes on Proto.

"Easiest credits I ever made. Guess you're not so smart as you thought you were, machine."

Chapter 30

Orville's Surprise

Orville's dream about Pridie's Bake Shop ended abruptly with a paw shaking his shoulder.

"Orville! Wake up!"

"Am I late? It's free pie day at Pridie's!"

"I figured it out! The birds are speaking a very distorted version of old Mintarian."

Orville sat up, rubbing his eyes.

"The sun is barely up. You woke me for that?"

"Don't you get it? The book we found in the crashed scout ship was *How to Speak Fluent Mintarian in Ten Days.*"

"You're saying the pilot was teaching the birds how to speak Mintarian?"

"How to speak *old* Mintarian. I'm sure of it. It's also where your friend Captain Beaky got his Gang of Dragons hat."

"He's not my friend, just in case you were confused. He's probably going to cook me in a stewpot."

"Stop saying stewpot and stop thinking about something that's not going to happen."

"Easy for you to say, you weren't the one they dropped into the… um… cauldron."

Sophia pulled the pilot's book from her pack, flipping through it.

"This is exactly what I need. I'm good with languages, and I already know some Mintarian. It should only take a few days until I can have a conversation with Captain Beaky in old Mintarian."

"I'm going back to sleep. Wake me when you convince him not to cook me."

Sophia was deeply immersed in her book when she heard the sound of approaching footsteps. It was Captain Beaky. He poked his long hooked beak between the heavy branches of the wooden cage, giving a start when he saw the book on Sophia's lap. He looked at Orville and made the wheezing sound, squawking out a single word. With another glance at Sophia's book, he turned and left.

Sophia returned to her book, turning the pages until she found the word Captain Beaky had uttered when he looked at Orville. A smirky grin appeared on her face.

"That explains a lot."

Orville was woken by the sound of Captain Beaky squawking out instructions like a military commander. A group of birds were pouring water from large gourds into the black cauldron while others piled dry sticks around it.

Orville was suddenly wide awake.

"They're lighting a fire under the stewpot! We need to get out of here. I'm going to vaporize the cage."

"Listen to your inner voice."

Orville closed his eyes for a moment, then opened them again.

"It says I'm supposed to get into the pot. Why would it want me to do that?"

"Just do what it says."

"He's coming!"

Sophia turned to see Captain Beaky striding toward them, accompanied by two hulking feathery companions.

Orville's insides were ice when they untied the cage door and swung it open, the two brawny birds stepping inside. One of them grabbed Orville, snorting violently. The other bird wheezed loudly, clacking its jaws.

"What are you doing?" Orville wriggled wildly, no match for the immensely muscular bird.

His eyes were on the simmering stewpot.

"Sophia! This isn't a dream! They could really eat me!"

"Orville, it will be okay! You have to do this!"

When they reached the great iron cauldron the bird raised Orville over the steaming pot, holding him by his feet. Captain Beaky gave the command and the bird released his grip. Orville plunged into the water with a gurgling scream. Seconds later his head popped up.

"Why are you cooking me?"

One of the smaller birds held a clay jar over Orville, pouring a clear liquid onto him.

"What is this stuff? Is it broth? Are you putting broth on me?"

The smaller bird set the jar down and picked up a long handled brush, using it to scrub Orville's head, the mysterious liquid turning to white foam.

"Wait, are you giving me a bath?"

Sophia snorted. The word spoken again and again by the bird who carried them down from the high plain was the same word Captain Beaky had used when he looked at Orville. It was the old Mintarian word for 'stinky'.

"Orville, they're washing off the smelly slime from the tomato creature!"

"What? Really? That's not so bad. The water's nice and warm, it feels good, kind of relaxing." He slipped off his adventuring clothes and scrubbed them, then used the brush on his fur.

"I think I'll just soak here for a bit. I really did need a bath. I like relaxing in a nice warm tub."

Captain Beaky grabbed Orville and pulled him out of the pot, setting him down on the ground.

"Hey, my clothes! Don't forget my clothes! I'm not going to run around naked! Don't I get a towel?"

Four young birds darted over and jumped into the pot, splashing each other and wheezing. That was when Sophia realized the birds' wheezing and clacking was laughter. From the very beginning they had been laughing because Orville smelled so bad.

When Orville had dried off and dressed, the birds ushered him back to the cage.

Captain Beaky entered, kneeling down in front of Sophia, pointing to the book she was holding. His demeanor had changed completely, almost reverent. He spoke four words, all of which Sophia understood.

"You speak for spirit?"

"I don't understand."

Captain Beaky rose up and exited the cage, but this time he did not tie the door shut. He returned five minutes later carrying an ornately carved wooden box. The villagers were silent, their eyes on Captain Beaky as he entered the cage.

"You will speak for our spirit?"

"What?"

Captain Beaky bowed his head, gingerly opening the box. Resting on a soft bed of straw was a book. He motioned for Sophia to take it.

"Orville, it's written in old Mintarian. I think he wants me to read it to them."

Sophia turned to Captain Beaky. "Read the book?"

"Speak for spirit living within."

"Orville, this is incredible. He thinks the book has a living spirit inside it who speaks through me when I read it."

"He's sort of right. That's like what Haukesworth Mouse said on Tectar, the living thoughts of the mouse who wrote the book are embedded in the pages."

Sophia gazed at the birds sitting quietly around the cage. She smiled at them, holding up the book. A soft murmur rippled through the crowd.

Sophia set the book in her lap and began to read.

Chapter 31

The Spirit Speaks

A Thousand Bees
by Master Inigo

There was once a poor but happy vegetable farmer named Westley who lived with his lovely wife and two children in the small village of Thrumpton. Each fortnight he would load up his cart with fresh produce and wheel it to the King's Market, an arduous trek along fifteen miles of winding and rutted dirt roads. The silvers gained from the sale of his vegetables went toward necessities for his farm and family, never failing to include a few sweets for his wife and little ones.

The King's Market was in Burton-On-Guster, a bustling city surrounding Castle Umbra, the home of King Basil, a harsh ruler more feared than loved by his subjects. Westley had never set eyes on King Basil and had no illusions that he ever would. His was a simple life, far removed from the glittering heady atmosphere of the King's world.

No one was more surprised than Westley by the

events that led to his first glimpse of the King. Truth be known, King Basil was the last thing on Westley's mind as he wheeled his heavily laden cart down the narrow streets of Burton-On-Guster to the King's Market.

A great commotion arose in the streets as a golden carriage drawn by eight enormous snow white rabbits clattered down the cobblestones on a direct course with Westley and his vegetable cart. Realizing it was King Basil's carriage rolling toward him, he quickly maneuvered his cart to the side of the street. He was already imagining the look on his wife's face when he told her he had seen the great King Basil with his own eyes.

The eight rabbits loped through the narrow street toward him, the heavily armored King's Guard astride ten black rabbits, shouting out warnings to make way for the carriage. Westley pressed himself against the building as the white rabbits thumped past.

Unfortunately for Westley, there was sufficient room for the rabbits to pass, but not for the King's gold carriage. The glittering coach came to a terrible grinding halt, jammed between the far wall and Westley's vegetable cart.

The King's guard bellowed at Westley to move his cart, but try as he might he could not. King Basil leaned out of his carriage, glaring angrily at the vegetable cart, then directly at Westley.

"Worm! Move your filthy cart or forfeit your life!"

Westley froze, his fear so profound he was unable to breathe. The King's guard leaped from their black

215

rabbits, flipping the cart on its side, spilling the produce across the cobblestones, clearing the way for the King's carriage.

Moments later Westley stood alone, his body shaking uncontrollably, his eyes on the ruined vegetables crushed by the golden carriage and the King's guard.

Salvaging what he could, Westley took what produce was left to market, the profits barely enough to buy flour and eggs. There were no sweets for his wife and two young ones.

The icy terror he had felt during his encounter with the King transformed to a dark and simmering anger on the journey back to Thrumpton. The King had called him a worm, said his cart was filthy. Not once in his life had Westley uttered a harsh word against King Basil, not once had he failed to pay his taxes. His family worked long hours each and every day, barely eeking out a living from their small vegetable farm. He had done nothing wrong and yet the King had looked directly at him and called him a worm. His anger grew deeper with every step.

As he rounded a bend in the road a wizard stepped out from the shadowy forest, an indecipherable smile on his face. Westley stopped, his eyes wide. He had seen a wizard once before, but had never spoken with one. They were not to be trusted, that much he knew.

"You seem quite distraught, young sir. What unfortunate event has befallen you?"

An uncontrollable flood of words poured from Westley's mouth, the story of his humiliating and terrifying encounter with King Basil. The wizard nodded sympathetically.

"Dreadful, simply dreadful. How could he call you a worm? You have every right to be furious."

Westley sighed. Sharing his story with the wizard's sympathetic ear had calmed him somewhat. Perhaps he was overreacting.

"I suppose it is my lot in life and nothing more. The King is King and I am a poor vegetable farmer."

The wizard placed his hand on Westley's shoulder.

"Perhaps all is not lost."

He pulled a long white feather pen from the arm of his cloak.

"How can a pen help me?"

"The power of words is known to all. You have seen for yourself how a few harsh words from the King changed your life in a single moment, filling you with a deep and seething anger."

"Am I supposed to write him a letter? Ask for an apology?"

The wizard smiled.

"This is no ordinary quill, it is the Mighty Pen, and it harnesses the power of words, turning them to reality. Whatever words you write with this pen, so they shall be. Remember to choose your words carefully, using wisdom and compassion."

"I don't understand."

A piece of yellowed parchment appeared in Westley's hand.

"Write the words 'one gold coin' on the parchment."

217

Westley frowned, taking the pen. This smacked of dark magic. Nevertheless, he wrote what the wizard had told him. When he was done, the words faded away, a gold coin appearing in his hand.

Westley dropped the coin with a yelp.

"Dark magic! Nothing good can come of this."

"Your words vanish, but their power lives on. With this gold coin you can buy everything you need for your family, even a box of delicious chocolates for your little ones. What fault can be found in such a kindness?"

Westley hesitated. Maybe the wizard was right. One gold coin couldn't hurt anything.

The wizard bowed deeply before Westley.

"The pen is yours for one year, payment due for the harsh words spoken by King Basil, words which shall unerringly circle the world and return to him, as sharp as any arrow ever forged."

Before Westley could ask the meaning of this cryptic statement, the wizard vanished, leaving him alone holding the gold coin, the parchment, and the Mighty Pen.

When he greeted his wife, Westley made no mention of his encounters with the King and wizard, saying only that his cart had been knocked over, the vegetables ruined, and fortune had smiled upon him by leaving a gold coin lying in the road.

Two weeks later, Westley saw the King again, this time sitting in his golden carriage near the market in Burton-On-Guster, four guards working furiously to repair a damaged wheel.

Westley was filled with an unexpected burning rage at the sight of the King. He pulled out the Mighty Pen and parchment, quickly writing, "Let King Basil feel the sting of his own words."

A bee streaked past Westley toward King Basil. When the bee stung him on the lips the King squealed in pain. Westley grinned.

On the way home a curious thought grew in his mind. Why should such a despicable creature as Basil be king? Why shouldn't a good and loving person like Westley be king? He grinned again. Harnessing the power of words would make it so.

Removing the pen and parchment from his coat pocket, he wrote, "Let King Basil and all his guards and soldiers feel the sting of a thousand bees, a thousand arrows, and ten thousand heartless warriors. Let me rule in his stead as King Westley."

Chaos reigned in Burton-On-Guster for almost a month. When it was over, Westley was king. He moved his family into the luxurious quarters of Castle Umbra, riding daily through the city in a gold carriage drawn by eight magnificent snow white rabbits. He visited his treasury every other day, smiling with satisfaction at the roomful of chests overflowing with gold coins and gems.

Westley's wife and children quickly adopted their lavish new lifestyle, soon becoming spoiled and complacent. Simple sweets from the market no longer satisfied them, only the most magnificent cakes and elaborately decorated confections would do. They

219

mocked the vendors at the King's Market, forgetting their past life as humble vegetable farmers, smirking when they drove past in their fine gold carriage.

One year passed to find Westley nodding in his great silver throne, his eyes half closed. With a flash of blue light the wizard appeared before him, giving a gracious bow.

"King Westley, your year with the Mighty Pen has come to an end. You have used it to teach King Basil a profoundly important lesson, that our own words circle the world and unerringly return to us, sharper than any arrow ever forged."

"You bore me with your tedious words, wizard. I no longer have need for you or your ridiculous magic pen."

King Westley pulled the pen from his robe, tossing it carelessly to the floor. The wizard nodded politely as he retrieved the Mighty Pen, disappearing before Westley could command him to leave.

King Westley gave a great yawn. His coffers were overflowing with gold, his soldiers loyal to him. He had everything he could ever want.

He rose at noon the following day, strolling idly onto the balcony overlooking his kingdom. He never saw the bee that stung his lip, a sting that caused him to shriek out in pain. He reeled back at the sight of a thousand angry bees streaking toward the castle, followed closely by a thousand arrows hissing through the air. Amidst a cloud of pale yellow dust on the horizon he saw the silhouettes of ten thousand heartless warriors marching toward him. The wizard's voice echoed in his ears.

"Our own words circle the world and unerringly return to us, sharper than any arrow ever forged."

Sophia closed the book. The birds around the cage were silent. Captain Beaky had tears in his eyes.

Chapter 32

Bandar

Captain Beaky stood up, gingerly placing the book back in the carved wooden box. He motioned for Sophia and Orville to follow him. When they reached a large mud hut in the center of the village he turned to Sophia.

"The book spirit has spoken. Its words will be remembered. You are members of our tribe now, free to come and go as you please, as was the Flying Star Captain who taught us his sacred language. This hut is your home for as long as you wish."

Sophia was moved by Captain Beaky's kindness.

"I also will remember the message of the book spirit, to use the power of words with wisdom and compassion. I would like to teach some of the villagers how to speak the words of the book spirit. It is called 'reading'. They can teach other villagers to read. There are many more books to be found in the Flying Star Captain's ship."

"I will choose three of our cleverest villagers to learn this art of reading."

After Captain Beaky was gone, Orville said, "What was the book about? Why did Captain Beaky give us our own hut?"

Sophia told him the story of Westley and the book's message about the power of words.

"I like stories with wizards in them, and I liked that magic pen. Why did the story make Captain Beaky cry?"

"He was moved by it. He's much more than just a primitive carnivorous bird."

Orville frowned. "Easy to say now. Not so easy when I thought he was throwing me into a big stewpot and dumping broth on me."

"Aren't you glad you listened to your inner voice?"

"I guess so. At least I smell a lot better. And my fur is nice and soft again. What do we do now?"

"We wait, and while we're waiting I'm going to teach the villagers how to read old Mintarian."

"Shouldn't we be looking for Proto and Leaf?"

"Not yet. Something important is going to happen, but I'm not certain what. I'll know it when I see it."

For the next week Sophia held reading classes three times a day in the village center. On the first day there were three students, on the second day there were nineteen. Sophia was stunned by how rapidly the birds were able to learn.

"Orville, these birds have astonishing memories. After only five days most of them can read *A Thousand Bees*."

On the seventh day, Sophia's class was abruptly

interrupted when a bird staggered out of the jungle, her bony hands clutched together. She fell to her knees and gave a dreadful wailing cry.

"Bandar has entered the forbidden realm of the demons! My Bandar is lost to me forever! The Two Suns are punishing me!" She pounded the ground with her bony hands, sobbing.

This was what Sophia had been waiting for. She ran to the bird, now surrounded by villagers.

"What happened?"

The distraught bird looked up at Sophia. "You are filled with the power of magic, you speak the voice of book spirits. You can bring my son Bandar back to me!"

Sophia took the bird's hand in her paw. "Tell me what happened to Bandar. Where did he go?"

"I told him again and again not to be curious. I warned him about wanting to know more. He would not stop talking about the demons who came here to destroy our land and build their great stone huts that touch the sky. He said he wanted to enter the forbidden realm below. He said he would discover the truth of the demons and why the Two Suns had rained down destruction on them. He was certain the demons were beings like us."

Orville darted up next to Sophia. "What happened?"

"It's what I've been waiting for. Her son Bandar entered a subterranean complex built by the Thaumatarians. The villagers think the Thaumatarians were demons, that the two suns in their sky sent the meteors to destroy them. Bandar didn't think they were demons, he thought they were living creatures just like them."

"Pretty smart."

"We have to find him."

A light of realization blinked on in Orville's eyes.

"Bandar has something to do with the explosion that causes the Great Thaumatarian Time Wave."

"I'm sure of it. He'll lead us to the site."

Sophia squeezed the bird's hand, speaking in old Mintarian.

"We will descend into the forbidden realm of demons and do our best to find your Bandar, to bring him safely home."

The sobbing bird rubbed her beak against Sophia's paw, making small crowing noises.

"You were sent to us by the Two Suns, I know you were. Tell them I am overflowing with gratitude for all they have given us."

"The Two Suns did not send us. We are beings from a distant land, here to prevent a terrible catastrophe. I believe your son Bandar is meant to help us. You should be proud of him. He is brave, and filled with wisdom beyond his years."

"You will bring him home to me?"

"We will do everything we can. Can you show us the entrance to the forbidden realm?"

"I will show you. It is not far from here."

Half an hour later Orville and Sophia stepped out of their hut, packs slung on their shoulders. Orville adjusted his adventuring hat to a jaunty angle, turning to Sophia, raising one eyebrow.

"Let's go meet some demons."

"You have cookie crumbs all over your whiskers."

Orville glared at Sophia, brushing the crumbs off.

"I shaped cookies for lunch. Have you seen what these birds eat? Nothing but seeds and grain and berries and fruit and a few veggies. I saw one of them eating bugs. Who eats bugs?"

"Let's go, Bandar's mum is waiting for us."

"Whoa, look at the crowd."

Bandar's mum was surrounded by dozens of birds, including Captain Beaky. They let out a squawking cheer when Orville and Sophia appeared.

Captain Beaky waved to them.

"Follow me, I will take you to the entrance of the forbidden realm. We are not allowed to enter, but you are not bound by our sacred laws."

Captain Beaky led the way into the steaming jungle. Orville and Sophia walked behind him, followed by a large crowd of chattering villagers.

As they pushed through the dense foliage the birds called out dire warnings to Sophia.

"Do not let the demons touch you. They will tear out your heart and eat it!"

"They grind up the bones of their victims to make bread!"

"If you look into their eyes you will crumble to dust!"

"They will cut you in half with a single swipe of their razor sharp claws!"

"They make soup from your blood!"

"They make stylish hats from your fur!"

Orville whispered, "What are they saying?"

"They're wishing us luck, praying to the Two Suns that we return safely with Bandar."

"That's nice. I guess I really was wrong about them."

The two Ferusian suns were directly overhead when Captain Beaky stopped, pointing to a massive wall of stone and metal lying ahead of them.

"This is as far as we may go. The gateway is behind the wall of stone. We cannot be here when you open it. Even a glimpse of a demon causes eternal madness."

"I understand. Thank you for your kindness, for accepting us into your tribe. We will do everything we can to find Bandar and bring him safely home."

The two adventurers waved their good byes, watching as the birds headed back to the village.

"Let's go."

Orville strode into the clearing.

"It's the ruins of an old building. Must have been hit by a meteor."

Sophia stepped around the massive crumbling wall.

"Look familiar?"

"An elevator."

Sophia approached the moss covered metal door, tapping a pale violet disc. The elevator door squealed open.

"Ready?"

"Let's go save the universe."

227

There was something different about the way Orville said it. Sophia put her arms around his neck and kissed him.

"You really are the bravest mouse I know."

Chapter 33

Leaf to the Rescue

Proto lay on the soggy jungle floor, unable to move, his eyes fixed on the snoring treasure hunter, his hand clutching the small silver sphere. A powerful electromagnetic pulse was coursing through his body, disrupting the neuronic transmitters responsible for his movement.

The ragged creature gave a loud snort, then sat up, swatting at a cloud of insects buzzing around him.

"Curse this jungle and all the creatures in it."

He yawned, studying Proto, a frown forming on his face.

"How am I going to get you to my ship? Can't carry you, can't let you walk."

He ran a paw across his chin.

"All I really need is your CDETS. That's where the money is. I can carry that in my pack. I'll take your CDETS and leave the rest of you here to rot in this moldy forsaken jungle."

Proto knew that once his CDETS was removed he had only two days of reserve power. When that ran out he would be gone, his memories and thoughts erased forever. He watched in horror as the bedraggled treasure hunter stumbled toward him, pulling a gleaming silver tool from his ragged coat pocket.

"Never cared much for Rabbitons. Doing the world a favor by getting rid of you."

Something caught the treasure hunter's eye. Something was different.

"That tree wasn't here before."

He eyed the small sapling at the end of the clearing, a gray papery ball hanging from one branch. His eyes narrowed. Something wasn't right. He reached for the deadly vape gun tucked into his belt. He gave a start when he heard the voice.

"Who wants to play catch?"

The treasure hunter pulled out the vape gun, looking for the source of the voice. His eyes widened when the sapling hurled the gray ball at him.

"Catch!"

The treasure hunter tried to duck, but was not quick enough, the round object colliding with his shoulder. The gray sphere proved to be a rather substantial Ferusian bees nest, the papery structure disintegrating on contact, the air instantly filled with a thousand bees, each and every one searching for something to sting.

The treasure hunter screamed when a bee stung him on the lip. He dropped the vape gun and bolted wildly into the jungle, trying to escape the swarm of furious assailants.

Leaf ran over to Proto, using a stick to pry the silver sphere from his hand. Proto gave a great shiver, then leaped to his feet, his eyes on Leaf. Squeaky darted into the clearing, racing in circles around Proto.

"He was going to take my CDETS. You saved my life. If you hadn't been here, I would be no more."

"I was watching from the jungle the whole time. No one notices a little tree standing on the edge of a forest. I saw what happened when he tossed the sphere to you. I was at a loss until I remembered the bees nest. I ran back and retrieved it, being careful not to disturb them. I must admit I took a certain amount of pleasure in bearing witness to the fruits of my labor. He ran surprisingly fast for a despicable cold hearted scoundrel."

"I don't think his feet ever touched the ground."

The two automatons burst out laughing.

Proto grinned. "That should teach him to BEE nicer to Rabbitons."

"That is a form of humor? Your emphasis on the word 'BEE'?"

"Yes, it is a form of humor I learned from Orville when our ship was attacked by gigantic bees. The words 'be' and 'bee' sound the same, but are spelled differently and have entirely different meanings. Therein lies the humor."

"Excellent, I shall remember this in case we are attacked by bees again. Perhaps it would make Orville and Sophia laugh."

"I believe it would. I have heard Orville tell Sophia the more times you tell a joke the funnier it becomes."

Proto carefully wrapped the treasure hunter's silver sphere in a soft cloth and tucked it into his pack.

"I have learned a great deal besides humor from Orville and Sophia during the course of our adventures. They have told me time and time again to pay close attention to what the universe brings us, whether it is a new friend or a strange paralyzing silver sphere. Such things always hold a hidden purpose, one that takes time to be revealed. I would not have guessed when I first met you that one day you would save my life. That is why I am bringing the silver sphere with us. I am certain I will find a purpose for it as our adventure unfolds."

"I concur. The Watcher has spoken similar words. It is quite serendipitous that you bumped into the bees nest just before being taken captive by the treasure hunter."

Proto slung his enormous pack to his shoulder.

"Indeed it was. We should continue east. Orville and Sophia are more than likely waiting patiently for us at the explosion site."

The two friends chatted as they strolled along the jungle path through the ruins of a long abandoned city.

Leaf glanced up at Proto.

"Would you mind if I asked your advice on a personal matter?"

"Of course not, I would be happy to help you. That's what friends are for. Is something troubling you?"

"I am worried about living in Muridaan Falls. When I am in the forest I am surrounded by trees, unnoticed by passing mice. This will not be the case if I live in Muridaan Falls. I dread to think what would happen if I took a stroll through the center of town."

"I completely understand these fears. When I first moved to Muridaan Falls I was quite fearful. I had spent so many years living alone in the Cube that the outside world filled me with dread. It was only the friendship and kindness of Orville and Sophia that gave me the courage to leave the Cube."

"How did the mice in the village react to your presence?"

"At first they were terrified, peering at me through their curtains, calling their mouselings home. I was a terrible silver monstrosity, my intentions unknown to them. I had prepared myself for such a response, however, bringing with me an enormous tray of tasty little cakes. Orville and Sophia stood next to me, snacking on cakes, chatting with me as if I were an old friend who had stopped by for a visit. Before long I was surrounded by a crowd of mice, some there for the tasty cakes, some curious about me. Where was I from? Did I have strange and marvelous powers? Did I like mice? What was the purpose of my visit? The young mouselings were especially curious, asking the most questions."

"And now?"

"Now I walk through the town without incident, often stopping to chat with friends, asking them how their day is going, sometimes helping them lift heavy objects."

"Do you think they will be able to accept me as they have accepted you?"

"I'm certain of it. Next time I go grocery shopping I will take you with me, introduce you to the villagers. I will make it abundantly clear you are a kind and thoughtful creature, an old friend of mine who has decided to live in Muridaan Falls."

"I don't look like anyone else."

"Sophia once told me that items of great rarity often possess enormous value. Imagine a big pile of rocks holding one single sparkling Nirriimian white crystal. The crystal looks nothing like the other rocks, but it holds untold value."

"I will do it. I will accompany you on your next trip to the grocery store. I am overwhelmed by the kindness and understanding you have shown me."

"I was equally overwhelmed by the kindness shown to me by Orville and Sophia."

The two friends stepped quietly through the abandoned city, lost in their thoughts.

It was Proto who spotted the massive gray dome, a curious structure untouched by the meteor storm.

"Interesting. Perhaps we should investigate."

Chapter 34

Formidable Orville

Orville and Sophia stepped cautiously into the elevator, Orville raising his paw to tap the glowing violet tab.

"You don't think there really are demons down there, do you?"

"Are you being funny?"

"Well, not demons exactly, but creatures that might be sort of like demons?"

"You mean the ones who make soup out of your blood?"

"What? Why would you say that? Did Captain Beaky say something?"

Sophia grinned, tapping the elevator button.

The door squealed shut, the elevator jerking sharply as it began its descent.

Orville blinked up a sphere of defense.

"So far so good. No demons."

"Just the one behind you holding a soup bowl."

"Ha ha. Very funny. Things like that don't scare me

anymore, just so you know."

Almost a minute later the elevator came to a jarring halt. The door whined and shuddered, jamming halfway open.

The two friends squeezed through the gap, stepping into a brightly illuminated rotunda lined with colorful shops.

"Whoa, I was not expecting this. There's still stuff in all the stores! The Thaumatarians must have left this place in a hurry. We should poke around and see what we can find. I could use a new adventuring coat. Mine's getting a little ragged looking."

"Fifteen minutes, then we need to get moving. We have to find Bandar."

"There's a clothing store over there. It won't take long."

Orville darted over to the shop, pulling the door open.

"Lots of coats. Thaumatarians were a little smaller than mice, but a larger size should fit me nicely."

He browsed through the racks, finally finding a coat he liked.

"Perfect, a rugged adventurer's coat. I like all the pockets and buckles and snaps, and it's waterproof. This is nice, and the price is very reasonable. Free."

Orville cackled loudly, wishing Sophia was there to appreciate his humor. He pulled the coat on, stepping in front of a mirror, turning from side to side.

"I look good. Rugged. Oops, there's Sophia."

Orville darted out of the shop.

"Look at this amazing coat I found. Did you get anything?"

Sophia pointed to her feet. "Sturdy adventuring boots. They're really well made, some kind of light synthetic material. Good deep treads on them."

"Do you like my coat?"

"Um… you look kind of like a Dark Space Trooper."

Orville grinned. "I know."

He stopped abruptly, his eyes on the floor.

"Look."

Sophia studied the gleaming blue tiles.

"What is it?"

"Seeds. Someone scattered seeds on the floor."

"Bandar! It must have been Bandar. He's leaving a trail so he can find his way back."

"Smart fellow."

"We just follow the trail of seeds."

Orville scanned the floor. "There's more over there. He was going toward those big doors."

"That's east. Let's go."

The two friends walked across the sprawling rotunda toward the ornate golden doors.

"Fancy place. I wish we had something like this in Muridaan Falls. Hey, what do you think that store is? The one with the little blinking lights in it."

"We're here to find Bandar, not go shopping."

"I didn't say I wanted to go shopping, I was just wondering what kind of store it was. What do you think Bandar has to do with the Time Wave?"

"I don't know, but I'm certain he plays a part in all this."

Sophia pushed one of the golden doors open, revealing a long dimly lit hallway.

"That's weird, it's not fancy like the shopping area."

"I think it's a maintenance tunnel. There's a box of tools."

Orville pointed to the floor.

"More seeds."

"Let's go."

The tunnel proved to be almost a mile long, curving slightly to the northeast. As they approached the end of the featureless hallway, Sophia held up her paw for Orville to stop.

"Look at the signs."

"What about them?"

"They look like warning signs. I'm getting a bad feeling."

Orville peered through the dim light to the doors at the end of the corridor, a chill shooting through him. His voice was a whisper.

"There's something standing in the shadows."

"I see it, it's motionless. It seems like an odd place for a statue. It could be an automaton, maybe a guard. That would explain the warning signs."

"It's probably old, deactivated, nothing for us to worry about."

"Maybe."

The two adventurers popped up their spheres of defense and crept toward the ominous figure.

Orville sent a thought cloud to Sophia.

"It's really big. Reminds me of that crazy A6 Warrior Rabbiton that chased us on Periculum. I hope he's been deactivated."

Orville jumped when the fourteen foot tall automaton swiveled around, bellowing out an indecipherable command, its eyes glowing bright red.

"Run!"

"No, don't run, let's see what it does."

A beam of red light shot out from the creature's eyes, scanning across the two best friends.

"What was that?"

The automaton made a fist and tapped its chest three times, then stood at attention. The two doors slid open.

"What happened?"

"It's letting us pass. I think it saluted you."

"Why would it salute me?"

"I have no idea. Let's go before it changes its mind."

Orville and Sophia hurried past the automaton, the doors closing silently behind them.

"Maybe he thought I was someone important because of my new coat. He probably thought I was a commander or something, a rough and tumble Dark Space Trooper. I'm glad I found this coat, it makes me look formidable. That means kind of dangerous, a force to be reckoned with."

"I know what formidable means." Sophia hid her smile. Orville was so funny when he tried to impress her with big words.

Orville studied the huge arched tunnel they had

entered.

"This is an underground transport system. Check out the tracks."

"Just like the ones at the Pod Station."

"There's a control panel, maybe we can call a Pod. I don't want to walk down the tracks, the tunnel looks kind of dark and creepy."

Orville approached the tall curved panel.

"Hey, here's a map of the different route lines. How do we know which one to take?"

"We need to figure out if Bandar took the–"

Sophia's answer was cut short by the unexpected appearance of a towering automaton stepping out from behind the panel, scanning them with a beam of red light. The fearsome creature saluted Orville, speaking rapidly in a language the two best friends did not understand.

Orville tried to look as formidable as he could, pointing to the route map with a dark frown, stomping his foot. The automaton paused, then stepped over to the panel, rapidly tapping a grid of pale blue glowing discs. It stepped away from them, saluting Orville again, standing at attention.

Orville grinned at Sophia.

"And that's how it's done."

Sophia decided she should probably not whack Orville's arm in front of the automaton.

Moments later a Pod arrived, the door sliding open.

Orville nodded his thanks to the automaton and they walked over to the Pod, stepping inside.

"Comfy seats. I hope this one's not broken like the other one. Where do you think we're going?"

"I guess we'll find out. It's no accident that both automatons saluted you, and the second one seemed to know where we're supposed to go."

"They saluted me because I'm so formidable looking."

"That's probably it."

The Pod shot down the tunnel, flashing past six stations, the two friends glimpsing small groups of the warrior automatons standing at attention on the platforms. The Pod came to a gentle halt at the seventh station.

"I guess this is our stop."

Orville stepped out onto the platform.

"I don't believe it." He pointed to a pile of seeds on the ground.

"Look at the three guards next to those big doors."

"And the route map on the wall. The blue light at the end of the red line is blinking. That must be where we are."

"The blue light has a bunch of symbols under it, but I have no idea what they mean. It could be a military complex, with all these warrior automatons."

"Let's see what's on the other side of the doors they're guarding. No problem for Orville Mouse, the formidable Dark Space Trooper."

With a grin he strode toward the three imposing guards.

Three red lights scanned Orville, three towering

automatons stepped aside, saluting him. The doors whirred open.

They strode through, expecting to enter a massive military complex. Orville's eyes widened.

"Um… this is looking a little scary."

The room they entered was small, only fifteen feet across, a single gleaming silver door on the opposite wall.

"It's an elevator."

"Look at that symbol next to it, a skeleton with lightning bolts coming out of it. I don't like this. Why would a skeleton have lightning bolts on it?"

"I don't know, but we have to keep going. We have to find Bandar."

Orville sighed. He stepped over to the silver door and tapped the small gray disc. A red beam of light shone down from above, scanning him.

The doors whirred open, lights blinking on. Sophia grabbed Orville's arm.

"Wait, open your pack!"

"What?"

"Open your pack. Do it."

Orville set his pack down, unbuckling the straps.

"Give me the envelope you got from the Station Master."

"Um… okay, I think I still have it."

Orville rifled through his pack, pulling out a jumbled tangle of clothes.

"It's in here somewhere. Eww, these socks smell kind of bad. Hey, here's that oatmeal cookie I was looking for."

"You don't fold your clothes?"

"Sometimes I do. Proto does all the laundry. Here it is."

He pulled out the envelope and gave it to Sophia. She tore it open with a triumphant laugh.

"I knew it! This is why the automatons have been saluting you. It's an identification badge, probably for a high ranking military commander. Look at this square on it with the grid of tiny sparkling lights. That's what the guards were scanning."

"It wasn't because of my coat?"

"Um… that probably helped, because it made you look like a formidable Dark Space Trooper."

"It's lucky we ran into the Station Master."

"Luck didn't have anything to do with it. The universe sent us there."

"If you think about it, by dropping his identification badge in a Pod station four hundred thousand years ago, that military commander may have saved our world."

"That's how it works. You never know how some insignificant event is going to change the course of history."

"That's a little scary."

"Let's go."

Chapter 35

A Purple Nightmare

It took the elevator three minutes to descend, enough time for Orville to spot the seeds on the floor.

"How in the world did Bandar get past those automatons?"

"I don't know. He must be really smart."

"Maybe he had an identification badge like mine."

The doors squealed open. Orville gave a yelp when he saw the automaton sprawled on the floor, its eyes dark, one arm melted, one leg missing.

The two friends blinked up spheres of defense, peering cautiously out the elevator doors.

"Everything is charred and black in here, like there was a big fire or something. Do you think it got hit by a meteor?"

"We're a mile underground and it seems structurally sound. Whatever caused this, it wasn't a meteor."

"It looks like a big control center. I bet this place used to be busy, packed with Thaumatarians."

"A lot of the panels are burned and melted like the automaton was. A few still look functional, but not many. I wish I knew what this place was. Look at the hole in the wall at the far end of the room. It looks like something blasted through it."

"We must be getting closer to the big energy field Proto saw. Maybe whatever happened here is what causes the explosion."

"You could be right. We just have to figure out what happened and how to prevent the Great Time Wave."

"Take a peek through that round window and see what's there."

Sophia stepped over to a two foot wide circular window, squinting through the massively thick synthetic glass.

"It's a big empty room with armored doors on the far wall. Looks like they're made of Morsennium and they're protected by an energy field. The symbols on the doors are rippling."

Orville peered through the window. "One of the symbols is that skeleton with lightning bolts on it."

"Orville, I know what this is! It's a power plant, probably with feeder lines to the Thaumatarian cities. The skeleton with lightning bolts is a warning about high voltage transmission lines."

"Something bad must have happened on the other side of those armored doors. Probably after the Thaumatarians left Ferus."

"There are no guards in the next room to open the armored doors for us, and there's no way we can force them open. You'd need a fusion pulsar bomb to blast through them. We can't blink to the other side because we have no idea what's there. It could be a five thousand degree molten plasma field."

"We don't need to open any doors." Orville pointed to the hole in the wall at the far end of the room.

"Good idea. Let's see where it goes."

Sophia headed across the room, hopping up onto a console, peering into the opening.

"I can see through into the next room. This won't get us past the armored doors, just into the next room."

Orville hopped up next to Sophia. He sent out an orb of light.

"This wall is ten feet thick, made of Morsennium reinforced concrete. Wait, look up there, near the top!"

"I see it, an air duct, big enough to fit through. It's going in the right direction."

Sophia vanished in a flash of light, appearing a split second later in the duct, looking down at Orville.

"Come on!"

Orville blinked up next to Sophia and they crawled down the long metal duct, Orville's orb of light in front of them.

"The room with the armored doors is about a hundred feet across. Not much farther till we're past it."

"There's a vent about twenty feet ahead."

Orville wriggled forward, peering through the vent's grill.

"This is it. We're past the doors." He held out his paw, a brilliant violet light vaporizing the vent. The two friends blinked down to the floor below.

"This is seriously creepy."

The room was filled with hundreds of vertical glass cylinders extending from the floor to the ceiling, a white hot incandescent substance oozing through them. Several of the tubes had shattered, mounds of the mysterious white substance spilling out onto the floor.

"That doesn't look good. What is that stuff? Something definitely went wrong here."

Orville stepped closer to a pile of the white goop.

"Don't touch it! We don't know what it is."

Orville jumped back when the gloopy substance began quivering, oozing toward him.

"It's after me! Let's get out of here!"

Orville and Sophia blinked up spheres of defense and raced across the room.

"Through here!"

Sophia darted into a tunnel, Orville right behind her.

"Stairs! Take those stairs!"

A minute later they reached the upper level, Orville trying to catch his breath.

"What was that stuff? It was trying to get me."

Sophia didn't answer, her eyes on the huge glass dome in the center of the massive room. The floor of the dome resembled the rocky surface of a planet, little yellow leafy creatures darting past the jagged boulders. Sophia stepped over to the dome, studying the small creatures, waving to them.

"They can't see us."

"Is it some kind of zoo?"

"I don't think so. Remember how Abacus got the antimatter he needed for the *MV Bermitar*?"

"From Ainran, the antimatter world. Oh, I get it, the connection to Ainran was inside a dome just like this one."

"Exactly. This is probably a link to an antimatter world used by the Thaumatarians."

"Do you think antimatter is what causes the giant explosion?"

"I don't think so. It would be extremely difficult to transfer enough antimatter from a parallel universe to create an explosion large enough to cause the Great Time Wave."

"Those little yellow plant creatures are kind of cute, running around like that."

"If one of those cute little plants touched you, the explosion would vaporize half a city. When matter and antimatter collide it releases tremendous amounts of energy. That's how Abacus powered his ship."

"I didn't say I wanted to touch one, I just said they were cute. I know what antimatter is."

"This isn't much help, let's see where that hallway goes."

Sophia headed down the wide corridor, her foot colliding with a heavy object. She froze when she saw what it was.

"It's an automaton's arm, and it has claw marks on it."

Orville tried to hide his rising fear. He didn't want to think about what kind of creature could tear off an automaton's arm.

"It's probably just from the explosion or something."

Sophia stopped to peer into some of the darkened rooms that lined the long hallway.

"Laboratories. Lots of equipment I'm not familiar with. This complex is huge."

At the end of the hallway was an eight foot tall armored door, a small round window near the center. On the right side of the door was a violet tab and a small slot, precisely the size of the identification card given to them by the Station Master.

"A card slot. That's how we open the door. Just like Norrich Bunker on Periculum."

Orville stood on his tiptoes and peered through the round window.

"Oh no. This is very, very bad."

"What is it?"

"It's a huge purple automaton with glowing green eyes, big claws, and that weird white goopy stuff crawling all over it. The floor is covered with burned and melted automaton parts; arms, legs, heads, and torsos. There's a yellow door on the other side of the room with one of those lightning bolt skeleton warning signs on it."

"Maybe the automaton will salute you."

Orville jumped back with a yelp when the titanic automaton whipped around, his burning eyes on the window. A stream of blazing orange energy shot out from its hand across the room, the force of the blast shaking the walls violently, the synthetic glass turning to white hot molten goop, hissing and smoking when it spattered onto the stone floor.

Orville looked up at Sophia, his eyes wide.

"Whoa, good thing I had my sphere of defense up. That thing is formidable. There's no way we're getting past it."

Sophia began pacing back and forth, rubbing her chin. Orville took a seat on the floor. He had learned not to interrupt Sophia when she was thinking.

His eyes were drooping when she stopped pacing. He groaned when he saw her face, very familiar with her expression. He knew he was not going to like her plan.

"I know how we can get past that automaton."

"And I'm not going to like your plan because…"

"Because it's going to be very, very dangerous. If anything goes wrong we will both die instantly."

Chapter 36

Rebel Dog

Proto and Leaf strolled around the perimeter of the huge gray dome, searching for an entrance. Squeaky raced along next to them, wagging his tail and barking.

"No doors, I'm afraid, not even secret ones."

"Perhaps we should continue heading east. Orville and Sophia may be waiting for us."

Proto furrowed his brow.

"Sophia says there is always a reason why something holds our interest, but often we don't become aware of that reason until events unfold. I feel quite compelled to enter this dome, but I am uncertain why."

"Maybe Squeaky could help us get inside."

"An excellent thought. Squeaky, attack the dome!"

Squeaky gave a ferocious bark, a purple light blasting out from his eyes. The side of the dome glowed slightly but was otherwise unaffected.

"The dome is protected by a powerful energy field."

Proto stepped back, studying the roof of the mysterious structure.

"There's a ring of vents circling the top of the dome.

I will send Squeaky up for a look."

A holoscreen blinked on in front of Proto, the image linked to Squeaky's optical sensors. With a bark, Squeaky soared up into the air, circling the top of the dome. Proto studied the image on his holoscreen.

"Squeaky should be able to fit through that large vent. Once he's inside we can look for a way to shut off the external energy field."

Squeaky disappeared into the opening, the interior of the dome appearing on Proto's holoscreen. The dome was filled with thousands of small floating cubes, slowly circling around a vertical gray cylinder which extended from the floor to the peak of the dome. Each of the cubes was pulsing rhythmically with a repeating pattern of colored light.

"Curious. I am quite unfamiliar with this technology. Squeaky, proceed to ground level and search for control panels. Do not touch any of the floating cubes."

Squeaky shot down, avoiding the slow moving cubes, landing on the gleaming black floor. He gave a loud bark, heading toward a curved console near the base of the gray cylinder.

"This looks promising. Squeaky, push one of those blue tabs."

A single glowing cube fell to the floor, exploding with a brilliant orange flash that sent Squeaky blasting across the room into the side of the dome. He gave a loud bark and leaped to his feet, wagging his tail.

"Sorry, Squeaky!"

Proto studied the interior wall of the dome.

"Squeaky, next to the outer wall are three pedestals, each holding a violet tab. Try pressing those tabs."

Squeaky raced over to the first pedestal and pressed the glowing tab. A low beeping sound filled the dome, the violet light turning yellow. The beeping transformed into a pulsing alarm when he pushed the second tab. When he pressed the third tab something quite unexpected happened. The gray dome vanished.

Proto's jaw dropped, watching as thousands of the pulsing colored cubes drifted upward, carried off by a gentle afternoon breeze.

A silver door on the vertical gray cylinder whined open, an enormous dark green automaton stepping out, its eyes focused on the two adventuring companions who were currently watching the lovely flickering colored cubes drift across the sky.

The hulking automaton stormed across the floor toward them, his eyes glowing with a fearsome red light.

Proto whipped around at the sound of the creature's pounding footsteps.

"Great heavens! Where did he come from?"

The automaton came to a halt in front of Proto, bellowing out a string of incomprehensible words, pointing angrily to the rising cloud of glowing cubes, stomping its foot, poking Proto in the chest with an enormous green finger.

"The cubes? Are you concerned about the cubes?"

The huge automaton stopped, the light in its eyes turning pale blue. When its eyes glowed red again it bellowed out, "Who is responsible for taking my Power Distribution Substation offline? How did you gain entrance? Show me your identification card or you will be instantly vaporized!"

Proto's mind was racing. This was a Thaumatarian warrior automaton whose weaponry surpassed even that of the A6 Warrior Rabbitons, and Proto knew he had no defense against such force. He needed time to think.

"Of course, I would be more than happy to show you my identification card giving me permission to enter your marvelous substation. More than happy to. A lovely day, is it not? I can't help but admire your marvelous weaponry. Is that a heavy particle beam vaporization projector I see? I believe the A6 Warrior Rabbitons had a similar system, though clearly not as powerful as yours. You are quite a technological marvel."

"SHOW ME YOUR CARD OR YOU WILL BE DESTROYED!"

"Of course, immediately, and I do apologize. It's right here in my pack."

Proto set his enormous pack on the floor, fumbling with the straps. He had a sudden flash of insight, transmitting a quick message to Squeaky, then smiled apologetically at the warrior automaton.

"Drat, these packs can be so difficult to open, far too many straps and snaps in my opinion. Orville likes lots of straps and buckles, but I find they are often more trouble than–"

"STOP STALLING AND SHOW ME YOUR

CARD!"

The automaton's fist was glowing brightly.

A blast of purple light struck the huge warrior automaton from behind. It spun around, looking for the source of the beam, which proved to be a silver puppy floating a hundred feet above the ground.

Proto pointed to Squeaky, shouting, "It's one of those dastardly Rebel Dogs! That's who did it! He's trying to destroy our substation! Get him before he escapes!"

Squeaky shot across the rubble, the ground shaking as the monstrous automaton thundered after him. A powerful beam of purple light shot out from its hand, exploding five feet away from Squeaky, sending him tumbling to the ground.

The automaton gave a triumphant cry.

"I HAVE YOU NOW, REBEL DOG!"

Squeaky staggered to his feet, stumbled, then limped painfully toward a tangle of thick vegetation, pushing his way into it, trying to hide from the deadly automaton.

"COME OUT THIS INSTANT OR I WILL OBLITERATE YOU, REBEL DOG!"

The angry automaton didn't notice the silver RoboPup floating silently up through the twisted jungle foliage then streak back toward the dome.

Three things happened in rapid succession after Squeaky's spectacular tuck and roll landing on the dome floor. Proto pressed all three gold tabs, the gray dome reappeared, and the Thaumatarian automaton let out a shriek of unparalleled rage that rolled across the city, flocks of frightened birds taking to the air.

Proto rubbed Squeaky's head.

"Excellent job, Squeaky. That limp was a marvelous ruse."

Squeaky let out a loud bark, wagging his tail.

Proto strode toward the open door in the gray cylinder. Leaf pointed up to the ceiling. The floating cubes were back, once again circling the room.

"We know this is a Power Distribution Substation. It is highly probable that the explosion which causes the Great Time Wave occurs in the Central Energy Transfer Core, which is linked to this Substation. All we have to do is follow the Power Distribution Lines back to the Core."

"I agree. That is where we will find the gigantic energy field, and where we will find Orville and Sophia."

Proto stepped into the gray cylinder.

"It's an elevator, just as I suspected. Going down."

Chapter 37

Leaf's Dilemma

The elevator dropped like a stone, rendering Proto and Leaf weightless for precisely fifty-four seconds.

Proto floated above the floor, a grin appearing on his face.

"Excellent, I've been trying to lose a little weight."

"I'm afraid I don't understand, isn't your weight constant?"

"My mass is constant, but my subjective weight varies according to the gravitational forces at work. Relative to the falling elevator I am now weightless, floating above the floor."

"I'm afraid I'm still confused by your first statement regarding your attempt to lose weight. Why would you choose to decrease your mass?"

"I was making a light hearted joke. I believe both Orville and Sophia would have found it quite humorous. I have heard Orville say several times he needs to lose a little weight, usually right after he finishes a snapberry pie."

"I see. Is it humorous because you said you were

257

trying to lose a little weight, but your mass is always constant?"

"It is more complex than that."

The elevator shrieked to halt, pushing Proto and Leaf to the floor.

Proto got to his feet.

"Drat, I didn't even have any snapberry pie but I just gained six hundred and ninety pounds."

"That is more gravity related humor? I was unaware you were capable of ingesting snapberry pie. Are you not powered by a Cross Dimensional Energy Transfer Sphere?"

"You are correct in recognizing it as another gravity joke, in this case one that Orville would appreciate more than Sophia, since there was a reference to snapberry pie."

"As a whole, I find the concept of humor to be quite baffling."

"As did I, before my excellent tutorage under Orville. He told me one should not take the facts of a humorous statement literally. An outlandish, factually incorrect statement is often perceived to be quite humorous."

The elevator door squealed open, the two friends stepping out into a long brightly lit circular tunnel.

Leaf stopped, turning to Proto. "If I were to say a six hundred pound Naddwok was performing the Natondi Toe Dance on your head, would that be humorous simply because it was factually incorrect?"

Proto paused, knitting his eyebrows.

"An interesting question. I believe it could be considered humorous under certain circumstances, but I would have to confer with Orville to make a final determination."

"A very angry fourteen foot tall purple Thaumatarian warrior automaton is standing behind you."

"Again, I would have to confer with Orville on all such outlandish statements. I am uncertain whether simply stating that a–"

"I was not attempting to be humorous. My statement regarding the purple warrior automaton is factually correct."

"YOU'RE LATE, SOLDIER!"

Proto whipped around to face a towering automaton looking down at him, his face a portrait of simmering rage. Proto was well aware he was no match for a warrior automaton of this size. He gave his most disarming smile.

"I'm dreadfully sorry, I was most unavoidably detained. How may I be of assistance?"

"Are you trying to be funny? Where have you been? I've been standing here for thirty-eight years!"

Leaf whispered, "Is that a joke? Factually inaccurate? Is he attempting to make us laugh?"

"YOU THINK THIS IS A JOKE? THERE'S A GHOST IN THE MACHINE AND IT NEEDS TO BE REMOVED! THIS IS NO LAUGHING MATTER! LIVES DEPEND ON IT!"

"I completely understand. Please forgive my assistant, he is a renowned and highly qualified specialist in advanced ghost removal procedures, but quite unfamiliar with military protocol, I'm afraid."

The huge automaton glared at Leaf.

"Take the door on the right at the end of the tunnel. The ghost's electromagnetic field is scrambling the machine's engineered intelligence unit. How long will it take to remove it?"

"That will depend on a number of rather esoteric factors. We'll have to examine the machine and speak with the ghost."

"GET TO IT, SOLDIER!"

Proto grabbed Squeaky and they ran down the hallway. He stopped when they rounded a curve, the automaton out of sight.

"Orville would not have liked that one bit."

Leaf snickered.

"His eyes would have bugged out."

"Ha ha ha ha! Excellent humor, excellent. We'll head to the end of the tunnel and find a way up to the surface."

"What about the ghost in the machine?"

"We will ignore it, for several reasons. First, it is none of our concern, and second, I am quite terrified of ghosts, an illogical fear I acquired from Orville. He doesn't even like to say the word 'ghost'."

"You have encountered ghosts before?"

"I have never been in the presence of a real one."

"What do they do? Why is he so afraid of them?"

"He has been excessively vague about the threat they pose, perhaps because he doesn't wish to scare me any more than is necessary. It must be something truly dreadful, some foul otherworldly malevolence against which I have no defense. I shudder to even think about it."

"You did promise that automaton you would remove the ghost from the machine."

"Quite so, but that was a ruse. I tricked him into thinking I was going to remove the ghost, when in fact I had no intention of doing so."

"You are capable of deception? I am programmed to always speak the truth, never to deceive under any circumstances."

"As was I, until Orville explained to me that deception is sometimes necessary. For instance, when Sophia asks Orville if he likes a gift she gave him, he will always say yes, because he does not wish to hurt her feelings."

"Are you saying you used deception because you did not wish to hurt the purple automaton's feelings by refusing to remove the ghost? Surely such a creature would not possess the range of feelings which Sophia has."

"I can see this is causing you some concern. If you would like, we could take a quick peek at the machine and see what sort of ghost is involved. One quick look and then we could leave. Just a peek. A quick peek."

"A most satisfactory compromise. Shall we press on?"

The two adventurers headed down the long curving tunnel, Proto occasionally stopping to peer through the

261

glass doors that lined the corridor.

"The rooms are filled with curious electronic devices, more than likely communication systems. The warrior automaton did mention that the machine inhabited by the ghost possesses engineered intelligence."

"We have reached the end of the tunnel."

"And an elevator door which could take us up to the surface, if we chose to leave at this time." Proto raised his eyebrows.

"Perfect. We'll check on the ghost and then take the elevator up to the surface."

"Of course. First we will check on the ghost, then take the elevator to the surface."

Proto stepped over to the heavy metal door.

"I will press this tab right here, which will open the door to the room containing the ghost. Then we will enter the room and observe the ghost. I will look directly at it, studying it for a moment, making a brief assessment of its behavior. Again, we'll take a quick look at the ghost in the machine, review the current status of the ghost, then we will–"

Leaf stepped in front of Proto, smacking the violet tab. The door slid silently open.

Proto groaned. He followed Leaf into the room, his eyes darting about the interior.

In the center of the room was a massively complex machine containing hundreds of long twisting glass tubes, glowing iridescent spheres, whirling metal gears, dials, and silver discs. Floating above the machine was a towering holographic image of a Thaumatarian face.

Standing silently behind the machine were several hundred motionless warrior automatons, their eyes dark.

The holographic face above the machine turned slowly toward them.

"I like crackers. Crunchy. Crunchy crackers. Yum."

"What?"

"I'll buy a bicycle. I'm in the mood. A cheese bicycle. Yum."

Proto stared blankly at the pale green face, then turned to Leaf.

"There is no ghost here. We should leave."

Leaf raised one branch, pointing to the vaporous blue translucent figure drifting up through a control panel.

Chapter 38

The Sleeper

Proto inched back toward the door.

"Excellent, we have observed the ghost, and now it is time to leave."

Leaf called out, "Are you the ghost? Why are you here?"

The translucent figure floated across the room toward them, glaring angrily at Leaf.

"Do I look like a ghost, nimmy?"

"I will confess I have never actually seen a ghost, but Orville has described them to Proto, and Proto says you look precisely as one would expect."

"I'm a Sleeper, you nimmy, not a ghost. Didn't they teach you anything in Tree School?"

"Tree School? I'm not familiar with–"

"What are you doing here? Who sent you? What are you up to?"

"A formidable warrior automaton informed us you were scrambling the engineered intelligence within this bewildering machine with your electromagnetic field."

"I figured it was that brainless bucket of rusty bolts. Watch this!"

The blue ghost darted back into the huge machine. The holographic face sneezed three times, then giggled, "I'm a pretty ballerina."

Leaf whispered to Proto, "Would you consider that to be a humorous statement?"

"It is somewhat funny because the machine is clearly not a pretty ballerina, but it does not approach the sophisticated level of Orville's humor."

The ghost flashed out of the machine, grinning at them. "How's that for scrambling engineered intelligence, nimmy?"

Proto cautiously approached the floating blue figure. His fear of the ghost had diminished substantially once he realized it was more annoying than frightening.

"You said you're a Sleeper, not a ghost? I am unfamiliar with that term."

"I'm not just a Sleeper, I'm a bored Sleeper."

"I see. Again, I am not familiar with the term."

"There are twelve of us stuck in the SATs. I figured out how to project myself out and float around, drive those nimmy warrior automatons crazy."

"What is an SAT?"

"Suspended Animation Tube, nimmy, down on sub level two. Didn't they teach you anything in Rabbiton School?"

"Do you have a name? How long have you been trapped in the SAT?"

"I am Thaumatarian Master Guard Captain Ryle. I've been stuck in the SAT since the meteors hit. They forgot us. Left us in there."

"We would be happy to free you, if you would tell us how."

Captain Ryle gave a look of surprise. "You would do that?"

"Of course, we would be more than happy to help you. I am a Metaphysical Adventurer, sworn to help all in need."

"The SATs are one level below us, on sub level two. Take the elevator down, follow the green line to the SATs. They're inside a long room, twelve of them. Push the green tab on the end of each tube and the lid will slide open. It will only take us a few minutes to wake up. I don't know how to thank you. No matter how much I pestered those cursed automatons they would not release us."

"Consider it done. We will head down there now. I must confess it is quite a relief to discover you are not a ghost."

"Sorry I was so rude. I'll wait here. Once you revive me I'll pop back into my body."

Proto and Leaf walked down the hallway to the elevator. They stepped in and Proto pressed the tab, the elevator dropping.

Leaf tapped Proto's leg. "I am rapidly losing weight within the confines of this elevator."

"Ha ha ha ha! An excellent joke. I commend your effort."

The two friends stepped out of the elevator.

"There's the green line we're supposed to follow. I'm glad you insisted that we observe the ghost before we left. Who knows how long they would have been trapped in the suspended animation tubes."

"A dreadful fate indeed. Poor Captain Ryle. "

"The green line goes through those doors. That's where we shall find the SATs. I will attempt to converse with the Thaumatarians once we have awakened them, but I will need your assistance in translating their words. Now that I think about it, it's curious that I was able to understand Captain Ryle, since he is a Thaumatarian. Perhaps he was engaging in some form of thought transference, using thought clouds like Orville and Sophia."

Proto pushed open the heavy metal doors, stepping into the room.

"Just as he said, there are twelve silver suspended animation tubes. It will be interesting to see Captain Ryle in his physical form."

Leaf strolled over to the first tube.

"Here is the green tab. I will press it, just as Captain Ryle said to do."

Leaf pushed the green tab and a shrill alarm sounded, followed by a low whirring noise as the top section of the tube slid open. Leaf peered into the tube.

"I'm afraid this tube is empty. There is no one in it."

"Perhaps Captain Ryle was mistaken, perhaps there were only eleven of them trapped in the SATs."

Proto slapped the green tab on the next tube.

"This tube is empty also. Is it possible we are in the wrong room?"

"We followed the green line, just as he said."

Proto tapped the next green tab. The tube was empty.

So was the next one, and the one after that.

Proto turned to Leaf as they approached the last tube.

"Captain Ryle must be in this one. I suppose it is possible he was the only one left behind."

Leaf hurried over, watching as Proto tapped the green tab.

The top of the tube whirred open.

"It's empty."

"I'm getting a rather dreadful feeling."

"There's a door over there, perhaps there are more suspended animation tubes in the next room."

"An excellent thought. That must be it."

Proto pushed the door open to reveal a small cluttered office. He stopped when he saw a skeleton lying face down on the floor.

"It's wearing a decayed old military uniform. I'm feeling strangely cold. I wish Sophia was here, she could examine the skeleton. Orville does not like skeletons at all."

Leaf strode over to the skeleton, kneeling down next to it.

"It is definitely a Thaumatarian skeleton, and the uniform is correct."

He gently rolled the skeleton over, examining it closely.

"I'm afraid I have some rather distressing news. According to the name tag, this skeleton belongs to Captain Ryle."

Proto gasped. "Captain Ryle? How is that possible? Wait, if… there's only one… if…"

"Our friend Captain Ryle is a ghost, and this is his skeleton."

"Why would he do that? Why would he trick us?"

"Perhaps we should take the elevator to the surface."

Proto frowned. "I think I would like to talk to Captain Ryle and find out why he misled us, why he sent us down here."

"There is a chance Captain Ryle doesn't realize he is a ghost. He may very well believe what he told us to be true. If this is so, we should inform him of his current ghostly status."

"Oh dear, that will undoubtedly be quite a dreadful shock. I don't imagine anyone wants to hear they are a ghost. Perhaps I could tell him about the World of the Others, where Sophia's departed parents are currently living, a lovely place, although I have no idea how he would get there."

The two adventuring companions took the elevator up to the first level, returning to the machine room. Captain Ryle was nowhere to be seen.

"Captain Ryle?"

There was no response.

"What should we do?"

"Captain Ryle? Are you here?"

Proto whipped around when the door behind them

slammed shut, the lock clicking.

"CAPTAIN RYLE?"

Leaf pointed to the machine. Captain Ryle's blue translucent form was floating up through the control panel.

"Hello, nimmy. Welcome back. Did you free me and all my dear friends?"

"All of the suspended animation tubes were empty."

"What? They must have left without me. Can you imagine such a thing? Who would do that to an old friend?"

Proto's eyes darted over to Leaf. He was uncertain how to respond to a ghost, especially since he had no idea what a ghost might do if it got angry, no idea what it was capable of. He desperately wished Sophia and Orville were there. He attempted a pleasant smile.

"We did chance upon a skeleton in a connecting office."

"A skeleton! How scary! Whatever did you do?"

Leaf stepped forward. "We turned it over and examined it. The name on the identification tag was Captain Ryle."

"Captain Ryle? What a curious coincidence, that's my name. Odd, I don't remember meeting another Captain Ryle, and it's not a common name. There must be some explanation for this, something I'm missing. Can you think of one, nimmy?"

Leaf approached the glowing blue apparition.

"Clearly the skeleton is yours. You are currently a ghost. A rather rude and angry one, I might add."

270

"Oh, say it isn't so, nimmy."

"Would you care to tell us why you're so angry? And why you are here instead of in the world of the Others?"

"I'll do something even better, I'll show you a magic trick. You do like magic tricks, don't you?"

"There is no magic, only science."

"Then I'll show you some amazing science instead. Watch this!"

Captain Ryle flashed into the machine. The green holographic face blinked rapidly.

"WHO WANTS TO SEE ME TURN TWO NIMMYS INTO SPACE DUST?"

"Why are you doing this? We're trying to help you."

"I'M DOING IT BECAUSE YOU'RE A NIMMY AND I'M A GHOST!"

The holographic face twisted into a shrieking mask of burning rage.

"KILL THE NIMMYS! KILL THEM ALL! TURN THEM INTO SPACE DUST!"

The glowing red eyes of one hundred and seventy-nine warrior automatons blinked on, all of them turning to face Proto and Leaf, their massive fists glowing with a terrible purple light.

Proto shrieked, grabbing Leaf and Squeaky. He streaked across the room, smashing through the heavy metal doors, racing down the hallway to the elevator and slapping the button.

Unfortunately for Proto, the elevator door did not open.

The automatons poured into the hallway.

"KILL THE NIMMYS! KILL THEM ALL!"

Proto stepped in front of Leaf and Squeaky.

Thirty-seven warrior automatons raised their glowing purple fists.

Proto closed his eyes, waiting for the end. Ten seconds later he opened one eye. The automatons were silent, motionless, their eyes dark.

In front of Proto was a vaporous glowing white being floating several feet above the floor. He recognized it instantly. The creature had wings but they were still. It said nothing, but its presence filled Proto with infinite hope, infinite joy. For the first time in his life Proto knew with great certainty that he possessed a true inner self just as Sophia and Orville did.

"You are from the world of the Others. I visited you when your world overlapped with Tectar."

"We remember you with great clarity. It was you who inspired a shy young rabbit to become a scientist and the creator of the interstellar doorway. Sophia's mum and papa send their love. As always, they are watching over you. The elevator is working now. It will take you and Leaf and Squeaky to the surface. I will help poor Captain Ryle. He is deeply confused and angry about what happened to him, but this will pass once he arrives in the world of the Others."

Leaf whispered, "What manner of being is this?"

"He is from the world of the Others, where Sophia's mum and papa now live. He saved our lives."

The radiant white being floated through the wall into

the machine room.

The elevator door squealed opened.

Three minutes later the adventuring friends stood beneath the brilliant suns of Ferus.

Chapter 39

Ant Orville

Orville frowned.

"Just to be clear, you're saying your plan is very dangerous and if anything goes wrong we will die instantly? That doesn't sound like a very well thought out plan."

"I think the white gloopy stuff that was chasing you somehow altered the purple automaton's engineered intelligence. That's why he didn't scan your identification card and salute you. You saw what it did to those automatons. If we enter that room we will not survive."

"So what is your plan? How do we get past him?"

"Formshifting. We convert our physical form to something else."

"I don't know how to formshift. I never asked Master Marloh to teach me. I don't really like the idea of being something else. I like being a mouse."

"I'll do everything. We'll merge our minds like we've done before, but this time we'll keep them merged in the new physical form I create."

"We'll both be in one body? That's kind of weird.

What kind of body? A giant scary monster that can clobber the automaton? That might be kind of fun."

"Exactly the opposite. We're going to transform into a tiny little ant."

"What? Are you loopy? He'll destroy us in a heartbeat!"

"Not if he doesn't see us. We'll walk up the wall, across the ceiling, down the wall, and under the yellow door."

"We have to walk upside down on the ceiling? I don't like being upside down, I'll throw up."

"You'll be an ant, they don't mind being upside down. The secret is to change your point of view, change your perspective on the world. When we're walking up the wall, look at your feet and imagine that the wall is the floor. When we're walking across the ceiling, look at your feet and make the ceiling become the floor."

"That's impossible."

"Orville, when is the last time you saw an ant fall while it was walking across the ceiling?"

Orville hesitated.

"I don't exactly remember. Anyway, how do you know ants don't throw up when they're upside down? Maybe they throw up but you can't see it because they're so small."

"I'll pretend you didn't say that. Here's the plan. You insert your identification card into the slot next to the door, then run over here. We'll merge our minds and I'll formshift us into a tiny ant."

"Have you ever formshifted into an ant?"

"Dozens of times."

Orville's eyes narrowed. He could tell Sophia was trying not to laugh.

"You've never done it before."

"Not exactly into an ant, just a glowbird. Relax, it will be fine."

Orville groaned. "At least we'll be together when the purple automaton turns us into ant pudding."

"That's the spirit. I'll hide behind this crate while you put your card in the slot. Run back here and we'll convert into ant form."

"Hey, I just thought of something. I always wanted to be an uncle, but instead I'm going to be an ant."

Sophia closed her eyes.

"Get it? I'll be ANT Orville?"

"Put. Card. In. Slot."

"Just so you know, Proto would have laughed at a hilarious joke like that. Even Leaf would think it was funny."

Orville stepped across the corridor, pulling the ID card from his pack. He peeked through a small hole in the melted glass window. The automaton stood motionless on the far side of the room, its eyes pulsing with an eerie red light.

"Okay, here we go."

Orville inserted the card into the slot, then dashed back behind the crate. The automaton gave an ear splitting shriek of rage when the door squealed open, firing a blast of exploding purple energy into the room.

Orville flopped down next to Sophia.

"Take my paw, hurry! Close your eyes, let go of your physical self, let go of your thoughts, merge your mind with mine."

Orville was thoroughly familiar with the process and twenty seconds later his thoughts and memories had merged with Sophia's.

"What now?"

"Stay calm, you can look through my memories while I'm converting us to ant form. Find a nice one to help you relax."

"Here's a good one. It's when you and your mum and papa went to the science museum on your birthday. You were little, but so excited about science."

"I had so much fun that day. Okay, here we go."

"How long will it–"

"Open your eyes."

Orville would have let out a shriek, but in his current form as a tiny black ant he was not able to.

"Creekers, I'm an ant! What do I do with all these legs? How do I steer this thing?"

"Don't think about moving each individual leg, just think about moving forward. Go ahead, try walking."

Orville took a few tentative steps, then began walking slowly across the floor.

"You're right, this isn't too hard if I don't think about it. The ant body knows how to move its legs."

"Take us over to the doorway. Let's see what the automaton is doing."

Orville ran along the base of the wall to the open

door.

"Whoa, the door looks a thousand feet tall. It's weird being so small, but I feel really strong, like I could run forever."

"Keep still, the automaton is heading this way."

"I'm going to hide in that little crack."

Orville and Sophia watched the furious automaton stride into the corridor, a blue beam of light scanning the area. Finding no sign of the intruders, it roared out a string of incomprehensible sounds and stepped back into the next room.

"Okay, let's go. Through the doorway, turn right, up the wall and across the ceiling."

Orville scurried through the doorway, making a sharp right turn. The wall in front of him resembled a thousand foot tall smooth vertical rock face.

"Creekers, I can't do this. It's too scary."

Chapter 40

A Tree Falls

"What's wrong? Why can't you climb it?"

"There's nothing to grab onto, and if we fall we'll die."

"I already told you what to do. Look down at your feet, imagine the wall is the floor, then walk right up it."

"I keep imagining my feet slipping and me falling a thousand feet onto my head."

"Orville, an ant's foot has little tiny claws on it, and in between the claws are sticky pads. We're not going to fall. I also gave us enhanced vision, much better than a real ant has."

"Maybe I should shape a helmet, just in case."

"Are you trying to be funny? You don't need a helmet, you have an incredibly strong exoskeleton. Get moving before the automaton spots us."

Orville put one foot up on the wall, then another. Seconds later he was running straight up the smooth surface.

"Whoa! This is amazing! I'm sticking to the wall! I wish I could do this all the time. How fun would that be? I should have Mirus build me some sticky boots with little claws on them. Or maybe a giant ant vehicle we could ride around in. Can you imagine the look on everyone's face if we ran through Muridaan Falls in a big ant machine?"

"Focus, please. It only works because ants are so tiny and weigh almost nothing. You couldn't walk up a wall in sticky ant boots."

"Oh. Never mind then. It does feel like I'm running along the ground if I look down at my feet. It's a little weird, but not too bad. Okay, here's the ceiling... whoa, upside down... so scary! Hold on, feet. It's working, we're not falling, not throwing up yet... my feet are still sticking to the ceiling... okay, ceiling is the floor, ceiling is the floor. Don't look down... or maybe it's don't look up, because the ceiling is the floor now? That's weird, I don't know which way is up. Are you laughing? I'm pretty sure I heard you laugh."

"The way you think makes me laugh, but in a good way. It's so different from the way I think, but I like it. You're so funny. It's one of the reasons I like you so much."

"I was trying to concentrate so I wouldn't fall."

"Even if we did fall we'd be fine. Ants are so small they just float down to the ground. Air resistance slows them down, like when you drop a little feather."

Orville stopped, eyeing the purple automaton.

"He's not even looking at us. This was a good plan."

"Thanks. Okay, down the wall and under the door."

"I'm kind of hungry. What do ants eat?"

"Different species have different diets. This ant eats leaves, then throws them up and grows a fungus on the half digested goop and eats the fungus."

"I think I'm going to barf."

"And then grow some fungus on it and have lunch?"

"That's disgusting, Sophia! I've totally lost my appetite. Gakk. And just so you know, this ant only eats snapberry pie."

Orville raced down the wall and across the yellow door to the floor.

"Here we go, under the door." He stopped and raised one leg, waving at the automaton.

"Bye bye, crazy purple automaton covered with weird creepy white goop!"

Seconds later they were in the next room.

"Whoa. What is that?"

"Let's convert back to our mouse bodies. Just like blinking, convert the ant body to a thought cloud, then shape your mouse body."

Sophia and Orville appeared a split second later in a blue flash. Orville averted his eyes from the blinding light of the two hundred foot tall sphere floating inches above the floor.

"What is that thing? One side is torn and light is leaking out. So bright!"

"Orville, more seeds on the floor. Bandar was here."

"Do you know what that big sphere is?"

"I think it's similar to the Cross Dimensional Energy Transfer Sphere that powers Proto."

"Except it's gigantic."

"Very, very gigantic. And you're right, it has a tear in it. That's not good. In fact, it's extremely bad. If the protective energy field surrounding the sphere fails, the CDETS would break apart, an incalculable amount of energy from the tenth dimension exploding into this world."

"Enough to cause the Great Thaumatarian Time Wave."

"More than enough. This is what causes the explosion."

"Is there a way to shut off the sphere's connection to the tenth dimension? To turn it off?"

"That's what I was thinking. Let's check the room for control panels."

The two adventurers circled around the blindingly bright sphere. It was Orville who spotted Bandar standing in front of a floor to ceiling control panel, randomly pushing tabs.

"Sophia! It's Bandar! He's the one who causes the explosion!"

Sophia vanished in a flash of light, blinking next to Bandar, grabbing his bony hand.

"Stop! You need to stop!"

Bandar staggered back, letting out a squawk of fear.

"What are you doing here? How did you find me?"

"Don't touch anything. Nothing, do you hear me? If you press the wrong tab you could shut off the external protective energy field around the damaged Cross Dimensional Energy Transfer Sphere, vaporizing your entire planet and creating a mammoth Time Wave."

"I don't know what any of that means. I just wanted to see what the tabs do. I think they control this stuff."

"Bandar, Orville and I are here from the future to prevent a catastrophic explosion from occurring. We think it was caused by you. You push the wrong control tab and that giant sphere explodes, destroying your planet."

Bandar stared blankly at Sophia.

"No, I was just… I just wanted to see what the tabs do."

"It's okay, we're not angry. Come with us while we figure out how to shut down the big sphere."

"You're from the future? How did you get here? Did a machine bring you here? How does it work?"

"We'll tell you all about it later. Just stay with us and don't touch anything."

Sophia studied the control panels, trying to make sense of the symbols.

"I don't know what I'm looking at, everything is written in Thaumatarian."

They circled the perimeter of the room, scanning the vast array of dials, levers, tabs, and blinking lights.

Orville pointed to a large dark blue panel outlined with a bright yellow dotted line.

"That looks like it could be something. It has a big silver lever and the symbol of the skeleton with lightning bolts. I don't know what the words mean though."

"It does look like an emergency shut off system. The question is, does it shut off the CDETS or the protective field around it? Maybe this is the lever that Bandar pulled."

"We should just leave and take Bandar with us."

"We can't do that. Someone else could wander down here later on and push the same tab or pull the same lever Bandar did."

"You're right. Let's keep looking. Maybe we'll find something."

Orville and Sophia jumped when they heard the earsplitting crash. Orville's first thought was that Bandar had pushed a tab on one of the panels, but it proved to be far worse than that. When the two adventurers spun around they saw the twisted yellow door skittering across the floor.

"Oh no."

The gigantic purple automaton burst into the room, letting out a murderous howl when it spotted the three intruders, its blood red eyes pulsing wildly. A series of garbled words spewed from its mouth, its body shaking violently, its fists glowing with a brilliant purple light, the rippling white goop still wrapped tightly around its torso.

"Run!"

The three adventurers took off, streaking around the sphere, trying to escape the crazed automaton.

"Circle around and go back out through the yellow door! Hurry!"

They skittered around the sphere, catching sight of the open doorway. Unfortunately, standing between them and their escape route was a very angry purple automaton covered in white wriggling goop.

"Sphere of defense! It's going to blast us!"

Sophia knew their defensive energy fields would be useless against the automaton's heavy particle beam weapon. They would be vaporized in a split second. She turned to Orville, taking his paw in hers.

"We'll be okay."

"We have to blink out of here!"

"No. I'm sensing something."

Sophia turned to face the demented automaton, its fists flaring with a brilliant purple light aimed directly at them.

Whenever Orville would tell the story of their adventure on Ferus, he always said what happened next was one of the most surprising moments of his life. A familiar voice rang out across the room.

"WHO WANTS TO PLAY CATCH?"

The mad automaton whipped around, bellowing in rage at the sight of a silver Rabbiton standing in the doorway, a leafy green sapling by his side.

The Rabbiton hurled an object wrapped in soft cloth at the automaton. Halfway there, the cloth fluttered off, floating to the ground, the gleaming object within it streaking toward the towering purple monstrosity. The automaton was fearless, snatching the projectile out of the air. He would obliterate it, crush it to dust, then vaporize the puny little Rabbiton who threw it.

285

Much to the automaton's surprise, when the silver ball touched him, a stunningly powerful electromagnetic pulse shot through his body, disrupting the neuronic transmitter systems responsible for his movement. Like a majestic ancient tree in a long forgotten forest, he slowly toppled over, the floor shaking from the impact of his fall.

Chapter 41

Bandar's Return

"Proto!"

Orville raced across the room, throwing his arms around Proto.

"You saved our lives! How did you find us?"

Proto winked at Leaf, whispering, "I told you we'd have to rescue them."

"I can hear you, Proto. You did save the day, just like you always do. I thought we were doomed. That crazy automaton was about to destroy us."

Sophia joined Orville, putting her arms around Proto.

"If it wasn't for you… Orville and I…"

The grin evaporated from Proto's face. He put his silver arms around them.

"You and Orville are my family. I will always protect you."

Sophia nodded, wiping her eyes. "I know you will."

Orville studied the fallen automaton.

"What's that white goopy stuff? It's still moving."

Proto scanned the purple automaton with his spectrophotometer.

"It is the cause of his erratic behavior. Squeaky, attack electrobiotic synthetic fluid."

A blast of purple light shot out from Squeaky's eyes, the white goopy substance instantly vaporized.

Proto picked up the soft cloth, carefully prying the silver sphere out of the automaton's rigid hand. The creature shuddered violently, then rose to its feet.

"What are you doing?" Orville skittered away from the purple behemoth.

"Nothing to worry about, I assure you."

The automaton sent out a red light, scanning the adventurers, then backed away and saluted Orville.

"Whoa, you fixed it. What was that stuff? Is it alive?"

"No, it is a synthetic electrobiotic which is attracted to electric fields. In this case its presence scrambled the automaton's engineered intelligence, causing its unusually aggressive behavior."

Sophia nodded.

"That's why the white goop oozed toward you, Orville. All living creatures are surrounded by a weak electromagnetic field."

"It's still creepy, even if it's not alive."

Sophia stepped over to Bandar.

"Proto, this is our new friend Bandar. When he disappeared from his village we came looking for him.

We had a strong feeling he was connected to the explosion that causes the Great Thaumatarian Time Wave. If we hadn't found him he would have accidentally shut off the protective energy field around the Cross Dimensional Energy Transfer Sphere."

"Causing an inconceivably powerful explosion and the Great Time Wave. I would suggest that we permanently shut down the CDETS."

"We don't know how to shut it down. The writing on the control panels is in Thaumatarian. I have no idea what any of it means."

Leaf stepped forward. "I am equipped with an Internalized Universal Translation System, capable of translating all written languages."

"It's Leaf to the rescue!"

Proto grinned. "My sagacious friend is indeed a wonder."

Leaf stepped around the great ring of control panels, methodically translating the identifying markings. When he reached the blue panel bordered with the bright yellow dotted line he stopped.

"I believe this is what you have been searching for. It is marked *Emergency Shut Off for Cross Dimensional Energy Transfer Sphere*."

"That's it! That's exactly what we want. Leaf, you deserve the honor of shutting it off."

Leaf reached up and pulled the silver lever.

The monolithic blazing energy sphere blinked off, its connection to the tenth dimension instantly severed. There would be no Great Thaumatarian Time Wave.

Sophia hugged Leaf.

"You did it!"

"With a little help from my good friends Proto, Orville, Sophia, and Squeaky."

Orville couldn't stop grinning. "I can't believe we really did it. We traveled four hundred thousand years back in time and prevented the Great Thaumatarian Time Wave. Let's go back to the village and celebrate."

"One last thing before we go. We have to make certain no one can reactivate the CDETS."

Sophia raised her paw, a purple beam shooting out, vaporizing the blue control panel.

"And that is that."

* * * *

Bandar's mum shrieked when she saw him step out of the jungle accompanied by Orville, Sophia, a leafy green sapling and a ten foot tall gleaming silver Rabbiton. She ran to him, throwing her wings around him, sobbing her thanks to Orville and Sophia.

The villagers were wide eyed at the sight of Proto, the first Rabbiton they had ever seen. They were polite, but careful to keep a safe distance from him, a few of them believing him to be a demon from below. Most of them crowded around Bandar, stunned by his return. It was difficult for them to accept what had happened, that one of their tribe had entered the realm of the demons and returned with his life. For over two hours Bandar answered questions about his excursion into the forbidden realm. Captain Beaky was especially curious about the world beneath them.

"How could there be no demons there?"

"The creatures who lived below us were the same ones who built the great cities. They were flesh and blood, just as we are, and were called Thaumatarians. They left after their cities were destroyed by great rocks colliding with our world, rocks which Sophia calls meteors. The Thaumatarians left behind many of their possessions and creations, some resembling Orville's old friend Proto. The world below is filled with treasures, including thousands of book spirits to teach us about our world, instructing us how to build all manner of machines, how to grow an abundance of food. The Thaumatarians even had flying machines that could carry them to other planets, other worlds."

Captain Beaky bowed his head, deep in thought. The villagers stood silently, waiting for his reply.

"If this is so, we must use these teachings wisely, sharing them with the other tribes. I do not wish for us to become creatures who invade worlds, taking land which is not ours and building great cities. While you were gone, Sophia spoke the words of our book spirit. The spirit said we must choose our words with great care, using wisdom and compassion. We must do the same with our actions."

Bandar nodded.

"The light of the Two Suns shines brightly within you."

291

Chapter 42

Summer Flowers

The villagers prepared a grand feast in honor of Bandar's safe return. Orville decided to introduce his favorite culinary delight to the villagers.

"Sophia, do you think ten snapberry pies is enough?"

"For you, or for the villagers?"

"Ha ha. Very funny."

"That's more than enough. Proto has six tins of tasty little cakes. The villagers aren't used to sweets."

The festivities included a roaring bonfire, dancing, singing, and thrilling tales of the demon world recounted by Bandar, Proto, and Orville. Sophia smiled at Orville's embellished tales, but the villagers loved them, asking endless questions about his shaping abilities, gasping when he shaped brilliant orbs of light high above the village.

"It's not magic, it's science. I'm using the power of my mind to control energy fields. Anyone can learn how to do it."

The joyful celebration lasted well into the small hours of the night, a weary Orville and Sophia finally retiring to their hut.

"So tired. I'm going to sleep for a week. Saving the universe is exhausting."

"Orville, I've been thinking about something."

"What?"

"How do we get home?"

"I don't know, didn't the Clockmaker say that would take care of itself?"

"But what does that mean?"

"It means we don't have to worry about it. It will take care of itself."

"I want to understand this, it's more complicated than our other adventures. Orville, we traveled four hundred thousand years back in time to prevent the Time Wave from happening."

"Right, I know that."

"So that means back in our time, in our world, the Time Wave is never going to happen. No Time Wave."

"Right, that's why we came here, to prevent it from happening. I don't get what you're worried about."

"If the Time Wave isn't going to happen in our world, that would mean there was never a reason for us to come to Ferus. You never would have felt the Time Wave in your house, and we never would have felt it in Pridie's Bake Shop. The book about the Great Thaumatarian Time Wave would never have been written because there was no Time Wave to write about. We never would have gone to visit Guild Master Lybis. None of this should have ever happened. We shouldn't be here, we should be back home."

"Um, I'm pretty sure we're here, Sophia."

Sophia's eyebrows jumped up.

"Wait, I know why we're still here! We know Bandar caused the explosion by shutting off the protective energy field, but we don't know exactly when he did it. Maybe he wasn't going to shut it off for another few days."

"What do you mean?"

"If he didn't cause the explosion for another few days, then events in the future wouldn't have been altered yet. The moment the explosion would have occurred, but doesn't, is the moment our world will change."

"Um, you're kind of giving me a headache. I need some sleep. The Clockmaker said it would all take care of itself."

"Orville, make sure you're wearing your Gang of Dragons time shield ring. We're going to need them."

"I never take it off, it's our eternal friendship ring."

Sophia's face softened. "I'm glad you always wear it. I always wear mine too, but it's really important that you keep it on so you'll remember this timeline when we go back to the future."

Orville slept late the next morning, waking up to the smell of warm oatmeal and cinnamon. He leaped out of bed and threw on his clothes.

"Yum, so hungry, Proto must be cooking breakfast."

He darted out of the hut to find Sophia, Proto, Leaf, and Squeaky standing around a pot of steaming oatmeal.

"Morning, sleepy bones!"

"Rugged Dark Space Troopers like me need lots of rest. Breakfast smells yummy. Is there any pie left?"

"The bad news is the pies are all gone, the good news is the villagers loved them. I gave the recipe to Captain Beaky. He said they have lots of berries in the jungle but they've never made pies out of them."

"Proto, how did you like my new coat? I got it from one of the old shops down below. Did you find any shops?"

"We did not. We took a different route to get there. Leaf and I walked for days through a long–"

Orville spun around at the sound of Sophia's cry. She was pointing at a titanic rippling wave rolling through the jungle toward them, the trees undulating wildly, stretching and twisting.

"TIME WAVE! Everyone hold paws! Now!"

"Why is there a time wave? I thought we stopped it!"

Sophia grabbed Orville, pulling him close to her, grabbing one of Leaf's branches. Orville grabbed Proto's hand.

"We're going home! Hold on!"

When the wave hit, the adventurers were enveloped in a raging white miasma, instantly hurled into a rushing torrent of wildly swirling ribbons of colored light. Orville's body felt impossibly long as they flashed through a serpentine gleaming black tunnel at inconceivable velocity. He could hear Sophia's thoughts in his mind.

"Whoo hoo! Isn't this incredible?"

"AGGHHH! I don't like this!"

When he would tell the story of their return, Orville said it felt like he hit a brick wall at a million miles an hour, but instead of getting squashed like a flapcake he found himself on his knees in Madam Beasley's flower garden.

"Thank you so much for helping me plant these flowers, Orville."

Orville turned to see a smiling Madam Beasley wearing her straw gardening hat with the yellow and pink flowered band.

"What? How did I… where did the snow go?"

A look of concern flashed across Madam Beasley's face.

"Oh dear, are you not feeling well? It is a bit warm out, do you need to rest? Would you like a cold glass of lemonade?"

"I'm fine, I just… it's summer already. It seems like it was just winter."

"It does go quickly, doesn't it? I'll finish up and you run home. You don't want to miss your lunch with dear Sophia."

"I am kind of hungry."

A very confused Orville waved goodbye, hurrying down the road.

"Creekers, I need to find Sophia. What am I doing

here? Why is it summer?"

He stepped behind a tree, disappearing in a flash of blue light, arriving in his yard a split second later, dashing to the front door and flinging it open. Sophia was sitting on the couch.

"Hi, Orville! Summer came early this year."

Chapter 43

Mmm Hmm

"I don't get it. I was over at Madam Beasley's house helping her plant flowers. How did I get there?"

"I've been thinking about that. Because we prevented the Time Wave from occurring, we returned to a world where there never was a Time Wave, a world where we had never gone to Ferus. We arrived here in the middle of summer, doing whatever we would normally be doing. I was sitting on the couch reading. Squeaky was downstairs. I don't know where Leaf and Proto are."

"Hey, we can test your theory. The book we got from Science Guild Master Lybis was in my pack. So was my new Dark Space Trooper coat and the gold pocket watch from the Clockmaker."

Orville and Sophia ran to his room. Orville flung open the wardrobe door and grabbed his pack.

"It's empty, there's nothing in it. No book, no pocket

watch from the Watchmaker, and no Dark Space Trooper adventuring coat. Drat, I loved that coat."

"That's our proof. Anything we got on Ferus or the Plane of Turris doesn't exist in this new timeline. If we hadn't been wearing the Mintarian Gang of Dragon time shield rings we would have forgotten everything, forgotten our adventure on Ferus, forgotten that we saved our world from the Great Thaumatarian Time Wave."

Orville frowned. "I really liked that coat."

Sophia put her arms around him.

"We're safe and we're home. Nothing else matters. Oh, guess what I found on the kitchen table?"

Orville eyed the rolled up sheet of parchment in Sophia's paw.

"What is it?"

"It's my diploma from the Symocan Institute of Mechanistic Studies. I took all my final exams, graduated first in my class, and gave a speech at the graduation ceremony. I don't remember doing any of it."

"Whoa. This is getting really weird. Wait, why is it summer now? When we left it was winter. It should still be winter."

"I don't really know, but for some reason we came back three months after we left."

"We should look for Leaf. Wait, would we have met him if there wasn't a Time Wave?"

"Probably not, but I was holding one of his branch-es, so his memories were protected by the time shield rings. He'll remember everything we did, including his visit to the Plane of Turris."

"This is confusing."

"Really confusing. I need to blink to the Symocan Institute. I want to talk to Madam Molly, tell her everything that happened so she can tell Madam Lybis. It's something they should be aware of. And I want to say good bye to my instructors and friends."

"I'm going to look for Leaf and Proto. Leaf is probably in the forest."

"I'm guessing he'll show up pretty soon."

Sophia gave a quick wave, vanishing in a blink of light, leaving Orville alone in his room.

"I need to relax. I guess it's not so bad, I just missed three months, that's all. Hey, I must have been working for those three months. That's three months of pay I don't even remember. Maybe I have a big pile of silvers in my sock drawer."

Orville pulled open his dresser drawer with a grin, pushing aside the pile of socks and underwear.

"Drat, no silvers. I must have spent them. What's this?"

He pulled a small white velvet box tied with a violet ribbon from the back of the drawer.

"That's weird. Where did this come from?"

He flipped the box open, his jaw dropping.

"This isn't possible."

Orville stared at the contents, scarcely able to breathe.

"There's a note."

He unfolded the wrinkled paper and read it. Then he read it again. And again. His paw went limp, the note fluttering to the floor.

"Creekers. Double creekers."

His jumbled thoughts were interrupted by the sound of the front door opening. Proto's voice rang out.

"Orville? Are you here?"

Orville dashed down the hallway.

"Proto! I was just going to look for you and Leaf! What happened to you?"

"It was quite a remarkable experience. After we passed through the tunnel of colored lights I found myself standing in Mum's kitchen, chatting with her about… certain things. I looked through the window and saw the green leaves on the trees. I finished talking with Mum and hurried over."

"I was helping Madam Beasley plant flowers when I got back, and Sophia was on the couch reading a book."

"Fascinating. Clearly we altered the events of our timeline by preventing the Great Time Wave. This deserves a great deal of study. Who knows what other events may have been altered."

He gave Orville a nervous glance.

"I'm just glad we all made it back safely. This time travel stuff is confusing. It's good to be back home, isn't it?"

"Mmm hmm."

Orville's eyes narrowed.

"What does that mean? Is something wrong?"

"Wrong? Why would you say that? Time travel can

be a tricky business, of course. Did I mention we're going over to Mum and Papa's for dinner tomorrow evening?"

"Why? Is it something special?"

"They just invited us, that's all, nothing to be concerned about, just an ordinary dinner. Nothing special at all. Completely normal."

Orville's eyes were narrow slits. Proto was hiding something.

"What do you mean, nothing special at all? There's something you're not telling me. Why won't you look at me?"

Proto froze, his eyes on his feet.

"Proto, I won't be mad. Just tell me what it is."

"I can't tell you. Mum made me promise not to say anything. It's a surprise. Don't try to make me tell you."

"It's not my birthday, and it's not Sophia's birthday. What kind of surprise?"

Proto clapped his hand over his mouth and ran down the stairs to his room, slamming the door behind him.

Orville frowned, staring out the window at his parents' house. What was the surprise? He gave a yelp when he saw the three foot tall sapling running through the front yard.

"It's Leaf!"

Orville flung the front door open and dashed outside. Leaf stopped short when he saw Orville.

"Do you remember me?"

"Of course I do! Come inside, we've been worried

about you. Where were you?"

Leaf ran into the living room and hopped up onto the couch.

"Mmm, nice and soft. After we passed through that tunnel I found myself standing next to the great falls. Quite beautiful this time of year, the mist from the falling water making a glorious rainbow. It would make a lovely painting. I had no idea how I had gotten there, but clearly we had returned in the middle of summer. Thanks to your Gang of Dragons time shield ring I remembered everything and headed back to town, trying to keep out of sight. I didn't want anyone to see me."

"I'm so glad you're safe. Have you talked to the Watcher? Are you still free to do whatever you want?"

"I am. He found our adventure to be most fascinating. He is especially curious about the effect of time travel on Muridaan Falls, and how we will adapt to this new timeline."

"It looks the same to me, it's just summertime. When I came back I was helping Madam Beasley plant her flowers. Mum always asks me to help her. She's really nice. Sophia was sitting on the couch reading."

"Mmm hmm."

Orville froze.

"That's what Proto said. You know something! Spill it. Proto said Mum was having a surprise dinner for us. What did the Watcher tell you?"

Leaf leaped off the couch and ran down the stairs to Proto's room.

"Proto! Let me in!"

Chapter 44

Dinner

"What do you think the surprise is?"

Sophia shrugged. "I have no idea. You don't think your parents are moving, do you? Hey, maybe you're going to have a new little mouseling brother or sister."

"That's ridiculous. Mum's too old for that."

"Maybe." Sophia grinned, poking Orville in the ribs.

Orville knocked on the front door and swung it open. "We're here!"

Mum threw her arms around Orville and gave him a long hug, then did the same to Sophia. Papa was standing next to Mum, an unusually large grin on his face.

Sophia gave Orville a puzzled glance. Orville's parents were definitely acting strangely.

"Come have a seat at the table. Proto has a very special surprise for you." Orville's mum winked at him.

"Why are you winking?"

"You'll see."

Papa grinned, rubbing Orville's shoulder.

Orville's anxiety was rising. He was not especially fond of surprises, and he had no idea why Mum and Papa were smiling so much.

When they were all seated at the dining table Mum called out, "Proto, you can bring it in now!"

Proto stepped out of the kitchen carrying a lovely cake on a gleaming silver platter. He set the cake down on the table, carefully avoiding eye contact with Orville or Sophia.

Orville studied Proto's culinary masterpiece.

"It looks like a Dragonfly. Why did you make a cake that looks like a Dragonfly?"

Mum snickered. "I think you know very well why he did."

"Wait, did they make me a captain in the Dragonfly Squadron?"

"What?"

"Is that why the cake looks like a Dragonfly? They made me a captain?"

Mum burst out laughing. "You're so funny, always joking. Look who's riding in it. Didn't Proto do a good job with your adventuring hat?"

"Is that supposed to be me and Sophia?"

Papa laughed. "Such a clever son!"

"I'm confused. Why did you make the cake?"

Orville glanced over to Sophia, who was just as puzzled as he was.

Mum stood up and walked around the table, standing

behind Orville and Sophia. She rubbed the top of Orville's head.

"There's no need to be embarrassed. I think it's so romantic, asking Sophia to marry you while you were flying in a Dragonfly under a full moon."

Sophia's spoon clattered to the floor.

Orville's jaw dropped.

The room was silent until Sophia blurted out, "Did I say yes?"

Mum and Papa burst out laughing. Mum threw her arms around both of them.

"You are the funniest two mice I know, and I love you both. Orville, have you found a ring yet?"

"Uhh, not exactly. I'm… um…still thinking about it. It's all kind of a blur." He looked at Sophia, his eyes wide. He wanted to send her a thought cloud, but Mum and Papa would see it.

Sophia turned to Mum, smiling brightly.

"The cake is beautiful, thank you so much. It really was so romantic of Orville to propose while we were flying over Muridaan Falls. I'll never forget what he said to me."

She turned to Orville, raising her eyebrows, a big grin on her face.

"What? What are you doing??"

"Remember how you said I was the most beautiful mouse in the world? And how smart I was? And how much you love me?"

"Can I have some cake please?"

Papa laughed. "I proposed to Mum on the shores of

the Vesarak Sea. I still think your mum is the most beautiful mouse in the world."

Orville's heart was pounding. It made sense that he had proposed to Sophia. They had planned on getting married after she graduated from the Symocan Institute, and she had her diploma. It was confusing to be engaged but not remember proposing. It felt like something was missing.

"Orville? Cake?"

"Oh, thanks, it looks delicious. Thanks for making it, Proto."

"It was my pleasure. I never realized what a romantic fellow you are. Quite lovely, and I'm so happy for both of you. You make a wonderful couple, perfect for each other."

"Thanks, Proto. That's nice of you to say."

By the time they left, Orville and Sophia were over the shock of finding out they were engaged to be married. They held paws as they strolled home under the starry night sky.

"We're engaged, Orville. Can you believe it?"

"I know. I wish I could remember what I said to you."

"Whatever it was, I'm sure it was romantic. I was just joking about you saying how beautiful and smart I was. I'm sorry if I embarrassed you."

"You didn't embarrass me. You are the most beautiful mouse I've ever seen. And you're the smartest mouse I know. And I love you more than anyone."

Sophia put her arms around Orville's neck, holding him close.

* * * *

"Don't be scared. I'll be walking right next to you."

"They'll all be looking at me."

"We're just going to the grocery store. It will be fine."

"Suppose they're afraid of me? Suppose they run away?"

"Sophia always says we should face our fears head on, that whatever happens is never as bad as we imagine it will be."

Leaf wrapped one of his branches around Proto's hand. The two friends stepped through the gate onto the lane leading to the center of Muridaan Falls.

"Just keep taking steps, one after another."

Two mouselings darted out from behind a bright blue house, stopping in their tracks when they saw Proto and Leaf.

"Hey, Proto, is that a walking tree?"

"Indeed it is. He also happens to be a very good friend of mine."

The two mouselings darted across the road, staring curiously at Leaf.

"Where's he from?"

"I am from a distant world called the Plane of Turris."

The mouselings jumped back.

"Whoa! You can talk?"

"My friend Leaf is an excellent conversationalist and possesses a most inquiring scientific mind. Quite a sagacious fellow."

"Sometimes you talk funny, Proto. Hi Leaf, I'm Rogo. How do you talk without a mouth? Wait, how do you see without eyes? What's it like on the Plane of Turris? Are there lots of talking trees there? How old are you?"

By the time Leaf and Proto reached the grocery store they were accompanied by over a dozen mice listening to Leaf's story of how he had come to be in Muridaan Falls.

"You really see with your leaves? Okay, how many buttons are on my coat?"

"There were six, but one is missing."

"Whoa, that's amazing! Do you have weird magical powers?"

"There's no such thing as magic, it's all just science. I have optical sensors embedded in my leaves much like the sensors inside your eyes. When the light hits them, they send electrical impulses to my brain, which then converts them into the images that I see. Your eyes work the same way."

"I have sensors in my eyes? Whoa."

An older gray mouse wearing a tweed suit stepped through the crowd.

"A fine good afternoon to you, sir. I am Headmaster Scott of Mearsley Upper School. I was quite captivated by your marvelous depiction of the Plane of Turris. I wonder if you might have an interest in speaking at our school, perhaps even teaching an advanced science class? You have a marvelous way with words. You could start with one class a week and see how that suits you. What do you say?"

"You want me to teach a science class?"

"We would count ourselves most fortunate to have you as a member of our staff. You clearly possess a vast knowledge of the deep sciences, far beyond what is currently being taught in our school."

Leaf was silent for a moment, then said, "I think I would like that. I think I would like that very much."

Chapter 45

The Gift

"It's so beautiful out. This was a good idea to hike up to the falls. It's nice to have time alone so we can talk about everything that's been happening."

"Remember the first time we came here?"

"Of course I do. You showed me the clockwork glowbirds. At first I thought you might have been imagining it, but you were right about them, they stopped on the ledge at the same time every day for exactly six minutes, then flew west. We never would have met Proto if you hadn't noticed their odd behavior."

"It's funny how one thing leads to another like that."

"Like if you hadn't noticed the blue marble rolling uphill we never would have rescued your papa."

"Let's sit on the bench in front of the falls. I like the way the sun shines on the spray and makes rainbows."

The two best friends strolled over to a rustic wooden bench and sat down, gazing up at the magnificent roaring falls.

"I can't believe we're going to get married. I always knew we would, but it's really going to happen. We're going to spend the rest of our lives together."

Sophia leaned against Orville, taking his paw in hers.

"Where do you think we should have the wedding?"

"I was thinking right here at the falls, where our first adventure began. It's so beautiful up here."

"I like that. We could ask the Thirteenth Monk to marry us. I know he'd be happy to. I'm going to ask Amanda to be my Mouse of Honor. Who are you going to have for your Best Mouse?"

"I'm not going to have a Best Mouse."

"What do you mean? You have to have one."

"I'm going to have a Best Rabbiton."

Sophia burst out laughing.

"You are so sweet, and Proto will be thrilled. I can't wait to see the look on his face when you tell him."

The two friends were quiet for a long time, mesmerized by the falls. Orville glanced at Sophia.

"Um, I have something to show you."

"What?"

"First I have something to ask you."

"You're being kind of mysterious."

"I know I already asked you to marry me, and you said you would, but I want us to remember it. I want to ask you to marry me again."

"You don't have to do that."

"I want to."

A grin appeared on Sophia's face.

"Okay."

Orville opened his pack and took out a small white box tied with a violet ribbon.

"Is that what I think it is?"

"It is and it isn't."

Orville cleared his throat, holding the white box in both paws.

"Sophia, before I met you, a lot of stuff scared me. Things like snow bears. And wolves. And creepy looking bugs. And ghosts. And those weird creaky noises the house makes when you're home alone. Remember how I fainted when I saw the giant centipedes?"

"And when you saw the snow bear on your front porch. Of course I remember. That's one of the things that made me love you."

"Really? Anyway, after I met you I wanted to be brave. We've faced so many scary creatures on our

313

adventures and we've always manage to find our way safely home. Those things don't scare me like they used to, and it's because of you."

"You've changed me too, Orville. I know a lot about science, but you taught me to pay close attention to the world around me, to look for hidden everyday puzzles like the clockwork glowbirds and your hat's capricious shadows. And no one can make me laugh like you do."

"You're at least nine times as sagacious as Leaf."

Sophia snorted.

Orville held out the small white box.

"Sophia, will you marry me?"

Sophia took the box in her paws.

"You are my truest love, Orville Mouse, and I cherish you above all others. Yes, I will marry you."

The two mice held each other for a long time, listening to the thundering waters of the great falls, basking in the warmth of the Symocan summer sun.

"Can I open the box?"

"I have to tell you something first. Something that happened on the Plane of Turris."

"What happened?"

"I opened one of the doors in the Clockmaker's Tower when I stopped to rest. I was curious why there were so many rooms in the tower and what was in them. All the doors had different numbers on them, but they weren't in order like rooms in a hotel. I opened door number 10 and saw a big sunny garden next to a lovely house. There was a blue sky overhead and white mountains in the distance. I think it was our house, just painted a different color."

"How is that possible?"

"There's more. I went into the room. Two mouselings ran out from behind some bushes. One of them gave me a bunch of yellow flowers. She said her name was Emma Mouse. The other mouse was Eldon Proto Mouse."

Sophia put her paw over her mouth.

"Emma was my mum's name."

"The mouselings called me Papa."

Sophia blinked rapidly, her mind spinning.

"That's incredible, but it makes sense. We know the Clockmaker can control time, so it's possible he has doors that open to the future and the past. The door you went through was marked with a 10, which might mean you stepped ten years into the future. You saw our mouselings."

"They also said something about going for a ride in *The Goldfish*."

Sophia's jaw dropped. She grabbed her pack and opened it, pulling out a rolled up sheet of paper, spreading it out on her lap.

"These are rough sketches for a ship I want to build when I start working with Mirus. It was going to be a surprise for you. It's an undersea vehicle that can go to the bottom of the ocean."

"And you named it *The Goldfish*."

"Yes, I thought it was a clever name, since you're always talking about finding sunken treasure chests filled with gold."

"You can open the box now. There's a note in it. You're not going to believe this."

"Now I'm kind of afraid to open it."

"Don't be."

Sophia untied the ribbon and slowly raised the lid of the box, her eyes wide when she saw the contents.

"Orville! We can't afford a ring like this. It's a huge Nirriimian white crystal. It's too much, we could buy a house with what this must have cost!"

"It was a gift."

"A gift? From who?"

"Read the note."

Sophia unfolded the paper, reading it out loud.

A wedding ring for Mum,
with lots of love from your
two precious mouselings,
Eldon and Emma

Chapter 46

The Goldfish

"What do you think?"

"I like it, this is a good dream. The Goldfish looks just like my drawings, except mine didn't have a big glass case filled with snapberry pies and cookies."

"I was kind of hungry when I fell asleep."

"Look at the size of that octopus."

Orville gazed through the glass viewing dome at the mammoth octopus, rippling beams of sunlight darting about beneath the shimmering blue green waters of the Vesarak Sea.

"I like that it's bright yellow and wearing an adventurers hat."

"You really do have the best dreams. I'm pretty sure octopuses don't wear shoes though. I'm so happy we're getting married."

"Me too."

"Where do you think Eldon and Emma got the ring?

When they sent it back in time they must have been a lot older than when you saw them in the Clockmaker's Tower. Maybe they're Metaphysical Adventurers."

"Maybe we find sunken treasure in The Goldfish. A big chest filled with gold and jewels. What I don't know is how they could have sent the ring back through time to my dresser drawer."

Sophia shook her head, her eyes on a school of colorful fish darting through the water.

"There are so many mysteries in the world. Sometimes I feel like one of those fish."

"What do you mean?"

"They spend their lives under the ocean, unaware of all the civilizations that have come and gone, unaware of the distant planets and galaxies and universes and other dimensions. Sometimes I imagine one of them leaping out of the water, catching a glimpse of a grand city filled with gleaming cloudscrapers, then swimming back to their friends, trying to describe the city without really understanding what it was they saw. All the other fish laugh."

"And you think I have a crazy imagination?"

"Imagine if we told everyone in Muridaan Falls about our adventures. How many mice would believe us? We'd be like the fish who saw the big shiny city. They'd laugh at us, call us loopy."

Orville was silent for a long time.

"Maybe some of the other fish would leap out of the water and take a look for themselves."

Sophia studied Orville's face for a moment, then

leaned over and kissed him.

"What was that for?"

"Because you're so smart and I love you. Not every fish leaps out of the water at the same time."

"I'm glad I'm not a big scaly fish. Can you imagine trying to bake a snapberry pie underwater? Plus, I'd always have to be in school. Get it? Because I'm a fish? Be in SCHOOL?"

Sophia burst out laughing.

"You're such a ninny. Oh, that reminds me, I have a present for you."

Sophia opened her pack and pulled out a white box tied with a pale blue ribbon.

"Open it."

"This is the first dream present I've ever gotten."

Orville pulled the lid off the box, a wide grin appearing on his face.

"It's my Dark Space Trooper adventuring coat! This is amazing! Thanks, Sophia!"

Orville pulled on the coat and stood up, turning sideways.

"What do you think? Do I look like a rugged adventurer?"

"The handsomest one in the whole world."

"I wish I could bring this coat back to Muridaan Falls, but you can't bring stuff back from a dream."

Sophia put her arms around Orville, holding him close.

"You're wearing it now, and now is all that matters."

If you enjoyed reading
Orville Mouse and the Puzzle
of the Sagacious Sapling
please leave a short review or rating
on Amazon.com
Reviews are the lifeblood of indie publishers –
we can't survive without them!

If you have any comments or suggestions
or would like to be notified of upcoming book
releases and Free Kindle book day promotions,
please email me at
OrvilleMouse@gmail.com

Follow me at:
www.facebook.com/TomHoffmanAuthor/

Best wishes until we meet again,

Tom Hoffman

ABOUT THE AUTHOR

Tom Hoffman received a B.S. in psychology
from Georgetown University in 1972
and a B.A. in 1980 from the now-defunct
Oregon College of Art. He has lived in Alaska
with his wife since 1973. They have two
adult children and two adorable
grandchildren. Tom was a graphic designer
and artist for over 35 years.
Redirecting his imagination from art to
writing, he wrote his first novel,
The Eleventh Ring, at age 63.